With Best
an old fr

Wilbur

Oct 8?

CARTER'S CASTLE

CARTER'S CASTLE

WILBUR WRIGHT

C

CENTURY PUBLISHING
LONDON

First published in Great Britain in 1983 by

Century Publishing Co. Ltd,
76 Old Compton Street, London W1V 5PA

ISBN 0 7126 0164 3

Photoset in Great Britain by
Rowland Phototypesetting Ltd,
Bury St Edmunds, Suffolk
Printed by St Edmundsbury Press,
Bury St Edmunds, Suffolk

*Dedicated to the Fitters and Riggers
of the 33rd Halton Apprentice Entry, 1936
— to those still with us, and the many
who have gone on ahead*

THE CASTLE OF FEAR

An imaginary castle in a forest near Saragossa. It represents that terrible obstacle which fear conjures up, but which vanishes into thin air when approached with a stout heart and a clear conscience.

> 'It sank before my earnest face,
> It vanished quite away,
> And left no shadow on the place
> Between me and the day.
> Such castles rise to strike us dumb,
> But – weak in every part –
> They melt before the strong man's eyes
> And fly the true of heart . . .'

C. Mackay, *The Giant*

AUTHOR'S FOREWORD

Much of the Cambodian historical sequence in this book is based upon fact. Angkor *was* betrayed to the Siamese: much of the wealth of the Khmer kings is known to have disappeared during that part of the fourteenth century, hidden to prevent it falling into the hands of the invaders. As did, in fact, much of the wealth and religious artifacts of the temples of Angkor Vat – treasure which, to this day, has never been found.

I do not defend the employment of reincarnation in the narrative: so much reliable documentation of the phenomenon is now available that it would be a brave man who denied at least the possibility of its existence.

If there is any single reason for writing this book, it is this: every lonely widower like Donald Carter dreams of meeting his 'Liane'. Very few are fortunate. Perhaps this story may make the waiting and searching just a little more bearable.

None of the characters and organisations mentioned in the text are intended to resemble any living person or company, and any such resemblance is purely coincidental.

I would like to convey my thanks to Ken Tooke, Foster Robson and many other ex-apprentices of the 33rd RAF Halton Entry, who have provided most welcome support and assistance over the years.

Wilbur Wright,
Southampton,
1982

PART ONE

PROLOGUE

The aeroplane concealed her age, like a raddled old whore, beneath new paint and décor. But at forty thousand feet she flexed, groaned, moved upon herself at joints and interfaces, her creaking protests lost in the jet roar. After her birth in Burbank in 1958, she hauled many thousands of passengers, under the United American flag, on internal routes with perfect safety; around 1963, however, she began running into trouble. At Kansas City, Missouri, multiple hydraulic failure precipitated a heavy belly-landing, after which she flew consistently out of trim, yawing to starboard. Every pilot tried to trim out the imbalance. None succeeded. Yet mostly the pilots took her as they found her, for apart from that built-in skid, 10026 was a good old girl who gave crew and passengers alike a nice smooth ride.

In 1968, a PLO bomb exploded midway between Athens and Beirut, ripping a six-foot hole in the body, through which a stewardess, three passengers and a soft drinks trolley disappeared forever. Patched up and rebuilt, 10026 went back into service, adding to her repertoire a steady porpoising motion in level flight, which trimming and weight distribution did little to correct.

The owners faced a simple choice: treble the sick-bag allocations and lose passengers, downgrade the old lady to freight-only status − or sell. Bought by a faceless consortium of Casablanca entrepreneurs, she became a pariah of the air routes, changing owners at least once a year. She would turn up in Honolulu and Havana, Dulles and De Gaulle, and the refuelling crews would nudge each other, grin − and surreptitiously cross themselves.

Six years later, she burst four main landing wheels at Darwin and collided on the ground with another 707 which had total brake failure – a real 'Murphy'. Mechanics dropped tools which rolled into inaccessible corners; spilled coffee leaked into electric junction boxes; a punctured main wheel would be replaced, then the one next to it would go flat.

And a year later, a green and over-confident West African sky jockey dropped her in from fifty feet on the approach to Lusaka: the 6-G impact wiped off her main gear, and she was towed away to a remote hangar and abandoned. In the normal way of things, she would have been cannibalised for spares – except that the hangar door happened to be open as Budd Larkin and Singles Gabor walked by. Budd and Singles knew that a similar model 707 had been broken for spares in the Arizona desert – and they knew how to lay their hands on the ship's documents – cheap. So some six months and a lot of hard work later, a Boeing 707 emerged like a resplendent butterfly from its chrysalis, in immaculate white with red flashing. Between times, she had shed her original number from the tail and 50,000 hours from her logbook. Her restorers had no need to advertise: at the price asked, they had to beat off buyers with a big stick, splitting a neat £400,000 and their partnership for all time.

Her new Chinese owners operated a small commercial outfit out of Seletar Airport, Singapore – and since they had no intention of operating further east than Borneo, or west of Pakistan, a Certificate of Airworthiness and passenger clearance were obtained at little extra cost. The one-time ugly duckling joined a little fleet consisting of two decrepit DC3s and a mellow old ex-BEA Viscount. The single 707 crew, paid largely in cash notes, had some difficulty in complying with maximum flight-time rulings, but solved the problem by keeping two flying logbooks. They were professionals, from chief pilot Eddie Wu Pak, down to Claudine, the jazzy French stewardess with the thin legs and big ass.

Around that time, the price of gold took off like a Shuttle booster, and Eddie Wu Pak took to wearing a canvas waistcoat with a solid gold lining; this multiplied his salary about ten times, and if Eddie had been told the job was worth another $5,000 a year, he would have said, 'I'll pay it . . .'

* * *

In the early summer of 1979, a chartered DC8 from Gatwick landed at Singapore. One of her engines had been wrecked by an in-flight fire and eventually fell off on final approach, narrowly missing a small village. The DC8 brought in eight adults and fifty-three children bound for Hong Kong, where several Service families were eagerly awaiting their arrival. The children were starting the seven-week summer vacation, and remained unaware of the turbine failure which had come so close to killing them all.

At Singapore, no replacement engine was available. In such circumstances, decisions are often taken which are regretted later. The local agent telexed Gatwick: a replacement 707 was available for charter locally – could he proceed? Gatwick agreed thankfully, drank one more cup of coffee and went back to bed.

There was one joker in the pack – the weather. Eddie Wu Pak stared at the sky as he got out of his car on the flight line. He knew the weather could and would be totally different 1,400 kilometres to the north, but he still squinted up at the low cloud. He was well aware that there was a big depression near the Philippines that could turn into a typhoon very easily, and in other circumstances he might have ordered a twenty-four-hour delay – but he based his decision to proceed on two factors: at 38,000 feet they would be well above the weather – and the twenty-four gold bars in his waistcoat weighed heavily on his mind. The Hong Kong Triad boys wouldn't take kindly to a cancellation – arrangements for getting the gold out of Kai Tak airport were costly and complicated, and if he fouled up, Eddie could reckon on spending the next four centuries standing to attention in a bucket of cement at the bottom of Hong Kong harbour.

He shrugged, briefed his crew, strapped the plane to his backside and started engines. All four started without incident. Eddie restrained an impulse to comment; he was aware that this old airplane had a mind of her own and ears behind every panel. He got departure clearance for All-Orient Flight HK 108, taxied out and made a long, smooth take-off to the west.

At 3,000 feet, the old 707 disappeared into the overcast, the roar of her engines fading into the far distance.

She was never seen again.

ONE

In the closing decade of the fourteenth century, a vast horde of invading Siamese hurled themselves repeatedly against the stubborn defences of Cambodia, ruled by the Khmer Kings of Angkor. Each time, they were repulsed with much killing, inflicted by the mercenary armies of Jayavarman VI, armies equipped and sustained by the savage taxation of the people of the kingdom. Further, the nobles of the court themselves sent out raiding parties into Siam, carrying off vast numbers of slaves to work on the roads and the fabulous temples of Angkor Vat.

But the people of Khmer had had a surfeit of the wanton extravagance of the court, dedicated as it was to the god Siva: a court in which the gold dish used to feed the king's hounds would keep a peasant family for ten years; a court that worshipped Siva, a god who demanded not only gold and jewels, but also endless sacrifices of new-born babes upon the temple altars. There was a new god, from the West, men whispered. A god who demanded nothing save belief and dedication: a god called Buddha.

Yes, assuredly, soon things were to change.

At the time I became involved with Flight HK 108, I had lived and worked in Singapore for twelve years. The Minister for Civil Aviation, Mr Lee Kuan Lok, was a close personal friend: we had flown Dakotas together out of Cox's Bazaar in Malaya during 1944 and 1945.

In 1956, I took off in a Beverley transport from an airfield near Oxford. For some inexplicable reason, a fuel non-return valve had been assembled the wrong way round, and while a Beverley could fly reasonably well on two port or two starboard engines, one needed sufficient height and speed to regain control. In this instance, I had neither. Four of the seven people on board perished, while I – unfairly, it seemed to me – emerged with nothing worse than two fractured legs and a shortage of serviceable teeth.

The resultant limp became a permanent feature, and I drew a red line in my logbook and spent seven reasonably happy years in the Directorate of Flight Safety, with frequent secondments to the Air Investigation Branch. I gained a great deal of experience of aircraft accidents in those years, but it was, at times, a harrowing business. Human bodies are soft and distressingly vulnerable to impact and exploding fuel.

After I retired in 1967, I was fortunate enough to be offered a position with British Flight Instruments in Singapore as local agent. Since my wife had died almost a year previously, there seemed no reason to refuse. I suppose, had Stephen survived the climbing accident in the Sierra Nevada, I might have reconsidered, but that happened only a year or so before Nancy died, and neither are subjects on which I like to dwell.

It was not until I had been in Singapore some ten months that I ran across Lee Kuan Lok again, at a dreary party thrown by a senior British resident. He was as pleased and surprised to see me as I was to see him. I noticed he had a few extra inches around his black cummerbund now, and the lines on his face were deeper; his flesh, too, had that puffed, shiny appearance common in middle-aged Chinese – but otherwise I was astonished to see how little he had changed.

We met for lunch at Raffles some days later, spending almost three hours over an extended and most enjoyable meal, and opening up some very old hangar doors in the process. I believe I drank rather too much of the potent Straits rice wine, which probably loosened my tongue. Lee was oddly interested in my accident investigation experience, and told me that the government branch responsible at that time was both under-manned and inexperienced. My arrival must have seemed providential to him.

Of course, I resisted all suggestions of taking Singapore citizenship: I was a British subject and intended to remain so. But Lee produced a quite viable alternative – a post as part-time but fully accredited consultant to his Investigation Department. Civil aviation and local airlines were booming. It is fair to say that, while the salary offered was very attractive, my decision to accept stemmed more from a real desire to re-enter the field in which I had spent so many years. And as I realised at the time, the additional income might even permit the purchase of a small light aircraft, such as a Piper Cub or a Comanche.

In the years that followed, Lee – I am pleased to say – appeared more than satisfied. My salary was reviewed at regular intervals and was easily earned; serious accidents were, luckily, rare at that time. Lee insists that this was in no small way due to the implementation of various suggestions I made towards increasing flight safety, but I am afraid that he tends to exaggerate at times.

One evening he came to see me in the small club hangar at Seletar, where I was working on the Cub engine in preparation for the Certificate of Airworthiness check, due next month. I took up a piece of rag, wiped my hands and we walked slowly to the bar. The sun was low on the hills, and already the runway lighting glimmered softly in the dusk.

He told me, over a long cool drink, about Flight HK 108. It had disappeared over the South China Sea, en route to Hong Kong, after taking off that morning with a total of sixty-one passengers and crew. One becomes hardened to human tragedy over the years of probing aircraft accidents, but I felt a sharp pang of sorrow when he told me that fifty-three of those lost had been children. It seemed that all contact had been lost a few hours after take-off. Lee Kuan walked over to the Far East map on the wall of the clubroom. We had the place more or less to ourselves – members who had flown that day had gone home, and the usual influx of evening drinkers had not yet begun.

'The last position report,' Lee said gravely, 'put Flight HK 108 some two hundred miles south-east of the Mekong Delta – well clear of Vietnamese airspace. They could have landed at Saigon – but communication is difficult with Vietnam at the moment.'

That was an understatement. I would have said 'bloody impossible.' I stared at the map. 'The weather?'

He paused. 'Not good. A big depression over the Phillipines, deepening rapidly – it's a full-blown typhoon now. Heading roughly north.'

17

I set my glass upon the bar. 'Local aeroplane?'

'The 707 operated by All-Orient.'

I said slowly: 'That one? They haven't had it long. Who was the pilot?'

'Eddie Wu Pak. Their chief pilot.'

'Well, he should know what he's doing. Been at it long enough. How long since they went overdue?'

'Three o'clock local time,' the minister said shortly. 'Tanks would be dry by then. But the tower lost contact two hours before that time.'

I put my forefinger on the map, in the middle of the South China Sea. A modern jet airliner could travel a long way in an hour – more than 600 nautical miles. In two hours it could be almost anywhere. Lee agreed.

'I know, Alan. Look – we'd like you to take over the enquiry.'

I rubbed my chin. 'They might get a bit stuffy back home,' I said, grinning. 'Things have been a bit slow lately for British Flight Instruments.'

'No problem,' he said quickly. 'I telephoned your London office this afternoon – got hold of a man called Tagart. He got a bit shirty, but suggested you take annual leave.'

I turned my head and stared at him. 'I'm much obliged. Actually, I had planned to take the Cub down to Darwin in easy stages, after the C of A check.'

He smiled blandly. 'I know. But you'll do it?'

I owed the cunning old sod a great deal, but would never have told him so. It made it that much more difficult to say no. There was also the fact that the loss of the Boeing was the most serious incident in recent years. I managed to persuade myself that the enquiry would open and close very quickly indeed. I had little to lose, much to gain.

When such an aircraft goes missing over one of the world's most vicious oceans, there is little real hope of finding it again. The only feasible landing places en route, by my reckoning, were the Paracel Islands and Vietnam itself. The former I could eliminate very quickly – but the latter was an unknown quantity pointing to a very early adjournment.

I was among the prophets. The hearing opened the next morning, Tuesday, and closed at noon on Friday, leaving me free to return to work on the Cub. The final report was brief and inconclusive, consisting mainly of negatives; there was no information of any kind from Vietnam (surprise, surprise) and no sighting of wreckage by shipping.

Lee brought me my personal copy a week later, neatly bound in a black leather folder. I turned to the final page, to read confirmation of our findings.

> The aircraft is presumed lost at sea with no survivors. In the absence of evidence to support either of the two most likely causes of the accident – mechanical failure or pilot error – and despite the loss of radio contact at an early stage of the flight, the Court records an Open Verdict, with the rider that it is the opinion of the Court that the pilot, Captain Edward Wu Pak, was ill-advised to undertake the flight in view of the weather conditions forecast for the route.

That was in early May.

In the first week in October, I received a telephone call from Lee Kuan Lok.

'Alan,' he said urgently, 'you remember the enquiry on Flight HK 108? Back in the Spring?'

I was caught unawares for a moment.

'The Boeing lost en route to Hong Kong?'

'Yes. You'll have to re-open it, Alan. A survivor has been found – Donald Carter. He turned up at Khota Baru, on the north-east coast of Malaysia.'

'Alive?'

Lee said carefully: 'Yes. We're flying him to Singapore today – you'd better go and see him in hospital tomorrow.'

I sat and thought for a moment. 'All right. I'll do that. How did he come to be at Khota Baru?'

There was a long pause. Then the minister said slowly: 'He crash-landed on the beach, with three other survivors. In a Dakota which has been missing for five years.'

TWO

There were mutterings of discontent throughout the land of Angkor. Worse, serious doubts gnawed at the minds of the people. If – as was said – the great god Siva was all-powerful, why did he require the raw sexuality of the court, the naked perversion, the temple orgies? Why did he need the destruction of new-born infants roasted over a slow fire? Why did he permit the plundering of the poor, who were required to pay their lords three-fifths of that which they earned – simply to swell already-bulging coffers? Why did Siva permit the waste of lives in mining the great rubies and emeralds adorning the bodies of court ladies and the apsara, the professional priestess-whores of the temple? Was it not so much better to believe in the frugality and love and comradeship of the Lord Buddha?

In the inns and markets and working places, men began to brood and whisper – and conspire . . .

I saw Donald Carter the next afternoon, in a small side ward of the general hospital. First, I was able to speak briefly to the doctor in charge. He was a Dr Ranjit Singh, a graduate of Guy's who had considerable experience of treating cases of exposure, gained in reception centres for the Vietnamese boat people.

He told me that Carter and three other survivors had been admitted the previous evening: a stewardess, and two others, a boy and a girl in their teens. I sat at his desk, smoking one of my long black cheroots: they are locally made, mild, with a bamboo mouthpiece, and they are my sole vice in old age.

I said, 'Do you know where they've been for the past six months, Doctor?'

He shook his head. They had been in no state to be questioned, he said, but after a good night of rest, they seemed in remarkably good condition – considering they had spent half a year in the jungle. They had all lost some weight and were suffering from malnutrition; in addition, Carter had a suspected back injury.

I said, 'Can I talk to him?'

'O, yes, Mr Napier,' the doctor nodded. 'We are sedating him last night and he is having a very good sleep. It will do him good to talk, I think.'

I got up from my chair. 'This is an official visit, Doctor Singh. I have to find out what happened to that aeroplane last May. It may take more than one session . . .'

'I am fully understanding, Mr Napier, sir. All I am asking is, do not make the patient tired.'

I smiled. 'I won't. Perhaps he'll be glad of the company.'

Donald Carter looked up from a newspaper. He was a lean, spare man, in his fifties, and his hair was sun-bleached, fading to grey at the temples. He had been freshly shaven that day: his cheeks and body were two shades darker than his chin, and I judged that he had let his hair and beard grow long. He lay back against banked pillows, wearing green hospital-issue pyjamas, and looked to me to be remarkably fit and well, despite the lines of strain around his eyes and mouth.

I said, 'Mr Carter? My name's Napier. I'm attached to the Ministry of Aviation, Accident Investigation. We've re-opened the enquiry into the loss of Flight HK 108 – ' He raised his eyebrows. 'Your Boeing flight to Hong Kong,' I went on. He nodded, laid down his newspaper and reached for the cigarettes on the bedside table. I lit his for him, and said I preferred a cheroot.

I sat back in my chair. 'Are you well enough to answer a few questions?'

He nodded. 'I'm okay, Mr Napier. But it's a long story – '

I smiled again. 'I have all the time in the world. I have a tape recorder with me – do you mind?'

'Go right ahead,' he said, amusedly. He had a broad, engaging grin and blue eyes with an unusual quality of penetration. I set up the machine on the table, switched on.

'When you're ready,'

He stared down at the cigarette in his hand for a long time before finally raising his eyes.

'You'd better have the full story,' he said slowly.

After his wife died in 1975, Donald Carter's life disintegrated inexorably, with quickening pace. He missed her, and he also missed the security and activity of Service life. Difficulty in acclimatisation increases in direct ratio to time served, and after twenty-five years in the RAF, Carter found civilian life a depressing jungle. For years, he buried his grief and nostalgia in a succession of underpaid, uninteresting jobs; he even stopped looking at the sky each morning. Gavin, his son, was at boarding school, and Carter gradually lost touch even with the small group of fellow cast-offs in the Ex-Apprentice Association.

He drifted listlessly from job to job, uncertain of the future, unhappy with the past. His wife Jean tried to help him as best she could – nagging, encouraging, even swearing at him at times and always providing maximum support and comfort. And always Carter would come in, throw his P45 on the table and head for the Sherry bottle.

So it went. Until suddenly, Jean was gone. The suddenness of it shattered Carter. The cancer had consumed her with the speed of a forest fire. In hospital, all they could do was make an exploratory incision, shake their heads, stitch her up again and send her home to die.

Afterwards, Carter went downhill very quickly. Gavin was now a flight cadet at Cranwell with a permanent commission. During that year his father aged visibly. He became careless about his surroundings and his person, ate only when hungry, drank a good deal too much, took a bath only when he could no longer stand his own stench. Intervals between shaves stretched from days to weeks. Eventually there came a time when Gavin, now a qualified transport pilot, drove down from his Wiltshire base alone to make a final attempt to get him back on his feet.

He made Carter change before going to the pub and once there, stared with distaste at his father across the table.

'Look at yourself, Dad! Walking round like a bloody tramp!

How long have you worn that suit?'

Carter shrugged.

'Christ, I'm ashamed of you. Can't you even wash a shirt? You'll start turning into one of those dirty old men in raincoats if you're not careful. I know you miss Mum, but –'

'Let's leave her out of this, shall we?'

His son took a deep breath. 'I'm damned if I will, you old goat. Mum wouldn't have liked to see you this way. My God, if I didn't keep an eye on you, you'd end up in the workhouse.'

Carter sniffed. 'They don't have them any more.'

'I wouldn't be surprised if they opened one specially. And what about that pigsty you live in? Can't you find a daily woman?'

The older man flushed. 'They're hard to come by. And they don't stay . . .'

Gavin sighed, finished his drink, got a new round in. They lit cigarettes and sat in uncomfortable silence for a long time. It wasn't just the clothes, Gavin thought. The Old Man was turning into – an old man? The once-dark hair was grey around the ears, a little thin on top; the strong hands that once had hoisted him overhead with ease were slim and bony and trembled at times. He felt the dull ache of pity – not only for his father but for the human race, doomed to so short a tenure on life. He drank a little beer, set the glass down.

'Dad – I've got some news. You're going to *have* to look after yourself. I've been given a posting . . .'

'Oh?'

'Hong Kong. Hercules squadron. I want to go, Dad – it's my first overseas tour. But . . . I could get released on compassionate grounds.'

Carter stirred in his seat. 'No need. It'll look bad on your annual Form 1369 – do your career no good. I'll be okay. What about the family?'

'We all want to go – Shirley and Peter too. But Shirl's worried about you, Dad – she thinks you don't get enough to eat.'

'Don't talk bloody daft.' Carter said equably. 'Anyone would think I had one foot in the grave.'

Gavin stirred uncomfortably in his seat. 'You out of work again?'

'Sort of. Couldn't stand that selling business – walking

23

miles, conning old ladies . . .' Carter frowned into his glass.

His son grinned knowingly. 'I suppose you gave the sales manager an earful?'

'Well . . .'

'I thought as much. Dad, you have to take the world as it is, not the way you'd like it.'

Carter scowled. 'There are three kinds of robin, boy. Robin Redbreast, Robin Hood, and salesmen, the robbin' bastards. I could tell you a few things . . .'

'You eating regularly?' Gavin broke in.

'Not much point cooking for one. And the price of take-aways – a pound for fish and chips . . .'

'You short of money?'

'Christ – of course not. I get by.'

Gavin finished his beer. 'You could get a home help, you know – on Social Security.'

Carter grinned. 'Something long and slim and full of gin?'

'Look, Dad – it's three years since Mum . . . I mean, she wouldn't want you to go on alone, you know. You're not past it – with a shave and a decent suit –'

'Thank you very much.'

His son sighed, exasperated. 'It's just that I'd feel better, knowing you were settled.'

'When do you go?'

'Four weeks. Spot of leave with Shirl's parents, then we fly out from Lyneham. Here – did you see the *Gazette* last week?'

Gavin's father sneered, took a sip of beer. 'Since when do I need to look at the *London Gazette*? Even if I could afford it?'

'Second ring came through. Substantive flight looie.'

'Well done. Have a beer.'

Gavin grinned. 'That's more like it. It's my shout. Look, Dad – we'll be away two years, but I'll be commuting a bit – I'll drop in from time to time.' He went up to the bar, bought a fresh round, sat down again.

Carter said 'Cheers.' Then: 'I don't want you getting your knickers in a twist, Gav. I can manage. I won't write every week, but I'll answer all your letters. A deal?'

'Okay . . .'

Gavin, uncertain and worried, concealed his feelings: there were ways of keeping tabs on the old boy. He glanced at Carter, and a poignant tide of emotion welled up within him, as he remembered how his father used to be: tall, straight, uniform well-tailored and smart, the pilot brevet above the double row of ribbons; the two rings and 'scraper' of the squadron leader – an analogy, old as flying itself, of the arrangement of rings upon an engine piston; Mother beside him at some garden party, flowery dress flapping in the summer breeze, elbow-length gloves, modest gin and tonic held close against the buffeting of passing guests . . .

He sighed, remembering. 'I still think you should find yourself a rich widder woman, Dad,' he said, half-serious.

Carter's eyes glinted. 'You want a knuckle sandwich?'

His son grinned. 'Reaction at last.'

'Drink your beer and shut up!'

'But –'

'Cheers.'

Gavin represented the third generation of pilots in the Carter family: his son Peter would be the fourth. Peter – or maybe Donald Mark Two, currently halfway down the production line and due for his first solo flight three months after his mother reached Hong Kong. Charles Auckinlek Carter's Camel had collided with an Albatross in 1918, yet he still had a life of sorts, in the depths of an old metal trunk – a fading collection of old logbooks, leather helmets, a silk scarf or two.

Donald Charles Carter was born with immaculate timing in 1919, seven months after his father was killed – thus ensuring that he would be old enough to volunteer for the RAF in 1939. He crossed the Atlantic with the first wave bound for American training schools, and came home with 15,000 others in the *Queen Elizabeth*, early in 1942.

In learning to fly, he discovered a very strange thing. The moment he left the ground for the first time in the Tiger Moth, he was terrified; yet the sheer surging acceleration of that run across Smith's Lawn, the initial rocketing climb, overwhelmed his fears. And it was just as well. Surrounded by forty jubilant ex-schoolboys, he would rather have died than ask to be relieved from flying duties.

Back in England, he began to learn to use the aeroplanes he had been taught to fly. Just as the involvement and complexity of flying training left no room for fear, neither did the operational training and the two tours of air fighting which followed. Provided the flow of new distractions continued, he was content.

There were times when he tried to analyse his terrors. What was it that caused that tension in neck muscles, that sick feeling in the gut, the tightening of scrotum and loosening of sphincter? Not fear of falling – once airborne, he had no sensation of height; the ground seemed equally remote whether he was flying at 10,000 or 20,000 feet.

Fire? The danger was there – but he discounted it. He knew what it meant to crash and burn. He had seen men with no faces and enormous courage – courage which he himself would never possess; but then, he was a trained pilot. There were two ways of putting an aeroplane on the ground: one of them involved being able to use it again. He had no intention of investigating the second.

It could be, of course, that there was a German shell or bullet with his name on it. But that idea, too, he rejected. Someone else's name maybe – but never Carter's. He believed that instinctively.

His instructors, naturally, recognised his problem, but continued with training. They knew from experience that highly-strung young men under pressure tended to fight extremely well, provided they had only themselves to worry about. His gunnery and aerobatic assessments carried the day: they recommended him for fighters.

Carter, despite his own misgivings, was neither a fool nor a coward. Cowards recognise their fears, succumb, run away. He recognised them, came to terms with them and lived with them – which is about as close as one can come to describing a brave man. With his move to a Spitfire squadron, a flood of new external distractions was released – most of them sporting black crosses – and for a very long time he found he was unafraid.

He stayed on after the war in a restricted-promotion career, but with increased leisure and minimal activity, the old fears returned in strength. He began to imagine that some vengeful Fate pursued him, and with very little encouragement he could have developed a persecution mania.

There were good grounds for his suspicions.

He applied, with a friend, for a helicopter posting to

Malaya, and came second in a shortlist of two. Three weeks later, his friend died when a helicopter main rotor snapped near Kuala Lumpur. On an instructor's course a year later, be brought down a Vampire fighter, reported it as 'flying like a brick shithouse'; a staff instructor took it up on test, and the machine broke up in mid-air, killing the pilot.

He began to feel depressed at that time. How *could* all this be simple coincidence?

Driving back from Cheltenham, his car blew a tyre, rolled through a hedge and caught fire: Carter emerged singed but intact. On a clay pigeon range, he bent to pick up a stray cartridge – at the instant the man on the next butt fired accidentally, shredding the fence a foot above Carter's bent back.

There is no law of averages. If twenty pilots fly twenty planes for a year, during which time each plane has an engine failure, there is no way each pilot will have one emergency apiece. A few pilots may collect one or two; two or three unfortunates may have more; perhaps half will escape scot-free. One man will have six or seven – and be dubbed 'accident-prone'.

In 1950, Carter found himself flying a Mosquito trainer from the south coast to Yorkshire on a day of frightening turbulence, bouncing around and fighting to hold level some 2,000 feet beneath the thunderclouds. An undercarriage door-lock failed: the door whipped open and the Mosquito headed groundwards in a violent near-vertical sideslip, out of control. Carter, fighting to bale out, found his head jerked back again and again towards the seat he had vacated. His radio microphone plug had jammed in the seat-frame. He saw the ground coming up very fast, and prepared to die.

The increasing speed ripped away the open door: the Mosquito lurched into a straight dive from which he barely recovered in time, swooping so low that the tail-wheel ploughed through soft soil and cabbages and was torn away.

To the day he died, Carter suffered a nervous twitch, as if he was dragging his head against some unseen hindrance which bound him to a doomed aircraft. He left the Service when the time came, threw away his medals, burned three fat log books.

If he never saw an aeroplane again, it would be much too soon . . .

THREE

Now the people of Angkor began to ask, nay, to demand in public, whether it might not be preferable to live, even temporarily, under the heel of a tyrant invader – for once his rape of the land was ended, he might extract far less in taxes than the kings and the lords of the court. Was it not possible that the Siamese invaders might bring wealth and prosperity once more to Angkor? Their armies, certainly, would need to be fed and bedded, their horses and their elephants tended, and their soldiers eased of the burden of their pay in the inns and brothels. But how much better, they reasoned, that a man should keep the greater part of his crop to feed his children and barter for those things he had never had, than that the treasure vaults of Jayavarman should bulge at the seams – as they did now, even after paying for the new-fangled cannon from great China to the north.

Liberation, quite suddenly, seemed close at hand . . .

Alone, Carter settled down into something resembling normality. He washed, shaved most days, found a new job as traffic manager for an oil distribution company, and began to refurbish his small house in Bassett, on the outskirts of Southampton. More important, he worked on reducing his drinking, because he knew he was halfway to being an alcoholic.

This frightened him considerably. The letters to and from Hong Kong helped him a great deal, and a month after the family left for the Far East, Gavin began to hope that his father was truly a changed man. But inevitably, after exhausting every possible means of preoccupying mind and body, the old fears returned, and Carter began to drink again. The intervals between letters stretched beyond reason, and on the far side of the world, Gavin gnawed his fingernails.

'Three weeks, Shirl, and not a word. He could be dead, for all we know.'

His wife Shirley looked up from her book. 'There must be something we can do. Can't you write to the Social Services?'

He stared gloomily. 'He'd never speak to me again.' He walked to the window, gazing out over the sparkling water towards Kowloon, where the tower blocks reared like stone-age dolmens against the setting sun. A red-and-white hover-marine moved like some giant dragonfly across the surface, packed with commuters, homeward bound. 'Besides,' he said, 'Dad's no invalid. He's fit enough.'

'Developing a bit of a pot belly, last time I saw him.'

'True. But otherwise I hope I'm in as good shape when I'm his age. You know, I think I'll have a word with Ted Hughes – Harry Hopkirk's navigator. He's going home Thursday, tour expired. Lives at Chandlers Ford, near Dad. I'll ask him to call in and drop off our last ciné films – it'll make a good excuse to check up on him.'

His wife sighed. 'He hasn't been the same since Mum died –'

'I know.' He turned to look at her. 'I wanted to ask you something, Shirl.'

'Like: should we bring him out here for a holiday?'

Gavin swung round, astonished and pleased. 'You must be a mind-reader! I'll have to watch what I think about in future.'

'I know already,' she said blandly. 'It's darts night at the club. But you won't have darts on your mind when you come home . . .'

He grinned. 'How right you are. About Dad: I can always get a concession fare for him. It won't cost much.'

'You really think we should, Gav?'

'Why not? He could come out with the school holiday flight next month, stay about eight weeks. Maybe we can get him straightened out in that time.'

Shirley nodded, watching the light fade into glorious pink in the open window. The night insects were already buzzing and whining; soon she would have to close the drapes. She thought it would be very good, not only for Donald Carter, but for Gavin; he worried too much about his father, and she had been the wife of a pilot long enough to know that happy, unworried pilots tended to die of old age and boredom, avoided accidents and lived a great deal longer in consequence. She watched with affection the broad shoulders and sturdy legs of the man who had fathered her children, and rested her hands instinctively upon the swelling curve of her pregnancy.

'Do it, darling,' she said softly. 'Do it – soon. Life's too short to spend it apart from the people we love . . .'

Donald Carter held cigarettes at the ready: the instant the NO SMOKING light went out, he lit up with indecent haste and settled back in the seat of the 707, staring out at the opaque greyness of the clouds through which they were climbing. He was oblivious of the mock groans from the adjacent seats: his thoughts were on other things, other times.

Debby Worthington sniffed. 'I do *so* hate the smell of smoke.'

'You smoke yourself – you're too young to know any better.'

'I do too, Colin Todd. I'll be fifteen next month – but I don't like it.'

'Being fifteen?'

'Oaf. Smoking, I mean.'

She reached up, opened the overhead vent and the cold current sliced through Carter's smokecloud; he turned, said, 'Sorry,' and put out the cigarette.

Debby smiled, nodded. The man in the next seat was human after all. His lined face was like the antique dresser at home, she thought – it had taken a few knocks in its time, but stayed in reasonable shape. He seemed – careworn? No – not exactly. She glanced curiously at him. His suit was badly pressed, worn, egg-stained; there were new shaving-cuts on the lined face. The blue shirt was new but soiled, and she could see a tidemark under his ear, where he had stopped washing. Debby experienced both pity and disgust. How could older people let themselves *go* like that? She began to wonder why he was on the flight at all: the only other adults were escorts and two new teachers bound for the colony schools.

When they had taken off at Gatwick, he had sat alone at the rear of the cabin, wrapped in isolation; at Singapore she had left the smoke-stained DC8 with him, and he had looked white-faced, shaken . . .

She turned her head away, looked at Colin. They had

travelled together several times. At first, he had taken the lead to which his two years' seniority entitled him, unfuriatingly superior, to the point of taunting. It didn't seem to matter now: she was grown up, wore make-up by choice and a bra of necessity. But he still persisted on treating her like a younger sister.

He was totally engrossed in his paperback, the cover of which depicted a three-decker of Nelson's navy. Debby knew it concealed an illicit porn magazine purchased in Singapore the previous night, but Colin read on in happy ignorance. Occasionally, he took a massive bite at his apple, pausing with full mouth over some garish passage in the book. She frowned, unable to understand the obsession of young men with sex and turned again to Carter.

'I'm Debby Worthington. This is Colin Todd.'

'Hi, Debby. Donald Carter. Colin – pleased to meet you.'

They shook hands self-consciously; his hand was cold and moist, and Debby resisted an urge to reach for a tissue. 'Col and I are going to Hong Kong for the holidays – eight whole weeks. Are you going to stay?'

'Only for a while,' Carter said equably. 'To see my son and his family. He flies transport aeroplanes.'

'Colin's Air Force, too,' Debby confided. 'My Dad's a major, in the Army.' She groped in her bag for boiled sweets, offered one to Carter; he accepted gravely and thanked her. She watched him surreptitiously as he fumbled to remove the wrapping. His fingers were long, brown, with noticeable knuckles, and they seemed to tremble periodically; she watched, fascinated, observing the traumas of the old. His hair was a little grey, eyes distant and surrounded by tiny wrinkles which shifted attractively when he smiled, yet he wasn't *really* old. He was tall – as tall as Daddy, even – and a bit podgy round the middle, but his voice was nice, deep and vibrant. She decided she liked Mr Carter. She disliked fat men – like Skull, the art master, who leaned too close to examine her work, who dropped chalk in the aisle so that he could look up her skirt.

Quite suddenly, Debby recognised intuitively the unease which Carter wrapped around himself like an invisible cloak: he was actually afraid! As the veteran of a dozen holiday flights, Debby found this vastly mysterious, intriguing; she stared down the length of the Boeing, taking in the subdued

31

lighting, spotless russet carpet, gleaming décor. They were still climbing through cloud: she found the panorama of normality pleasing and reassuring.

Some forty seats were empty – mostly aft, where she sat. Passenger control on boarding had been superficial, and they sat where they chose. Soon adults were undergoing some harassment from the younger children, and the stewardesses weighed in to help. Debby crunched her sweet satisfactorily, parking a piece in each cheek, watching the movement within the cabin. Four of the staff were recognisably Chinese – small, lithe, bow-legged creatures in flat-heeled shoes, hiding behind toothy smiles. One was a gaunt Sino-American blonde with a grating voice and nicotine-stained fingers, who seemed to be in charge; the sixth was a slim, black-haired girl of startling beauty. Not Chinese – Debby couldn't yet distinguish between the half-dozen races she had encountered in the East. The girl could be Vietnamese, Laotian, Thai – perhaps even a Phillipino; her face was an integrated medley of parabolic curves, encompassing cheeks, eyes, chin, small, sculpted nose.

Debby thought herself ugly, and was constantly searching for the ideal on which she could plan her own metamorphosis; the tall stewardess came very close to it. The schoolgirl was young enough to crave beauty, old enough to be envious: she watched the way the Asian girl moved slickly within the blue gaberdine uniform, and sighed for the years that must pass before she, too, could move thus. She winced, watching the narrow, nipped-in waist, the superb, almost exaggerated breasts.

Colin nudged her in the ribs. 'I fancy that!'

'She's old enough to be your mother,' she said contemptuously.

'Rubbish – she's only about twenty –'

'And the rest, fatty. You can't tell, with these Eastern women.'

Colin grinned wickedly. 'You know what they say about them?'

'It's probably rude, and I don't want to know,' she said tartly. 'And don't think you're fooling anyone with that paperback, Colin Todd!'

He grinned guiltily. 'You're too young to understand . . .'

'Filthy beast!'

'Wait till you're a bit older –'

She turned back to Carter. 'Do you like flying?'

He was silent for a moment. 'I've done a lot of it, at one time and another. It's not a thing I liked or disliked – just a job.'

The schoolgirl, mature beyond her years, sensed he was hedging, but hesitated to probe further. 'I used to be scared stiff,' she said presently, 'but I'm all right now.'

Carter nodded. 'Everyone is, to start with. It takes some people longer than others to get used to it.'

She thought about that. Best not embarrass the old fellow. She glanced at him, caught his eye and smiled, and the innocence and candour of her youth caught at his heart and he turned away, watching the grey mists fleeting past the window. Old age was ten per cent self-pity and ninety per cent jealousy, he thought . . . That, and irrational envy. He had lived most of his life to the full, enjoyed it; yet he begrudged these children the future he would never see. By the time he had been ten years in his grave, they would be raising families: what wonders would those children see, in the century to come? Sixty or seventy years, he thought drowsily: such a short time, really. Deduct the first eighteen years of school, the last ten before physical disability sets in, and one was left with perhaps thirty years of *life* . . .

The design, he thought numbly, was incomplete, flawed. Mankind deserved a hundred years at peak . . . what wonders could he perform then? And memory should be inheritable . . . if one could be born with the knowledge and experience of one's parents, learning from their mistakes, steeped in the depths of their love . . .

He fell asleep, a faint smile around his relaxed mouth.

Within the port wing of the Boeing, close to the root end attachment points, a double row of titanium bolts passed through spacer tubes to secure a massive steel member, nestling in channels of extruded light alloy. Around several of the bolt holes in the metal, tiny cracks radiated outwards, concealed beneath the large plate washers of the bolt assemblies, and by the thick anti-corrosive coating on the metal itself.

Between one pair of bolts, upper and lower, two cracks wandered randomly but inexorably towards each other. As the

33

mainplane flexed in flight and upon landing, the cracks extended almost imperceptibly, a millimetre of movement requiring hundreds of flying hours, and the metal absorbed infinitely small quanta of energy from the imposed stresses. This process had been in train for many thousands of flying hours, and the energy was not dissipated entirely in heat, or electrical energy, or momentum. It was stored within the nuclear lattice of the metal itself, which would eventually change in characteristics, becoming crystalline in structure, brittle, and with almost none of the strength and elasticity of the original metal, of which it would become an isotope. When that happened, very little force would be necessary to break the metal. This process, metal fatigue, was well-known to the Boeing engineers in Seattle, who had produced years previously a system of inspections involving removal of the bolts and the use of X-ray spectroscopy to identify any change in the metallic structure.

The old aeroplane had changed both owners and identity. Her new engineers believed, from the aircraft logs supplied by Larkin and Gabor, that these and other inspections had been carried out properly. Indeed, they had – but on a disintegrating wreck of a 707 in the Arizona desert.

On the previous flight, the cracking process had accelerated enormously, reducing by one half the distance between the advancing cracks. An hour after take-off on this flight, the spar metal underwent an abrupt and significant change in structure. The colour changed instantly to a pale, powdery grey and the cracks raced towards their final rendezvous. With each successive positive and negative deceleration, the wing structure began to groan, the noise remaining inaudible above the slipstream and jet roar. One of the bolts, now resting in an ever-widening channel, began to rotate, and at intervals it blurred visibly in violent reaction to the subsonic vibrations within the wing.

Thirty-eight thousand feet below the Boeing, the sea rolled and tossed uneasily beneath the towering cloud banks, reacting to the pressure wave of the storm front eight hundred miles to the north, across the China Sea.

34

FOUR

Thus it came to pass that the Siamese came down from the hills like the waves of the Eastern Sea, pouring across the plain to the walled city of Angkor. But the city was already betrayed: the gates, the secret tunnels, the canal network were all open to the lethal horde – opened by renegade Buddhist priests who cared nothing for the fall of Angkor, but only for the rise of the Lord Buddha, and also by the merchant princes and adventurers who most expected to gain from the occupation. Before the people of Angkor were fully awake that dark midnight, the streets were filled with the screams and blood of the slain and the flash and slash of curved bronze swords, stained bright red in the stark moonlight. Fires glowed throughout the city, and along the western horizon flames clawed skyward from Siamese campfires and burning villages alike. The people of the city fled, but found no refuge: they died where they fell, with a single question unanswered upon their lips. The mighty, the invulnerable city of Angkor had fallen. But how?

Eddie Wu Pak was uneasy. All pilots have a sixth sense for danger, an innate awareness defying description, that warns them when something may be amiss. The image taking root in Eddie's mind was more than a hunch, less than a premonition. Yet pilots are realists too: ask them if they believe in extrasensory perception, and they will walk away in disgust. Maybe it was the weather, he thought numbly . . . But then he thought of that canvas waistcoat and the soaring gambling debts that it alone could pay off. He *needed* this trip just to break even, maybe leave a little working capital. Climbing out of Singapore, he tried to justify his decision in the light of the forecast weather, and found it hard. That damned typhoon up near Manila could move any which way, and alternative landing sites were hard to find around Hong Kong.

And now the aeroplane herself. He made another slow, methodical scan of the instruments; they were climbing in cloud on autopilot, passing 20,000 feet. The altostratus contained scattered 'cobblestones' – regions of heavy turbulence which made the plastic beaker on his console vibrate jerkily towards the edge. Wu Pak shifted uneasily in his seat, turned to the flight engineer.

'Any problems, Charlie?'

'Board all green, skipper.' They spoke in English, the *lingua franca* of the airways.

The pilot nodded absently. He looked at the co-pilot, monitoring the instruments.

'I'll take it now, Chang.'

'You have control, Captain.'

Flight deck protocol was observed scrupulously – Eddie ran a tight ship. He released the autopilot, resting hands and feet lightly upon the controls, absorbing the forces and movements shifting in ceaseless patterns through the Boeing. He adjusted rudder trim slightly, trying yet again to eliminate the built-in skid to port; failing as always. He ignored the gentle porpoising – it was something the crew disliked, but accepted, after the ground engineers came up with no answers at all.

Eddie Wu Pak thought about all these things, well aware that the aeroplane wasn't a hundred per cent. Nothing, other than trim, that he could pin-point: in fact the old girl performed above specification in some areas of the flight envelope. And yet . . .

He shrugged, engaged the autopilot, handed over to Chang and lit a Marlboro. Very soon they broke through cloud-top, still tail-down in the climbing configuration. The sun overhead gave a strange luminosity to the irregular cloud-tops; at 30,000 feet, they formed a roughly level plateau, horizon to horizon. Scattered along the northern skyline, mountainous cumulo-nimbus clouds of vertical development were bursting like nuclear explosions. The upper air was unstable: once triggered, the thunderheads reached 40,000 feet within minutes.

'Nasty, Chang.'

'Yes, Captain. With luck, we'll clear the tops. If not –'

'Then we'll work round them. The vertical winds in those things are unbelievable. But we're not at full load. We can make forty-two thousand feet if we have to.'

The co-pilot nodded impassively. He had flown with Eddie Wu Pak long enough to realise that the captain was worried. Not about the rough weather ahead – they had flown through worse conditions before. Chang frowned a little; Eddie's mood was catching.

Eddie stood up, stretched, spoke briefly to the flight engineer again and went aft on his customary walkabout. He found Dolly Feng in the aft galley, talking to the new girl brought in to replace a surprised and very pregnant Claudine. Eddie looked at the small waist, long legs, and liked what he saw. It might be nice to get this new girl in the same kind of trouble.

'Captain, our new girl – Liane Dang Ko.'

The girl put a hand forward nervously: he noted the long, slim fingers, translucent nails – fingers which seemed boneless and capable of bending far back towards the wrist. She flushed, and her pale lemon skin seemed to take on the glow of fresh honey. Eddie retained the hand, complimenting her.

'I was trained as a ceremonial dancer, Captain, as a child. The finger exercises were most painful, but we learned. My parents died when I was small, and I lived at the dancing school.'

The pilot blinked. 'You must dance for me, sometime, Liane.'

She hesitated. 'I have not danced for years, Captain. Excuse, please. It is necessary to keep up with the exercises and movements.'

Eddie nodded. Plenty of time, little bird. 'You think you will like this crew?'

'Oh, yes, Captain. I think so.' Her English was grammatically correct, but stilted and spoken with a lilting accent.

'So. Tonight in Kowloon, we will all eat together – all the crew.'

Dolly Feng shot a glance at the young girl: the lashes were long and dark on smooth cheeks. This one isn't for you, Eddie Wu – stick to your bar girls and the footloose American women in down-town Hong Kong. She looked at the captain.

'The weather is not good?'

'We'll miss most of it, Dolly. Fly over it, if we have to. The landing forecast is good.'

Dolly Feng's lips tightened dubiously. Eddie wondered again what the hell had gotten into the crew on this trip. Doll was strong, experienced, full of guts – yet even she had a frail, pinched look about her. Nerves? Strain? He allowed his old confident smile to break out, but later, back in his seat, he lit another cigarette and watched anxiously as the storm clouds came marching from the horizon towards the scudding Boeing.

Donald Carter dozed lightly on the fringe of wakefulness, aware of the noise and activity in the background as a dull, hypnotic resonance; at times, it faded into absolute silence and he hovered on the periphery of sleep like a lost soul in limbo, until he jerked in nervous reaction and the noise came flooding back.

When had he last flown? Fourteen, fifteen years ago? It didn't seem as long as that. That final week of service . . . He remembered the last flight in the two-seat Lightning with Jock Hammond, his lifelong friend – a big, raw-boned Scot with gnarled, delicate hands and the biggest Mess bills in the business. The film of memory began unwinding: the titanic boost down the runway in reheat; vertical climb to 30,000 feet; a smooth, co-ordinated aerobatic sequence with tight 6-G turns; the constriction of G-suit around legs and gut, holding back the blood-flow to the feet; rocket climb to 60,000 feet; smooth acceleration to Mach 2; meteor-like plunge to sea level; the slow, relaxed stooge back to base . . .

After they landed, Carter had walked away from the aeroplane without looking back. But there was a hollow ache within him; some part of him, he knew, was still up there in the high altitudes.

He stirred in his seat, restless and unhappy. He was stiff and a little sore. Beside him, Colin and Debby talked, as children do, of adults asleep nearby.

'He's quite nice really, Col.'

'But scruffy.'

'Oh, foof. He's all right. I think he's all alone – never mentioned his wife. He's got a nice smile.'

'Never mind his smile. Do you want a look at my book?'

'What a dirty little man you are. I say, did you see his hands shaking?'

'So are mine. You should see this . . .'

'Idiot.' She shoved at him with her shoulder. 'Do you think he's afraid of flying?'

He considered. 'No. Most people have shaky hands. I remember Gran Walters before she died –'

'How old was she?' Debby stared at him.

'About eighty.'

'Mr Carter's not that old – not yet.' She giggled at the thought.

Carter closed his eyes, sensing the glance she shot his way.

Colin sniffed. 'I dunno. Everyone over thirty is old. I've decided not to grow up. Waste of time.'

The girl said softly: 'He says he's flown before – as a job. No,' she announced, 'he's not scared. It must be something to do with the muscles. My hands sometimes shake when I lift something heavy.'

'Mine shake when I read a book like this. Look, Deb – what about that? You'd hardly think that would be physically possible, would you?'

'What? Oh, you beast, you made me look. Men *are* disgusting.'

'All men?'

'And boys. Show me that again . . .'

The silence stretched into minutes. Carter sank a little deeper into sleep, chin low on his chest. He groaned quietly at long intervals, and his hands, palms upward in his lap, twitched spasmodically. Sometimes his head jerked sharply to the right and the escape hatch would not open . . . he could see each separate cabbage in the field, swelling in the windscreen, and pieces kept falling off the aeroplane, until he sat in sickening horror in a glass capsule, fitted with controls connected to nothing, and fell down the endless vault of the sky, screaming silently.

Most flight emergencies originate in some minor and insignificant occurrence, in itself is only a temporary inconvenience; it is only when if forms the first in a series of associated events that fate becomes involved. At a certain stage, the aeroplane reaches a point of no return at which the situation becomes irretrievable: up to that point, given immediate and correct remedial action, escape is still possible.

The Boeing was doomed because a flight mechanic should have replaced eighteen inches of old iron locking wire on the cabin condensation drain plug – but that would have involved a half-mile walk in the heat of the day. Instead, he used the old wire again. Too often twisted and strained, it broke at the locking lug, allowing the plug to rotate slowly for almost two hours. Then the cabin pressure exceeded the resistance of the few remaining threads and the plug blew out with catastrophic violence.

At 38,000 feet, cabin altitude was maintained at 8,000 feet by pumping in air. When the plug blew out, however, the occupants were instantaneously raised effectively through 30,000 feet, to a region of very low air pressure and intense cold, with insufficient oxygen. The effect on the passengers, and particularly upon the children, was devastating.

Eddie Wu Pak reacted very quickly. He disengaged the autopilot, slammed the plane into a 45-degree bank, threw himself forward on the controls and forced the 707 into a steep dive, heading for thicker and warmer air. In the cabin, adults and children were flung against seats and roof, and the tide of panic burst its banks in a universal, terrified scream.

Up front, Eddie and Chang fought their own battle against the old enemy – gravity. Veteran of a hundred emergencies, the captain slowed all engines, lowered some landing flap, got the wings level, dropped the main gear. The forward speed slowed, the vertical rate of descent built up and they entered cloud at 30,000 feet, flight deck and cabin already thick with the grey fog of condensation. On instruments, the pilot left Chang to concentrate on the internal problems; the compass was swinging wildly, and he used coarse control movements to stay near their original course. On the way down, he made a rough mental calculation of their position: south-east of Saigon, over the sea, outside Vietnamese airspace.

The headlong descent slowed, stopped and the Boeing

levelled out at 14,000 feet, within ten degrees of its original course – an outstanding feat of airmanship by any standards. Eddie sent the flight engineer down into the hold to investigate.

'We have a hole you could put your foot through, skipper. Looks like the condensation drain valve blew out.'

Eddie Wu Pak winced. 'Can we make a temporary repair?'

'Let's hope so. That sea's too rough for swimming. I'll check back with you.' The engineer collected his tools and went below again.

The captain checked with Dolly Feng. 'What's the score, Doll?'

'Awful, Captain. Some of the kids are hysterical. We're doing all we can.'

'Sure. Anyone hurt?'

'One woman has a broken leg. Two kids with split heads . . . nosebleeds. It could be worse. What the hell happened?'

'Explosive decompression. If we can seal the hole, we can work up cabin pressure, get back to altitude. I –'

He never completed the sentence. The Boeing, ploughing along through turbulent stratus cloud, had no chance of avoiding the thunderhead buried within. There was a brief sensation of sinking, followed by a raging climb that pinned the crew to their seats, cutting off Dolly Feng in mid-screech. The aeroplane vibrated, surged, twisted with insensate fury, fighting the vortex of air currents, the almost-solid rain, enveloped in a hideous globe of thunder and noise and blue light.

The lightning bolt hit the forward radio antenna. Carter, pinned in his seat, heard it as a dull explosion, jerking him into a paralysis of fear. Millions of volts flooded the aircraft systems, jumping circuit-breakers, starting a dozen small fires. The cabin lights failed instantly, yet the long fuselage was lit almost continuously by searing blue-white fire from the lightning, which flickered all around through the churning storm clouds. There was a reek of ozone and burning rubber and vomit and the old half-remembered stench of fear. Medical authority denies its existence; those with experience *know*: the body exudes its own sour, fetid redolence, a rancid excretion of hidden sweat glands that lingers on skin and clothes for many days.

Beside him, Debby wailed and buried her head in his

shoulder. Shaken and disoriented by the stroboscopic nightmare of light and darkness, Carter held her tight, pressing her oxygen mask close to her face.

The flashes came almost without interval, and Carter absorbed the stark unreality of the scene; the stewardesses, caught as if in some weird light projector, progressing jerkily through movements like demented marionettes in some alien cartoon. He saw the mouths of children gaping. Already it seemed an eternity since the storm broke.

He had been fully aware of the enormity of the emergency from the moment it began, and he had fought to secure oxygen masks for himself and the children, holding them in their seats by brute force until he got their belts fastened around them. But now he sat, frozen in a cocoon of terror, feeling the precious thousands of feet winding away beyond recovery, he was rigid in the grasp of fear such as he had never known, passing into some unknown dimension of dread. His very being contracted into a tight, impermeable ball of tension, from which he could look forth upon his body abandoned to its own resources. Then, slowly, he began to relax inside his silver egg, aware that the world might burst asunder into oblivion, but he would remain, locked inside his own personal survival capsule. It was a reaction as old as humanity itself: had he been lying down, he would have curled his body in a foetus-like facsimile of life in the womb, within which dwelt the only real security mankind could ever know.

Time had no meaning. His eyes recorded the sequence of light and shadow, but his brain ceased to transmit signals in terms of duration or meaning. The sphere contracted still further and became immeasurably strong, and inside it he slipped into the non-sleep of pseudo-death.

The crew fought the electrical fires until the last flickered and died, using every appliance they could lay their hands on; the compartment was filled with the fumes of burning rubber, seared molten plastic.

Eddie Wu Pak sat hunched in his seat, coughing harshly, watching the few remaining instruments. Everything electrical was shot; only the Turn and Slip, altimeter and airspeed indicator remained on which to assess aircraft altitude. The flight engineer had completed his temporary repair, and the altitude was creeping slowly back up through 18,000 feet. They had breached the worst of the storm, but lightning still flickered eerily in the grey depths, and the turbulence persisted, jarring and hammering at the aeroplane through the tendrils of cloud silhouetted against the blue fire. They had no accurate indication of heading: the gyrocompass rotated madly, out of control, and the small E2 emergency compass was little better; it oscillated violently through an arc exceeding ninety degrees.

'Charlie – status?'

The flight engineer came forward, leaning over the centre console. 'Not good. All electrics out. Engine instruments shot, but we seem to be getting full power – no problems there. All fires out – and we are also out of extinguishers.'

'Any systems left? Radios? Radio compass?' Eddie asked dully.

'Not a goddam thing, Skipper. That flash really cleaned us out. Hydraulics seem okay, but we've no instrumentation.'

'Shit. This thing is going to shake itself to pieces if we don't get out of this crap soon. Chang – any idea of position? Did we get a Mayday out?'

'Negative, Captain. No time – we'd hardly gotten straight and level when that flash hit. We were about 200 miles off the Mekong Delta when the shit hit the fan. Say, thirty minutes ago.'

Wu Pak nodded slowly. 'Check. We were close to course at the bottom of the hill – between 020 and 030 degrees. We could be anywhere between Borneo, Manila and Hainan Island by now.'

'What are you steering now?' asked the co-pilot tightly.

'God only knows, Chang. That damned E2 is going round like a roulette wheel – and I don't feel lucky. I'm working her round to a westerly heading; we'll never make Hong Kong at this altitude, and if we climb, maybe that patch over the hole will blow again. I figure our best bet is Saigon. If we hold this heading for an hour, we should be over land. I'll let down slowly in about thirty minutes. With luck, we'll come out over the sea near the Mekong Delta.'

Chang nodded. 'Better call it Ho Chi Minh City, Eddie. There'll be no red carpet for us there. You want I should take it for a while?'

'Not yet. She's a bitch in these conditions . . . Go check with Dolly Feng.'

Suddenly the storm burst around them in renewed fury, ramming the engineer up against the roof. He came down asprawl, with blood spewing from an arm gashed on a sharp edge. He was swearing, half-crying in fear and frustration, clawing at the First Aid kit.

Eddie Wu Pak tried to think about the weather: clearly this was no ordinary thundercloud. Hell, they were going up and down like the drawers of a Chinese whore at New Year. That goddam depression had worked itself up into a king-sized typhoon . . . If only they had got a Mayday out . . . If only they could break out into clear weather . . . If only . . . Eddie grinned wryly. *If* your aunt had balls, Eddie Wu, she'd be your goddam uncle. He would have to let down soon, he told himself – but shied away from the thought. Even the Jap Kamikazes wouldn't let down through cloud when they got lost. Hold course for another twenty minutes, maybe. It wasn't good, but in this kind of situation, multiple emergencies one after the other, he had the tiger by the balls and couldn't let go. Whoever heard of an airplane with so much trouble and still flying?

He grinned cynically, and lit another cigarette with difficulty. Someone, he thought despondently, was calling in the markers on Eddie Wu Pak. He stretched mightily in his seat, watching the instruments, aware of the co-pilot and engineer working on a swing-down radio panel. Keerist . . . it was rough out there. One more lightning strike, one more fire, and it would be premature retirement for Eddie Wu Pak.

In the galley, Carter stood drinking a brandy, listening to the tumult outside the thin metal walls. The place was a stinking shambles of spilled food and drink, débris swirling to and fro around his feet. He felt jaded, battle-weary. For a man of his age, he thought dazedly, he had taken some beating. He had left Debby and Colin to help the cabin staff and between them, he and the Asian girl Liane had worked like demons, pacifying children and getting them into their seats, where they could yell their heads off in comparative safety. They found a woman passenger groaning in the aisle, a leg twisted awkwardly beneath her; Carter helped the stewardess lift the woman into her seat, watched her remove one of the woman's stockings and use it to lash a fire-axe splint to the leg. Liane found brandy in the galley store, made the woman drink four miniatures; maybe it was against all medical practice, but it had the desired effect: soon she fell into an uneasy sleep, and they left her.

Back aft in the cabin, Carter had time to look at the girl closely. Her nose had bled copiously and her right temple was swollen a deep purple colour. The long dark hair was disarranged: she put up a tired hand to straighten it, abandoned the attempt.

'You okay now?'

'Yes – thank you, Mr Carter.'

'Donald.'

She smiled wearily; the wide generous lips, rose pink, parted to reveal even white teeth. With Carter, she turned, staring down the long cabin, where some degree of order had now been established.

Carter turned back to the girl. 'You'd better let me fix that bruise. It doesn't look too good to me. And we could do with another drink – '

'Go back to your seat, Mr Car– Donald. I'll bring it to you.'

'What about your head?'

'I'll be fine. Please – ' She smiled tremulously.

He stared at her doubtfully, nodded shortly and walked back to his seat. He turned to watch the girl moving towards the aftmost galley, bracing herself against the violent motion of the aeroplane. Saw her reach a doorway, sway, lean against the frame. He moved quickly, got an arm around her, made her sit down in the tiny jump seat in the galley. He soaked a towel in water, wiped away the dried blood from nose and lip, cleaned up the head injury, gave her a brandy and found one for himself.

'Head aching?'

'Only a little – '

'Double vision?'

'No. I tell you, Mr Carter – '

'Donald.' he said again, grinning cheerfully. 'Just checking you had no concussion. But you should stay in here for a while – that was a bad knock.'

The girl shook her head. 'I have to go . . . The children – '

'— are perfectly all right,' he said easily. 'Panic's over. Take it easy — I'll be back in a moment.' He went forward, located the senior stewardess, learned her name. 'Miss Feng? Donald Carter. Look — I have your girl Liane in the aft galley. She took a bad knock on the head, but she'll be fine after a rest. Do you need her right now?'

Dolly Feng wiped her hands on a paper towel. 'No. Keep her there for a while, will you? Things are more or less under control here. How bad is she?'

'No concussion, but badly shaken.'

Dolly nodded. 'She's lucky, Mr Carter. We all are.'

Carter said: 'That's right. The pilot did well. I was in the game for years myself. Would he mind if I spoke to him?'

Dolly waved tiredly at the flight-deck door. 'Be my guest.'

He went through, closing the door behind him. In the cramped dark cabin, flash-photographed on his vision every few seconds by bolts of lightning, the pilots sat motionless.

'Name's Carter. Pilot myself for many years. Anything I can do?'

'Mr Carter. Thanks — no. We lost cabin pressure, but my engineer made a temporary repair — he's down below checking it out now. How are things back there?'

'Don't even ask,' Carter grunted. 'We'll be late in Hong Kong?'

'We can't make Hong Kong. Don't have the altitude. We can make Saigon okay — heading that way now. Plenty of fuel. Only . . .' The pilot hesitated. 'Only . . . we have no radio after that lightning hit.'

Carter stared at him, appalled. 'But we got a Mayday out, surely?'

'Negative. Happened too fast. We're shot on all bands, fella.'

Donald Carter was silent for a long moment, digesting an unpalatable fact. 'Weather?'

'Lousy. We've no aids to get down at Saigon, no landing forecast. We can let down soon, lose altitude out to sea, come back in under cloud. We'll hit the coast somewhere . . .'

In the dark cabin Carter bit his lip. 'Lucky we were out at sea when we took the dive. There's some very solid green clouds on the mainland.'

'Damned right. It was real rough for a while.'

They stared at each other in unspoken understanding. 'Good luck to you, Captain,' Carter said.

'Nice to talk to you, Mr Carter.'

'Tell me,' the old pilot said stiffly, 'no bullshit. What are our chances?'

The captain turned back to his controls, shrugged his shoulders once: there was no need of amplification – Carter read him loud and clear. Dazed and uneasy, he stumbled back to the galley, made sure Liane was resting and made her drink a little coffee, lukewarm from the rapidly-cooling urn. At intervals the cabin staff came in for supplies, smiling tiredly, making tense little jokes at which no one laughed. He could sense their fatigue and anxiety; they were all skating on the thin edge of hysteria, doggedly summoning up every last ounce of stamina and courage. His heart went out to them.

It made a difference, keeping busy. How well he knew it. He looked at Liane, who stood swaying loosely as the plane hit more turbulence, both hands cupped around the coffee beaker, hair-strands dark and gleaming, hanging randomly over a shoulder. He could see the lines of strain around the wide, mobile mouth; the corners drooped a little and a little tic appeared intermittently under her right eye. He tried to draw her mind away from their problems.

'Been flying long, Liane?'

'About three years, Mr – I mean, Donald.'

'With this crew?'

'No. This is first time with them. Before, I was with Captain Charles on the Viscount. He's an American.'

For some obscure reason, Carter felt discomfited, but the feeling passed immediately. He thought about the girl's voice – low, musical, with an odd lilting accent and an occasional misplaced emphasis on certain consonants.

'Your family in Singapore?'

'No. I lost my parents when I was a little girl. My uncle took me in – he was a teacher at the dancing school in Battembang.'

'Battem – which?' he said, puzzled.

She laughed. 'In Cambodia – Kampuchea now.'

He smiled. 'I get it. What happened to your parents?'

'They . . . died when I was six. My uncle said they were killed by the government.'

'I'm sorry,' he said softly.

She stared at him, eyebrows raised, unaware of the convention. 'Why should you be sorry, Donald? It was not your fault.'

Carter smiled. The girl began clearing up the galley, and as he helped her, he saw that her skin was unusually smooth, a pale, delicate shade of lemon; her lashes lay long and luxuriant upon her cheeks, natural and untouched. He had little experience of Asian women; he was only vaguely aware of the TV version – short, flat-footed, snub-nosed, with oddly-shaped eyes. This girl – woman, rather, for she must be in her late twenties – had a beauty which caught his breath, and a quality about her he had never before encountered. He glanced at the short, tight uniform skirt, split in the fashion of a cheongsam for ease of movement; it accentuated the small waist, the oblique slope to rounded hips, the long elegant legs.

She was almost as tall as he was: around sixty-nine inches, yet her small-boned body was lithe and balanced. His eyes returned again and again to the sensitive oval face, the large, luminous eyes: they had the slightest hint of angularity, characteristic of her race. In London she could have taken the fashion world by storm – yet here she was, working as a servant on some nondescript Third World airline . . . She was beauty in a strange, alien mould, and he felt uncertain, disturbed by her presence.

Carter, he told himself ruefully, you're too old to understand women of this age – any age, maybe. There was a vast ethnic and time barrier between them, and he had no yardstick by which to assess the emotions in her pale, composed face.

He left her there, groping his way back to his seat. The lightning still flickered in the cloudy depths, and the violence of the turbulence seemed to be increasing. He spoke briefly to Debby and the boy.

'Mr Carter?'

'Yes, Debby?'

'Are we going to die?'

He looked upon the face of the girl, compassion gripping his heart. She was old enough to understand the truth, but too young to absorb the fearful consequences; it was a time for prevarication, false optimism. Besides, much could happen in the hours to come . . . He checked his watch. They had been airborne for four hours.

'I think we'll be okay, Debby. The cabin pressurisation is

holding. The captain thinks he'll get us down all right, probably at Saigon. He's very experienced. But keep strapped in — it's still very rough. Hang on to me, if you like.'

Debby smiled uncertainly, gripping his hand; her fingers were damp, cold with fear, and he knew she was close to breaking. Colin Todd sat rigidly and mutely terrified, staring into infinity with teeth clenched so hard that the jaw muscles looked like knotted cord. Carter thought the boy did not look too good at all, but there was nothing he could do about it. Seat-belt tight, Carter sat back, bracing himself against the violence of the storm, watching the play of St Elmo's Fire around the wingtip, listening dully to the pounding of his own heart in his ears.

FIVE

The Lady Indibaraja awoke fearfully in her room, staring at the ceiling of her room and the flicker of reflected flames where no flames should be.

'My Lady.' Suriya, the woman servant, shook the shoulder of her mistress — an act which would merit instant disembowelment in other circumstances. 'The Siamese are in the city! We must hurry, my Lady. The Lord Yasovarman awaits in the outer courtyard.'

The princess frowned in the dim light of the tapers. So soon? It can only mean treachery, she thought helplessly.

'Help me, Suriya. My blue robes . . . The leather walking sandals. And my jewels, in the sandalwood box. How soon before the dogs arrive?'

The girl hesitated, close to tears. 'Within the hour, my Lady.'

'And my father, the king?'

'Lord Yasovarman says the king is at the temple with the palace guard, there to fight until the end.'

'Great Siva help us, girl. Lead the way. Quickly . . .'

'I . . . I am afraid, my Lady.'

'So am I, Suriya. But no Siamese dog shall see it. Hurry . . .'

Some ten minutes after Carter resumed his seat, the reactions of the Boeing underwent a significant change. It began to resonate in waves of a periodicity of about one minute, after the fashion of a railway carriage bogey passing over rails. The change in tempo and sensation penetrated Carter's rêverie. At the same time, they flew into very heavy rain, and the clouds took on an eerie glow, a luminescence born of the incessant lightning.

Carter could feel the play of opposing G-forces in the seat of his pants: the switchback was becoming more severe, and he knew the pilots would be fighting the turbulence with every ounce of their skill, guiding the plane over the worst hurdles like a thoroughbred horse. He could see the great port wing, sweeping back from the root end near where he sat: it was flexing to a frightening degree, like the limb of some living creature under torture. Never, in all his experience, had he seen a structure distorted so much and so often. He thought again of all the narrow escapes he had had throughout his flying career; all the times when he had cheated the Nameless Ones who had haunted him so long. Perhaps now, they would find their final victory, here, in some unknown corner of the sky above an alien sea.

Numbly he gazed out at the hellish panorama of savagery raging around the Boeing. Then abruptly he sat up, found a tissue, wiped the window clear of condensation.

No – he had not been mistaken. He wished to God that he had. In the instant between two lightning flashes, the appearance of the wing had definitely changed in some way. He waited for the next flare – and was sure.

Along the joint of wing and fuselage, rivets were popping. With each flash, a few more black holes replaced flush countersunk rivets – sometimes singly, at other times in a group. Even as he watched, stunned, a row of four neat holes appeared. He raised his eyes, staring fearfully along the length of the wing. Great God in Heaven! In addition to flexing, it was also twisting – not much, perhaps only a few degrees at the tip – but enough. There could be only one end to that, he thought grimly.

Donald Carter sat back, feeling curiously calm. He closed his eyes and speculated. Would he die when the aircraft broke up, mangled in tearing metal wreckage? Or would he survive long enough to experience the long nightmare fall through miles of cloud to the sea below? He saw himself being thrown clear into the freezing belly of the clouds, floating dreamily amid a welter of fragments, still strapped to his useless seat; imagined the ephemeral instant between emerging from the cloud-base and striking the concrete-hard sea below . . .

Remarkably, his fear had gone, replaced by a consuming ghoulish curiosity. *How long?* He shot an appraising glance at the wing joint. A few more holes . . . A few more minutes. It could go in thirty seconds, or it could last thirty minutes. And he was the only one of all the souls on board who knew that they were about to die. Suddenly, the magnitude of the turbulence shocks they encountered assumed vast importance.

His mind drifted back over the years to a bright March day in 1945, somewhere south of Bremen in Germany. At 25,000 feet. His Tempest squadron was operating sixteen aircraft out of Volkel airfield in Holland, against fighters launched from the Osnabruck airfield complex to attack the incoming stream of American B17Gs and B24 Liberators bound for Bremen.

The day, he recalled, was glass-clear, the white-brown carpet of Germany laid true from horizon to horizon. 'A' Flight peeled over into a long, shallow dive to intercept the group of Me262 jets taxying on Rheine Main airfield, five miles below; Carter took 'B' Flight north, to cover the bomb run of the American groups.

More than thirty years later, the scene remained as brilliant and sharp in his memory as if it was being flashed onto a cinema screen: a single block of sky, a five mile cube, virtually filled with bombers, flak, fighters, parachutes, bombs, débris, burning aircraft, flares.

A B17, both port engines on fire, broke away from its group, sideslipping to keep the flames at bay; Carter saw three, four parachutes open like white fungi behind it. Suddenly a black Me210 slid shark-like through the little knot of survivors, hammering cannon shells into the stricken bomber. Carter wondered dully why the German bothered: that one would never see the fields of East Anglia again. He was too distant to help: he could only swear brokenly at the sheer bestiality of it all.

The port wing of the B17 folded back, almost gently; it began to break up. The entire tail section aft of the gun blisters separated from the rest and glided away in some grotesque parody of a real aeroplane. Carter watched: it assumed a weirdly stable attitude, descending in shallow, wide orbits towards the ground so far below. He thought wryly that the tail gunner could be the only survivor – if he could just fly the damned thing down to earth.

Fly it?

Carter's eyes opened wide and he stared out into the hellish guts of the storm. It would never work . . . And yet . . . And yet . . . It was, he reflected, a simple case of shit or bust. He had nothing to lose. Worth trying? By God, he thought, damned right – if only because it gave him something to do, instead of just sitting there, waiting for the worst.

He got out of his seat awkwardly, nodded at Debby and Colin, went aft to the galley. Liane was alone, working with little enthusiasm.

Carter said urgently: 'How do I get into the tail section?'

'The . . . tail?' she said, uncomprehending.

'For God's sake,' he said violently, 'show me! Where does this door lead?'

She hesitated, finger to lips. 'It's – I'm not sure. A cargo space, I think. Or for the mechanics. I think it is empty – all baggage is in the hold. Why?'

He bit his lip, trying not to look at her. There was no option.

'Look, Liane, you mustn't panic. I've been a pilot all my life – I know about aeroplanes. This one is just about finished – the wing joints are cracking up. Do you understand what I mean, girl?'

Her eyes opened very wide. 'You are saying we are going to die?'

'Maybe. Maybe not. There's a chance . . . People have survived things like this, usually when they're sitting near the tail. How do we get in?'

'There is a key, I think – here.' She opened a bulkhead panel, took out a small square-section T-key. It fitted the two holes in the door. Carter twisted, pulled, and it came open. It was dark and bleak inside, and Liane found an emergency torch in the galley store; they went in together.

Twelve feet long, tapering from ten feet wide at the door bulkhead to less than four feet at the aft end, the compartment was filled with cable looms, control rods, and electrical and hydraulic pipelines; the metal floor was fitted with recessed eyebolts for lashing down cargo, and several hanks of inch-wide canvas webbing were neatly stowed on the bulkhead. Across the far end of the compartment stretched a massive shelf: the centre section of the huge tail plane.

Donald Carter took a last look around, and followed Liane back to the galley.

'Time's short. Just do as I ask and no questions. Go and get the boy and girl sitting next to me – quietly, no fuss. Get them in here. Find all the blankets, food and torches you can. We'll strap ourselves down back there and pray the tail end holds together. Hurry now – '

He walked steadily and without haste up to the flight deck. 'Captain?'

'Mr Carter – what now?' Eddie Wu Pak's face was lined with strain.

'Bad news,' Carter told him. 'You've got serious problems at the port wing root. Rivets popping everywhere – and the wing's twisting badly. A sort of flutter. Any chance of finding smoother air?'

'Such as where?' Wu Pak yelled above the tumult. 'Thanks a lot – it's just one more problem on top of all the others. We have no electrics, we're lost, unable to climb. I'm starting a let-down soon. Best get back there and hold on!'

'But the wing – '

'We'll have to take a chance on that. But thanks for the warning. In case we don't make it – God go with you . . .'

Carter stared. The captain grinned tiredly. 'I'm Chinese, but I went to a Christian school. Much good it did me!'

Leaning against the door for support, Carter smiled just once more. 'You're all right, Captain. If anyone can get us down, you will.'

He turned, left the flight-deck. It was odd: he was no longer scared. He smiled a crooked smile, and went back through the cabin to reassure the harassed women and frightened kids. There was nothing he could do to help them really – he wasn't even sure why he thought the four of them might survive. But he did what he could, with a smile, a brief word here and there, a look of confidence that was less than skin-deep.

It just wasn't going to work, he told himself frankly. He and Liane and the kids would die along with everyone else, so there was no point in hoping. He was as good as a walking corpse already. In some strange way that struck him as funny. Another odd thing: he found that decisions were getting easier to take all the time, maybe because they would not affect what was about to happen. Only . . . He frowned momentarily. Just think of it: very soon, he could be seeing Jean again! Imagine! It was an ill wind.

The others were already in the tiny compartment, and Debby and Colin's eyes were asking questions he could not answer. He took a last look down the length of the main cabin in the fading light, then closed the door. The torchlight showed white, strained faces. He made them sit down against the bulkhead.

'We've very little time left. This thing is going to break up very soon. Don't ask me how I know. We have just one chance — a very slim chance — back here. Often, in cases like this, the tail comes down in one piece. If we lash ourselves down very tightly on the floor, heads towards the door, we may just come down with it. But don't take any bets. Liane — how many blankets?'

'Nine, Donald.'

'Okay. Quickly, now.'

They folded blankets, made four rough palliasses; Carter secured each of the others to the deck with webbing straps until they could not move a finger and placed a roll of blanket under their heads. Liane was last. As he pulled the loop of material tight under her heaving breasts, he muttered a brief apology. She smiled wanly in the torchlight, her eyes bulging with fear.

In one corner, he tied down the small bundle of stores Liane had collected, before taking his position beside her. He worked frantically, getting the webbing tight across legs, thighs, chest; finally, with one arm free, he found the torch, worked the arm under a strap and took a final look round before switching it off and jamming it under his knee.

The Boeing was groaning now like some half-butchered animal. The end could not be far off. There was nothing to say, nothing to do but pray, and that had never been Carter's style. With mouth dry, heart pounding, palms wet, body soaked with sweat, he lay there, waiting . . . waiting . . .

Eddie Wu Pak fought the storm to the last, but never lived to collect the credit he so richly deserved. Carter's information about the wing had meant little to him, except to indicate a way this nightmare might end. Descending slowly, the aeroplane reached 15,000 feet, ran into a shear plane of vertical winds and fell like a stone for a thousand feet, before slamming into an updraft moving at close to 180 miles per hour. They might as well have collided with a brick wall: the accelerometer needle wound round to 7-G, and jammed; the port wing bent slowly upwards through 45 degrees, twisting half a turn, before fracturing at the root end. The entire process took less than two seconds: the doomed plane yawed violently to starboard, and then equally hard to port. This reversal of stress snapped the fuselage at the aft end, just forward of the tail plane. Still in cloud, the aeroplane began to break up, rolling very fast and shedding the remaining wing and engines. A stream of bodies, seats and equipment vomited from the open end of the cabin, until the whole pulsating wreck broke into a thousand tragic fragments. It is doubtful if even a large bomb could have destroyed the aircraft so completely. Such is the titanic strength of the air, at 600 miles per hour.

Freakishly, the nose section and flight deck still held together, and the pilots went down strapped to their seats, side by side. But the flight engineer shot into the void like a bullet from a gun, disappearing into the grey mists on his way to join his ancestors.

In the tail, Carter and the others were subjected to a hideous nightmare of sensations that lasted an agonising four minutes. As they tumbled in a three-dimensional whirlpool, their heads whipped cruelly back and forth with the sharply-reversing forces, bodies compressed agonisingly under webbing straps which became steel bars. Through it all, a bitter chill and dampness oppressed them, and they could hear a background pandemonium of thunder, whistling winds and the clatter of hail upon the metal surfaces of their coffin. Carter became aware, too, of the sibilant hiss of air over the structure of the tail – the only indication that they were really moving and not suspended in some sensory purgatory. He sensed that they were plunging ever downwards, and wondered dully what awaited them below: sea or sand, country or city, mud or forests, or mountains. Too late, he remembered the lifejackets stowed under every seat, and groaned at the prospect of a watery grave.

There were times, in that endless fall, when they seemed to slow and stall, hanging suspended while the airflow appeared to slow and stop. Carter's ears had long since abandoned all attempt to distinguish between up and down, and at times he winced in pain from ears aching from pressure imbalance. He opened his mouth to scream, joining the others in a unison wail of terror.

They fell through endless aeons of time, light years of space. Ludicrously, Carter found himself irritated beyond measure to find that it was taking so long to die. He would have preferred to go quickly and cleanly, and he spared a brief thought of grief for those who had already gone ahead, and those with him who were about to die. Unseen in the black hole, he wept tears for the dead of all time.

Many days later, when they returned to the place where they finally came to rest, Carter saw at once that only divine intervention could have saved them. And being totally without religious beliefs of his own, he experienced an uncertainty and bewilderment which stretched his mind on a rack of indecision for long years afterwards.

Reconstructing, he saw that they had lost altitude in the manner of a falling leaf, descending obliquely in a shallow dive, until a shift had occurred in the balance of lift and drag upon the tail plane. This shift had been followed by a gentle climb, a semi-stall, a sideslip in the reverse direction, and again a shallow glide.

The shattered tail section dipped below cloud, skimming diagonally across the valley and into the upswing as it approached the steep, jungle-clad slope. At 200 feet above the rocky ridge, it slowed, rotated gently, started the glide back, following the curvature of the slope. The speed was low – perhaps only 60 miles per hour – when it ploughed through the slender treetops and bamboo thickets, sliding ever more slowly, remaining upright, but swinging with mindless violence on impact with the trees of the forest along its track.

Carter's straps slipped a little, then gave way. He slid clumsily down the metal floor, ramming his head against the unyielding bulkhead. Incandescent fire flared before his eyes, and he was aware, fleetingly, of intense pain, before he dived headlong into a whirling vortex of silence.

SIX

Prince Yasovarman waited impatiently in the dark courtyard.
His guards stood apart, staring fearfully at a night sky red with
flames, listening to the roar of cannon beyond the city walls.
When the women appeared in the archway, he strode forward,
led the way into the mile-long tunnel, heading for the causeway
and the road to Angkor Vat. Angkor Vat – the miracle of the
world: a temple a mile square, with walls towering fifty feet
above the plain, every inch elaborately carved to depict the
history of the Khmer kings, since the time of Siva himself.
Within the inner citadel, the king awaited them in a vast room
with polished copper floor, shutters open to the smoke and
stench of battle, now drawing ever closer.

'My Lord,' he said, laying a hand on the shoulder of Yasovarman, 'I knew you would not fail me. But your duty is not yet
ended.' He beckoned Indibaraja closer. 'Below, my goldsmiths
are melting down the treasure of Angkor; others are extracting
the jewels from the palace plate and crowns, the sacred vessels
of the temple. The molten gold runs even now into deep
underground channels in readiness for the time when Angkor
will rise again. But you, Yasovarman and my daughter, go east,
to the land of the Chams and the great delta. With you goes the
treasure itself – three carts loaded with jewels such as the world
has never seen.'

'And you, O King?'

'Here,' Jayavarman said grimly. 'Here was I born, and here
shall I die. But you, Indi my child, must guard with your own
life those things which shall identify you on the day you return.
This, my elephant ring; this, the great statue of Siva – and the
treasure itself. And if any should then dispute your claim to the
Khmer throne, there is yet one more proof. That which you
bear upon your body, as do all females of the royal blood: the
War Elephant . . .'

'But father –'

'Go in peace, Indibaraja. And in peace return . . .'

58

It was dark, and the rain smashed in endless fury against the metal roof. Carter lay still, totally confused, wrapped in blankets. It felt as if his head had been split down the middle. He could hear voices somewhere in the blackness; he fumbled for he knew not what, and touched a warm face.

'Jean?'

'Mr Carter? Thank God you're still alive! It's Colin — Colin Todd! Are you all right?'

That, Carter told himself sourly, was a moot question. He grimaced, remembering. He could hear Liane and Debby somewhere out there in the darkness. Groping, he found a torch and switched it on. As he sat up in the dim light, the shadows started whirling and gyrating sickeningly around him, but soon things began to steady themselves. Turning his head with difficulty, he found himself staring at Liane high above him, her eyes wide and shining. Painfully, he clambered up, fumbled at her straps.

'Liane — are you hurt?'

'No, only my neck. It hurts when I move . . .'

'Mine too. Colin — you there? How's Debby? She all right?'

Debby answered him herself. 'I — I think so. Can you get me loose?'

'A minute, girl . . . A minute.' He freed Liane from her straps, made her hold the torch and then released the others. 'Easy now, don't wriggle around, Debby, or you'll slide down. Hang onto this loop . . . good. Nearly done.'

Soon they were stretched out on the tilted metal floor, clinging to webbing straps, staring at each other in total disbelief in the stark light, unable to comprehend that they were all alive. The door key was lost somewhere, down at the bottom; Carter crawled down, groped around — and there it was. Opening the door was not so easy: he had to call Colin up to help take the weight, then heave it over the point of balance. It crashed out of sight and the blessed rain sleeted in, warm and somehow reassuring in its discomfort. Hurriedly, they stacked the blankets in a sheltered corner before scrambling out.

They would have to do something about the way the tail section was lying, but for the moment all that mattered was that they were still alive. They crawled out into the downpour, slipping on the thick mat of vegetation underfoot. The slope was precarious, steep, the clouds low overhead, and they stood mutely in the grey half-light of the rain forest, drenched to the skin, faces raised to the sky whence they had fallen. Thunder rolled and crashed overhead. They were lost – so lost that they did not even know in which country, or continent, they had landed. But it did not seem to matter very much. They stood close together, constantly touching to seek reassurance, shaking with delayed reaction.

They had survived. Against all the odds, they were alive.

Towards dusk, the rain stopped and a light, watery sun peered through the clearing overcast. In the fading light, the ground steamed slightly, and they saw that they were surrounded by thick, green, rain-soaked jungle, from which came a deep, orchestrated humming from a hundred different species of insects. They heard unidentifiable animal sounds; birds of many colours and small monkeys moved through the trees, and from nearby there came the sound of running water. They sweated in the high humidity.

A gamut of smells drifted on the wind: rich-rotting undergrowth, brief traces of perfume from exotic flowers. They saw orchids, azaleas, a vividly-etched red and orange flame tree standing out brilliantly against the dark background.

Carter stood alone, debating priorities, while the others talked in muted whispers of impersonal things – the forest, the rain, the heat – shying away from emotions and anything to do with aeroplanes and falling. They were not quite ready even to think about their escape, let alone talk about it.

The tail section was their only shelter: they would have to move it to a more level position. Sluggishly, as if unwilling to fight the lethargy which threatened to envelop them, they levered away with bamboo poles, and by the time darkness came, they were able to retreat into their lair like jungle animals. Their only torch was failing now. Carter made them drink their fill from the flask of cold coffee Liane had brought along, and they wrapped the damp blankets around themselves. Predictably, Colin and Debby paired off, and Liane sat in a corner against the slope of the floor. The door stood open a few inches, and Carter could see her face in the dim light, she caught his eye, smiled wearily, face stained and lined with fatigue and shock. Her dark hair was limp upon her shoulders, and the white uniform shirt clung damply to her body, a long tear from the side seam down to her waist. Above the dark rim of blanket, Carter saw the stark whiteness of a bra, an inch of brown skin.

'Get some sleep, Liane. Tomorrow ... Tomorrow, we'll see. At least, we're alive.'

She turned her head towards the sleeping boy and girl.

'They'll be fine,' he said tiredly. 'They're young. It's a great adventure for them.'

'But I think of all the others —' Her voice was husky, uneven.

'Don't,' he told her bluntly. 'It does no good. We couldn't have saved them, you know that. Try not to think about them. In time, you'll forget.'

For a long time she looked out of the door at the waving elephant-grass, the darkness of the forest beyond. In the end, she lay down and drifted into a restless sleep, haunted by dreams of nameless horror that still lingered on the brink of memory when she awoke the next day.

Donald Carter lay awake for some time, listless and un-happy. His mind wandered aimlessly, his memory replaying terrifying images of the break-up, the descent ... The wound on his head throbbed dully, and his thoughts explored labyrinths of speculation. Where were they? What country? Could he keep them all alive until they were rescued? Could they walk out of here? What dangers faced them in the jungle? Uneasily he listened to the enigmatic noises of the night.

Carter could hear the slow, measured breathing of the sleepers; Debby groaning and sighing with each exhalation, the boy grinding his teeth in unknowing frustration. The night wind soughed in endless patrol through the rain forest, and through the narrow aperture of the door, one or two stars glowed — unknown, strange stars, obscured at times by straying tendrils of cloud. They were so large, those stars: floating beacons in a mystery-wrapped universe.

His last thoughts, before sleep drowned him, were of Jean, dead these three years. But he found her face difficult to recall precisely: oval cheeks and oblique eyes seemed to superimpose themselves nebulously, like a strange Identikit picture con-stantly rearranging itself before the eyes of his mind.

Carter awoke, cold and stiff, staring at a stark sunbeam like a pillar of fire on the curved metal wall opposite. He blinked, stretched lazily and winced: every bone ached abominably. Liane lay motionless beneath her blanket, a still, shapeless bundle; the boy and girl lay stretched out, blankets thrown aside.

His watch had stopped at some point during that nightmare yesterday. Where in hell *were* they? Alive, certainly – but to all intents and purposes dead to those who waited in Hong Kong: the kids' parents . . . Gavin and Shirley . . . Liane's – what? Was there a husband waiting for her in some tropical airport?

He began to think back to the flight. According to the captain, no distress call had been made. The flight, he recalled from the airport wall map, had been entirely over sea – in which case, a search of this area was unlikely. The pilot had said they were heading for Saigon . . . Maybe they were on the Asian mainland, or perhaps an island? Further than that, he could not guess. One thing was for sure: no one would be coming to look for them. If they ever got out of this God-awful place, it would be by their own efforts. No Seventh Cavalry would be coming to the rescue . . .

Strangely, once he had accepted that, Carter felt much better. Sitting still, waiting, the recommended practice after crashing, was a non-starter: they could move, explore, advance or retreat. There was no future in worrying about the future: it would be hard enough just surviving from day to day.

Jungle survival . . . His thoughts went back to training days, and he began racking up the problems: heat, humidity, lack of salt; food shortage. Impure drinking water. Bugs. Snakes. Prickly heat, malaria, dysentery – all the old nasties of the tropics.

Speculation was a waste of time at this stage; he fumbled in his jacket, found cigarettes: the pack was damp, unusable. He got up carefully, laid out the cigarettes in a line on the warm, sunlit floor to dry. They steamed gently. Pleased, he sat with legs crossed, thinking. One thing stood out: no more flying. Ever! He had pushed his luck too far and let *them* get too close. *They* were everywhere. *They* were the ones who left pieces of timber on workshop floors, with lethal nails pointing upwards; arranged loose-ended electrical leads for people to trip over, left banana skins on pavements, jagged slivers of wood

on timber, unrecorded defects in apparently serviceable aeroplanes, oily patches on hangar floors. Loose heads on hammers, low beams to catch unwary heads . . .

Murphy's Law in action.

But Murphy only skated round the edges, Carter mused.
Somewhere around the corner, *they* watched and waited and
manipulated, scoring names from lists with malevolent glee. It
was certain, in his view, that *they* would have been very upset
to see him wriggle free at the fateful moment . . .

Upset? He grinned, turning a cigarette over to dry out
thoroughly. *They'd* be bloody livid – and *they'd* be after him in
full strength now.

Well, okay. *I dare you, you bastards,* he muttered. *I'm onto
you now . . .*

'Donald?'

'Liane . . . Sleep all right?'

The girl was sitting up now, blanket around slim shoulders,
knees drawn up close to her chest. 'A little. Your head – it
hurts?'

'Only when I larf.'

'Please?'

'Never mind. Did we bring any food with us?'

She nodded, groped behind her in the corner; the plastic
carrier, freed from its straps, held an assortment of goodies:
cigarettes, biscuits, potato crisps. A few liqueur miniatures,
some chocolate.

Carter grinned, pleased. 'Could be worse. Anything else?'

'Some coffee in the Thermos. Perhaps two or three litres. But
it will be cold –'

'Hell, we can warm it up. And make hot chocolate – if we
can get a fire going. Come on, you kids, show a leg!'

They sat up, bleary-eyed, hair tousled, flushed with sleep.
Colin yawned. 'What time is it?'

'My watch stopped,' Carter said. 'Any offers?'

Debby sniffed. 'I make it half-past three.'

'You're worse than me,' Carter said cheerfully. 'We'll have
to guess – let's say seven-thirty. Come on, let's have a look
around.'

The wrecked tail section lay in a small clearing, partly of its
own making: a steamy haze lay close to the ground, and the
metal skin glistened with condensation. It had come to rest on

a steep jungle-clad slope upon which they stood with difficulty, staring at the alien panorama around them. The sunglare was dazzling, and Carter, thigh-deep in thick elephant-grass, shaded his eyes under a flattened hand.

Wet thickets of fern, bamboo and coiled vines surrounded them; lush, shaggy undergrowth, agleam with water droplets and the sheen of foliage – a profusion of yellow-green, blue-green, red-green, under canopied banana-trees, laden with hard green fruit. Vines as thick as Carter's arm were bent upon strangling palms, living and dead jacaranda trees, and there was a rank, overpowering stench of chlorophyll and rotting vegetation – ancient smells filled with the essence of a thousand lost generations of growth. Club moss infested the skeleta of once-proud trees – banyan, neem, jacaranda, and many more whose names were unknown to them.

They stood transfixed: Colin had shed his jacket in the steamy air and was now wearing a blue short-sleeved shirt and charcoal-grey trousers, already stained and torn. Debby's green shirt was ripped at one shoulder, a fragment hanging down over the short black skirt; she was barefoot, and her underarms were already dark with sweat.

Carter turned slowly, scanning the vista of mountains and forests. Behind them, the steep slope terminated at the base of a high, rocky escarpment, stark grey walls of granite laced along the ridge with trees and brush. The wall curved away into the distance to encircle the valley below, an almost circular depression with a flat floor a thousand feet below them. It was probably volcanic in origin, he judged, and some five miles across, seven in length.

At the foot of the escarpment, the jungle slopes fell away steeply in verdant growth, like some giant crinoline skirt, to the valley floor. Across the flat, overgrown plain, a river snaked a devious course, sections glinting in iridescent ribbons where they caught the sun; far away to the right, the stream disappeared, it seemed to Carter, into the rocky face of the escarpment near a huge 'V' in the forested slopes. In many places around the valley, thin feathers of waterfalls showed creamy-white in the clear, warm air.

On the flatland below, beyond the river, there stretched a long strip of vegetation in lighter shade, in stark contrast to the multi-hued undergrowth around it. For one blinding moment,

Carter thought it was an airfield, but he changed his mind a millisecond later.

It *couldn't* be: too overgrown. It might have been an airfield at one time. No – perhaps an air strip, a single, cleared rectangle, hacked from the forest. Shading his eyes again, he took another look, ignoring the questions being flung at him from the others.

God's teeth . . . It was true. On the left of the strip, flat roofs of buildings – two, three, four, in mottled camouflage, almost invisible, betrayed only by the sharp angularity of outline. And beyond . . . His eyes narrowed, searching. Beyond, the outline of an old-fashioned hangar, a low, sweeping arc, ground to ground, festooned with brush and grass. Staring until his eyes ached, he could make out the darker segments of open rectangular doors in the side facing the strip.

He turned – a tall, spare figure in crumpled cavalry twill trousers, check open-neck shirt, suede shoes now black with moisture.

'Hold it! Hold it! Look – you can see for yourself. That was an airstrip once – but don't build any false hopes. It's been deserted for years . . . Derelict – that brush on the strip is as high as a man. But it seems the best place to go: we can't stay here, that's for sure. It won't go away – first we'll build a fire, heat up coffee and chocolate. Then . . . We'll see.'

An hour later, with the sun higher and hotter and the sky a clear, brazen mirror reflecting its heat, they stumbled away downhill, blankets rolled and tied with webbing straps to form backpacks. Carter led, the girls behind, Colin Todd as rearguard. The pilot was worried more about Liane than either of the others: she coped adequately with her tasks, but sluggishly, with an air of puzzled detachment that Carter thought was a very bad sign. They were all suffering from delayed shock, and unfortunately the natural palliatives of rest and sweet, strong tea were in short supply right then. Liane would have to take her chances until they found shelter of sorts – and if this was the rainy season, which seemed likely judging by yesterday's cloudburst, they had only a short time to find it.

Initially, Carter thought they might have three, four miles to go. The estimate was wildly inaccurate. For a start, the greasy slope was too steep for direct descent, and they were forced to traverse to and fro, following an oblique course and avoiding the dense thickets of brush and bamboo. In the process, they had to ford half a dozen streams again and again. The few game trails they came across were enmeshed in sodden tangles of undergrowth. Twice, small deer scrambled across the path in blind terror; swarms of flies assaulted them, attacking every bare inch of skin. Within an hour, they were near exhaustion, wilting in the heat and humidity, fighting the jungle at every step. In the end Debby sat down and burst into tears and open rebellion.

Carter sighed. It was no more than he had expected. He was reasonably fit for his age, but low on reserves: he had deliberately set a slower pace to favour the girls, and found it just as difficult to maintain. He made Debby drink some cold coffee, took off her shoes and stockings, dried them as best he could and watched Liane put them back on again – Debby was very near collapse. They rested for ten minutes, then set off again, more slowly.

Carter chose the route with care, but even so, after another hour he was beginning to feel a steel band of pressure tighten across his forehead. Fighting for breath, drenched in sweat, he found a clear spot beneath a mature banyan tree and ordered another halt. The girls fell asleep instantly; Colin, perhaps the fittest of them all, sat with head bowed between his knees, sucking in air like a drowning man. Carter stared at his team despondently.

A menacing throb within his own chest told its tale: this was no time or place for a heart attack, he told himself angrily. He lay back, breathing hard, a large heart-shaped leaf from some plant like wild rhubarb between his face and the sun. He slept restlessly and intermittently, waking very much the worse for it.

By noon, the ground levelled out. They stopped by a ledge where a brave stream broke free from its runnel, tumbling into a deep pool. Without a word they plunged in bodily, washing away the accumulation of sweat and dirt in their clothes, revelling in the cool, fast-flowing water. Afterwards they lay on the flat granite slabs, clothes steaming dry in minutes, ate a little fruit and watched Colin trying to catch a fish or two in the pool.

Carter caught Liane's eyes, smiled. 'You know this country, Liane?'

'I think so. The rain forest is the same in Kampuchea, Laos, Vietnam . . . I can show you the fruits to eat, the berries my people use for sickness.'

'That's something, at least. Animals?'

'Not so many. Deer we have seen. Elephant – they work in the teak forests. Many small monkeys – and snakes. Bad snakes.'

'Poisonous?'

'Yes. The green one we saw today – no. It is eating birds – birds and eggs. Cobras – not so many in the mountains. The long black snakes – very bad.'

He nodded seriously. 'We'll have to be careful. We have nothing for treating snakebite. What about dangerous animals? Tigers?'

'Not many here now. In Assam, Upper Malasia, yes. More dangerous, the spiders – some very bad.'

Carter looked gloomy. 'Thanks for nothing. I'd better warn the kids. Those clouds are building up. Time we were moving.'

Progress became painfully slow. Carter chafed at each delay, stifling in the humid air – it felt as if he was drinking it, rather than breathing it. They had 'guestimated' the time that morning, but by his reckoning it was ten minutes short of three in the afternoon when he finally lurched round a bamboo thicket and saw the river, some yards ahead. It was fifty feet wide, and the burble of the water against rocks was music in their ears: the current slowed at level spots, before tumbling into deeper pools full of green shadows and flat sandstone boulders. Wading in thigh-deep in the shallows, they crossed in pairs – Carter and Debby, Liane and the boy.

Soaked, dog-weary but exultant, they stood on the far bank, sobbing for breath – and the heavens opened. Broad leaves giving inadequate head shelter from the pounding rain, they fought their way into the derisory shade of a jacaranda tree.

'We'll have to keep going!' Carter bellowed, above the tumult of rain and thunder directly overhead. Lightning played on wet, frightened faces, staring at him, wild-eyed. 'Take your packs off – use the straps to keep together. If you get lost, stand still – don't go rushing about. Let's go!'

Doggedly they thrashed their way through trackless brush, endless mazes of whipping bamboo, stinging thorn, clinging creeper, sodden fern and bracken. Beyond speech, past caring about anything except the next step, his senses stunned by the violence of the storm, Carter agonised over direction. Visibility was less than a yard, and the rain was heavy beyond belief; his only guide was the oblique slant of the rainflood, from right to left: he staggered, reached for the next tree ahead – and suddenly there were none. He lifted his eyes: ahead, a sea of young brush and elephant-grass, chest high, a marked delineation extending away on both sides.

The airstrip . . .

They gathered around him, shattered caricatures of humanity. 'This is the runway,' he yelled hoarsely. 'Buildings that way – not far – stay close –'

They nodded mutely. Carter plunged away along the strip boundary, wading waist-deep, breaking a trail through heavy underbrush, feet sinking into thick, gooey clay; he knew it was going to take one last, frightful effort. Behind him, Colin yelled frantically: Debby was down, her face an inch from a footprint already filled with water, Liane kneeling beside her, water flooding down her dark, bedraggled hair. Colin got an arm under Debby's shoulder, Carter at her waist, and they half-carried, half-dragged her onwards, while she cried helplessly, struggling against their restraining arms. At one point Carter sank to his knees, head bursting, and they had to wait wordlessly, like statues, until he got back to his feet. On they went, blinded, deafened, desperately seeking some last reserve of strength, falling, finding their feet again, eyes and mouth, nose and ears filled with water and chaos.

They mustn't stop now, Carter screamed at them. If they stopped, they would die . . .

The hut loomed up through the water-curtain like a sudden supernatural apparition: Carter squelched his way across what was once a gravel path, climbed stiffly and carefully up rotted timber steps onto a débris-filled verandah. Water cascaded from a score of holes in the slatted verandah roof. Resisting a crazy urge to knock, he pushed open the door and staggered inside, the others close behind him, out of the relentless downpour.

They stood open-mouthed, the rain beating a devil's tattoo on the roof overhead, unable to believe, to absorb what they saw before them.

SEVEN

Most of all, Indibaraja remembered the hands. Hands that stripped her, rinsed the henna from her hair, removed the kohl from her eyes, clad her in the humble clothes of a merchant's wife – for as such would she travel. Yasovarman, in equally modest clothing, led forth the tiny procession of three bullock carts, a handful of guards, the young elephant upon which Indibaraja rode behind silken curtains. They proceeded slowly, at the pace set by the patient beasts between the shafts, and on the third day after quitting doomed Angkor Vat, they breasted a low hill and looked down upon Lake Tonle – forty miles long and fifteen wide at its broadest point. That same night, they boarded the ship that waited for them, a slim vessel with sails and twelve slaves at the oars, which accommodated with ease the carts, the bullocks and the dozen passengers. All through the night, the cadence of the drum kept them awake, for there was no wind to help them on their way, and in the evening of the following day, they came ashore at the southernmost tip of the great lake. In the night, Yasovarman and his men fell upon the boatmen, burying their bodies in the hold under many rocks, before sinking the ship in deep water. With the sun rising above the mountains to the east, they climbed slowly up the winding hill to the summit of the first ridge, and passed from sight and into history.

After living through twenty-four impossible and indescribable hours, Carter felt nothing could throw him any more – and he was so wrong.

The room – office – was furnished, almost dry; the roof, he discovered much later, was sealed with a flexible and water-proof plastic coating. A brace of rotting reed mats lay upon the plain wood floor, and in a corner a warped bamboo pole supported the remnants of a United States flag, standing in a cut-down oil drum filled with gravel.

Two cane chairs. A low glass-topped coffee table, stacked with mildewed magazines – he recognised a *Saturday Evening Post,* long out of print. Two wallcharts hung from twisted timber frames like half-stripped wallpaper.

On the right stood a long, rusted steel desk, flanked by two filing cabinets riddled with corrosion. There were two wire baskets on the desk, another on the floor, all three filled with rotting paper intermixed with leaves and débris.

Behind the desk, the remains of a man sat through eternity in a metal armchair. Only the bones remained, flaked with grisly fragments of skin and muscle; much of it, including the skull, had fallen to the floor. The torso was still contained within an open flying jacket of brown leather, adhering to the rib cage; on the left upper arm, some unidentifiable blue and yellow badge, and on the sagging chest, a yellow leather name tag, faded and indecipherable.

The olive drab shirt hung in tattered strips, and skeletal arms met on the desk top in a huddle of finger and wrist bones. A dull, corroded automatic pistol, a Colt .45, lay inches from the wasted hands. Carter moved slowly round the desk, peering at the skull on the floor. There was a hole an inch in diameter above the left eye, and another, much bigger, in the back of the skull. He put two and two together, made far too many and looked away hastily.

On the floor near the desk lay the dried, shrunken skin of a black snake, some six feet in length; the head was missing, the hide shredded and stringy at the neck.

Now the picture was complete. Carter absorbed it in seconds, but calming Debby down took a great deal longer: she screamed, dropped her blanket roll and bolted out into the storm, Carter and Colin in hot pursuit. She fought like a wild thing, hysterical, screaming, her body slick in the pounding rain. They dragged her back into the shelter of the verandah, but she refused to go a step further. In the end, Carter left the boy with her and went back inside.

'Liane?'

She waited patiently, face pale but composed. 'I am here, Donald. Do not be afraid . . . Dead men harm no one – only the living.'

He filed that for future reference, nodded approvingly. 'Give me a blanket ... No – I'll do it. Tomorrow, we'll bury this poor sod properly – meanwhile, he has to be moved.'

As he gathered up the pitiful débris, his mind was calm and unruffled, the storm a muted background to the scene. He knew he could not unloose the hysteria that was yammering away at his mind.

'I can see it all now, Liane. He must have been left behind ... No way out ... Then the snake – maybe he couldn't face hours, days of agony alone, waiting for the poison to ... He killed the snake, but it did him no good, poor bastard –'

Picking up the tiny bundle, he collected the snake by the tail, went out of the back door onto the verandah and hurled it into the far distance. He stopped for a moment, looking around: each of the four huts was connected to the other by a bamboo bridge, four feet above ground; he went down, pushed the bundle under the hut, wiped his hands with a shudder and went back.

Liane had been busy: the floor was clear when he returned, and the waste-paper basket in the corner had been filled. The rain was perhaps a decibel less noisy on the roof, and he brought the children inside and closed the door. It was no time for propriety: they all stripped to the buff and he built a fire in the small stone hearth fitted in one wall.

Debby averted her eyes from the desk and continued to avoid it studiously in all the days that followed. Now, she huddled in a blanket against the wall, watching Colin drying and folding blankets to make her a bed; she refused food, but managed a drink of water before lying down. She slept instantly, her young face fixed in a permanent frown, lips working. Carter thought grimly that it was going to be a long time before the kid got straightened out.

He fed the fire again, using the old cane chairs, and hung their clothes up to dry; Colin sat against the wall beside Debby, utterly drained by that last frantic effort. He had a blanket round his shoulders and his eyes were closed to blank out a world that suddenly seemed to hold too much for one person to absorb.

Carter, in bare feet and Y-fronts, got up from the fire, staring at Liane in her white bra and panties. He grinned tiredly. 'If my son could see me now!'

71

She found some string, rigged up another line and hung her skirt before the crackling fire.

'Your son – he is married?'

'Sure. Seven years now. He's a pilot, too – in Hong Kong.'

The Asian girl was silent, staring into the flames. 'You – your wife?'

Carter said briefly: 'I lost her. Three years ago.'

This time it was Liane's turn to apologise: 'I'm sorry, Donald . . .'

'Don't you start!' he said ruefully. 'It was a long time ago. Funny . . . First you miss them, yet you can't remember what they looked like. Then you get over missing them – and the memories come flooding back. We had a long time together.'

She nodded, understanding. 'I know. I will never forget my own father and mother. I was only six, but my uncle often told me about it. My father was in the government – I do not know what he did.'

'What happened?' he said gently. He lit two cigarettes, gave her one.

'He disappeared one day, along with many others in his department. They say he disliked what the government was doing and spoke out. Some, they never found. My uncle searched for a long time, and when he came out of the forest, he found my mother dead in the garden. I went to live with him in the dancing school.'

Carter gazed for a long time at the glowing tip of his cigarette. Then:

'Your . . . husband?'

'I am not married. There have been . . . men. Rich men. They came for me, with jewels and money in their hands. Promises of dresses and big houses. But none brought the gift I wanted.'

Carter looked up. questioningly.

'Love,' the girl said simply, and flushed.

Carter grinned again. 'Makes the world go round, I suppose. But don't miss out – find someone. Have a family . . .'

'Like yours?'

'Sure! Take Gavin – I raised him, sent him to school, and what does he do? Joins the Air Force, gets married and moves to Hong Kong. I came out to see him – and hey presto! Here we are.'

She smiled, eyes twinkling. 'You British! You know in the East we call you "round-eyes"?'

'That's nice,' he said equably.

She looked at him with oddly affectionate eyes. 'That is what I mean, Donald. We know your humour, out here in the East,' she said seriously. 'I have woman friend in Hong Kong who was in Burma in the war. She tells of the British prisoners – how they work until they die on the Japanese railway, but always with a joke. You know the Japanese could not understand this thing?'

It was the longest speech he had heard from her. 'It baffles me, too, a little,' he admitted.

Liane smiled, rubbing a hand down her calf near the fire. 'Tell English joke,' she commanded.

'Now?'

'Please.'

Carter stared at her, somewhat taken aback. 'Christ,' he said weakly, 'this is a hell of a time to start telling jokes.' He considered, briefly. 'All right. There was this old Cockney couple –'

'Please?'

'From London. The wife says to the husband, "Do yer luv me?" He says, "yus". And she says: "Go on, then. Knock us abaht a bit . . ."'

Liane waited patiently, staring at him.

'That's it,' he said brutally.

The Asian girl put a hand to her head. 'I do not understand, Donald –'

He grinned. 'Take too long to explain. Here: your shirt's dry – put it on and I'll fix you a bed. Tomorrow is another day.'

She turned her head, shirt half on. 'Please, Donald – you will sleep close? I do not think I am afraid but I will be happy, I think.'

'Okay,' he said softly. 'We can keep each other warm – like those two.' And he nodded at the recumbent pair in the corner.

Liane came to him trustingly, and they stretched out upon the folded blankets near the fire, another blanket covering them, her head resting in the crook of his arm. The sun was down, the rain had stopped, and all around, the forest was stirring. He lay quietly for a while, watching the fireglow fade, listening to the soft breathing of the girl beside him, feeling her

73

warm body close to his own, and wishing he was thirty years younger.

Unaccustomed as he was to sleeping on floors, he felt very stiff and sore when he awoke – but at the same time rested, relaxed.

The hut was cool, silent, an odd mixture of makeshift and modern: the metal windows were rusty, the timber structure lined with unpainted weatherboard and decorated with graffiti; the trusses and purlins of the roof were exposed. An electric bulb hung from the end of a white cable – he traced it with his eye until it disappeared through the far wall. A Far East map on oiled paper was stuck on the same wall, and beside it, a large-scale map of the Vietnam–Laos–Cambodia area. Carter nodded, pleased: at least that narrowed it down a little.

He padded across the floor in bare feet, drank a little water, and stood, hands on hips, studying the maps. He lifted a forefinger, traced a dotted line from Saigon, north-west towards the Dangrek Mountains near the Thai border. The line ran up through the Vietnam–Cambodia border country near Takeo, to an area with very few towns and villages, hachured to indicate high ground. It stopped in the middle of that area, and many lines radiated from that point to unnamed locations in Thailand, Cambodia and Laos.

So *that*'s where we've ended up, he marvelled. He shook his head in disbelief. Distances and headings were shown: in the open, thinly-populated patch, someone had scrawled 'Here Be Dragons'. There was damn little else, that was for sure, Carter thought numbly. They were hundreds of miles from anywhere, deep in the high rain forest, surrounded by rolling virgin ranges covered with thick jungle, uncharted rivers . . .

He bit his lip sharply and went out onto the verandah. It was damp, steaming in the morning sun, which was now showing a full shape above the eastern escarpment. The day was cloudless, perfect, the air cool and fresh, and he stood there, breathing deeply.

Liane came to stand beside him, securing the stained but dry skirt at her waist.

'Hi,' he said evenly. 'Sleep okay?'

She grimaced. 'Not much. The floors are very hard here.'

'They're hard everywhere. We'll sort out something better for tonight.'

Liane's eyes followed the valley rim, above the trees. 'Where is this place?'

He took her inside, showed her the map, speaking softly for the sake of the sleeping boy and girl. 'I think it was an American air strip in the war. They must have moved out very quickly at the end – was it April, 1975?'

'May, I think.'

'May. Okay. God knows how that poor sod got left behind – not that it matters. We are *here*' – he jabbed a finger at the map – 'way up in the border country. I think we may even be inside Cambodia.'

'Kampuchea now.'

'Whatever. I know this: we're bloody miles from anywhere.'

Liane frowned. 'There will be people looking for us?'

'Not a chance.' He told her about the Mayday message that was never sent. 'We must be hundreds of miles off track.'

'Perhaps someone will see the aeroplane?'

'No way,' Carter said firmly. He laid a finger on the map again. 'Look – the wreckage must stretch over fifty miles of mountain. They could search for months without finding anything in these forests – and besides, they don't even know we're here, on land.'

'It is very bad,' she said worriedly. 'But it is not far to walk to Saigon? Such a little way on the map –'

He grinned. 'Bloody sight further on the ground. Through jungle – full of lions and tigers –'

'No lions,' she said stoutly. 'But the people of the mountains are very bad. They are poor – they kill travellers for what they can steal.'

Carter smiled. 'I've been in hotels like that . . . Let's talk about it later. It's time we got these lazy kids out of bed.'

Over the last of their chocolate, heated over a small fire with water added, Carter put Colin and Debby in the picture.

'Obviously we can't make any plans. First, we go through this place – every inch of it. Anything we can use is a bonus. If that pistol works, I might be able to bag one of those small deer.' He avoided Debby's eyes. 'The first priority is survival. The second is getting out of here. Now listen: we have no doctors here, so we can't afford scratches, ulcers, sprains, colds or snakebite. We all stay fit and we all stay together. No wandering off ad lib – we go in pairs everywhere. Do you read me loud and clear?'

Three heads nodded.

'Okay. Let's take a look round.'

In the next hour their situation improved immeasurably. The adjoining hut proved to be partitioned, a dining area with a Formica-topped table and half a dozen chairs at one end, leading to a kitchen almost filled by a rusted gas stove, worktop, storage cabinets. Beyond, a storeroom – and Carter's eyes gleamed.

'Treasure!'

Treasure indeed: Dexion shelving held vast supplies of canned goods, sealed packages, crates of bottles; best of all, a dozen Tilley lamps with fuel.

'Colin – know how to light these lamps?'

'Yes. They have one in the boathouse at school.'

'Fine. Get half a dozen or so working – two in the sleeping hut, the rest in here. Then see if you can find anything to catch the rainwater; the river may be clean, but I'm taking no chances. There's coffee in those jars, and I can see breakfast coming up. Let's see what we have here . . .'

Over the squeals as the girls discovered fresh delights, Colin stuck his head round the door and said: 'Don, I've found a stack of gas bottles round the back. If we can get that stove working, we could have a hot breakfast!'

Breakfast was indeed hot – and delicious. Porridge oats with hot canned milk, fried corned beef with scrambled dried eggs, and unlimited coffee. Carter sat back, lit two cigarettes, gave one to Liane, and ignored a pleading look from Colin. 'You're too young – wait another year.'

Debby said: 'Oh, foof, Mr Carter – Donald. We've smoked for years. Be a sport –'

He grinned, pushed the pack towards them. That breakfast was too good to spoil with petty argument. They were in much better shape this morning: Debby had made an effort to control her hair, and her face and hands were reasonably clean; Carter suspected Liane's influence there. Colin wore only trousers and shoes, and Liane had knotted her shirt up under her breasts for coolness – it was already warm and humid. The Asian girl had lost much of the strain and bewilderment of yesterday: the bruise on her temple was fading, and her hair was swept back into a pony-tail, secured with an elastic band from the office desk drawer. Looking at them all, Carter felt considerably more confident.

'Well, we won't starve. There's enough food here for months – but there's to be no waste. No over-eating, no raiding the pantry: fair shares all round. Liane can show us what we can get from the forest, and I don't want you kids experimenting. We ought to keep the canned goods for emergency only.'

'You talk,' Colin said gravely, 'as if we're going to be here for years.'

'We won't get out tomorrow, that's for sure,' the older man said phlegmatically. 'We'll be spotted eventually – and we can build a signal fire. That may be a waste of time – there could be scores of jungle fires with all that lightning about. But if anyone sees or hears an aeroplane – light the fire.'

He paused, gathering his thoughts. 'Liane – can you and Debby manage the catering?'

The girl smiled brilliantly. 'I will enjoy it, Donald. Perhaps we can find some wild rice – I could make some of the dishes of my country.'

'Sounds good. Okay, Colin, we'll have a prowl round today and see what we can do about sleeping arrangements – that floor was damned hard last night. Debby, can you keep some kind of diary? I reckon today must be Thursday, somewhere around the twentieth of the month.'

'I'll try. If I can find paper and pencil.'

'Good,' Carter said comfortably. 'Let's work on the principle that we'll be here at least a month, maybe more. If we walk out, it'll have to be in the dry season, at the back end of the year. Of course, we *may* get lucky . . .'

Carter put his glass back on the bedside table and looked at me with those penetrating blue eyes.

'We didn't get all that lucky, Mr Napier,' he said slowly. 'We were in that valley darn near six months. But I think it was the best time I ever had. It was a beautiful place – fantastic trees and flowers – and apart from the rains and the morning fogs, the weather was wonderful.'

He stared at the wall opposite for a long time, and I thought I could see tears in the corners of his eyes. But that was stupid. After all, he had survived a major air crash, come out of the jungle after six months, and brought three other survivors with him.

There was no reason for him to cry. None that I could see.

EIGHT

For many days they travelled to the east, heading for the Cham country through plains and mountains. They bypassed Kon-pong Tham at the head of the river valley, a hundred miles from their starting point, and began the long, tedious climb through the foothills of the high mountains. Twice, they were ambushed by thieves, and twice, Yasovarman drove them away. In the second attack, the men from Angkor were ready: all nine of the raiders were killed, seven in battle, the others after capture. According to the custom of the time, Yasovar-man impaled them on sharp stakes buried in the ground, bound and gagged, their feet barely touching the soil. They would live until their tired muscles finally collapsed – and then they would die, slowly, in agony, and all who found them would know them for the thieves they were. Yasovarman took their horses, moved on, and on the morning of the twenty-second day, they stopped on a high plateau above a lush gorge. Staring down, they saw an immense crocodile of men, horses, bullock carts, elephants – an army on the move, heading for Angkor. The vultures, Yasovarman thought bitterly, were gathering; there would be no sanctuary for them in the Cham country. The people from the delta were invading the Khmer lands them-selves, like jackals intent on picking up the scraps left by the Siamese tiger . . .

When I sat down next morning, Donald Carter seemed unwell – yet I could not put his condition down entirely to reaction following his ordeal. As he spoke, he shifted position frequent-ly in his bed, seeking a more comfortable position, and I saw him wince at times.

It had been, he began, a time which none of them would

forget. Survival was not difficult: supplies were adequate, and they had companionship, too, as they worked together to build up their odd little society. They found large stocks of American cigarettes, even a box or two of very good cigars, a little stale but quite palatable to Carter, after they had been wrapped in moist leaves for a day or two. There were times, in fact, when they were very happy, he told me.

The way back started that very first day – and Donald Carter did not like the shape of it at all.

It came about in this way.

After breakfast, he and the boy explored the remaining huts, one of which proved to be a bunkhouse with spring frames under rotting mattresses; the girls brought in huge bundles of dried rushes from the bank of the river, stitching up rough paliasses which proved to be excellent beds. The fourth hut was a spares and materials store, and it was jammed to the doorway with boxes, cartons, packages. There was nothing of immediate interest there, so they continued their search.

The hangar was something very different. Some hundred yards distant, they had to wade through the deep wet brush to reach it, and as they did so, Carter saw that the arched roof had been cunningly overlaid with soil, in which grass and brush grew luxuriantly. From the air, he suspected, the building would be all but invisible, even to stereo-photography. The roof soared forty feet above ground level.

They stopped at the grey-green camouflaged sliding doors; there was a gap of four or five feet, and they walked cautiously through into the dim coolness of the building. Instantly, a raucous horde of multi-coloured birds took flight, streaming out through the doorway into the sunlight, showering streams of droppings as they went. Carter and the boy ducked, laughing, until the last screeching bird disappeared, then turned to survey the silent, echoing hangar. On the far wall, beams of sunlight streamed in through four plastic-covered apertures. Carter stopped dead in his tracks.

'My God! What the – ?'

Colin gaped. 'An aeroplane!'

For a single moment, Carter saw salvation on three rubber wheels. Then, sadly, he ran his fingers through damp hair and sighed.

'Once, maybe, Colin. It's a wreck now.'

The old DC3 was painted olive drab and grey camouflage on the upper surfaces, the paint almost hidden by a thick layer of guano. It had sat there, brooding through the long years, like some ancient stuffed bird in a museum, poised eternally on the threshold of take-off. Along the fuselage, in white block lettering, were the words AIR AMERICA. On the nose, beneath the cockpit window, was a cartoon drawing of a lush blonde in bed, a knife erect in her breastbone, and beneath it: THE DYING WHORE. Carter grinned, remembering wartime days.

He began to walk critically round the Dakota. The landing flaps were fully down; both main tyres were punctured, the main wheels resting upon cracked and perished rubber hanging in strips. The side windows were cracked, the main cargo door missing; the port engine seemed to be intact, but the starboard was minus propeller and cowlings, and surrounded by an aluminium servicing platform. Carter climbed three or four steps until his head emerged above the metal floor; he saw toolkits, oily rags and an apparently new cylinder assembly, still wrapped in oiled paper.

Climbing down stiffly, he went on round the aeroplane, Colin following hot on his heels, full of questions, but loath to intrude. Carter rubbed a questing toe in the congealed pools of hydraulic fluid on the concrete floor, pulled tentatively at the port propeller blades. The resistance was solid, without a trace of movement. He grimaced.

'Seized solid, Col. It's had it – in a big way.'

'You mean – ?'

'It'll never fly again. They probably left it here because it was scrapped. Look at it. Rust everywhere. Oil leaks. Everything locked solid.'

Colin looked doubtful. 'It doesn't seem *too* bad, Don.'

'It doesn't? Listen, it would take ten years and half the mechanics in the Douglas factory to get this heap of crap off the ground. Come on – we're wasting time . . .'

A small box of an office occupied a corner of the hangar; an open-topped store made from wire mesh in the other corner. Carter pushed open the office door with difficulty and went in. Rotting piles of mildewed publications lay on a desk an inch thick with débris; service manuals, fragments of Form 1, the servicing log used to sign out an aeroplane as serviceable.

There was a big metal toolbox against one wall: he slid out the butterfly trays of spanners, wrenches, screwdrivers and pliers – all were heavily greased and in good condition. Who had accumulated this kit? The dead man? He sensed some strange story here – tragic and hidden through the years in this quiet valley. At the height of the Vietnam War, six, seven years ago, this place must have buzzed like a monstrous hive. Overnight, it had been deserted like some jungle *Marie Celeste*, and a dead aeroplane and a dying man had been left behind. *Why?* He shook his head, disturbed and uneasy in the presence of things he could not understand.

The hangar office bore mute testimony to the industry of those departed men: a filing cabinet, locked; a small shelf with an electric kettle, coffee jug, sugar bowl, the latter swept clean of the last grain by marauding ants. A portable typewriter, irretrievably jammed, a metal table and two wire baskets filled with shredded paper . . .

Back in the hangar, he found the girls listening to Colin's explanations.

'It's all beginning to fit in,' Carter told them. 'Air America – that was the cover name for the CIA air transport organisation. They ran it like a civil airline, mostly on secret missions from bases like this. Remember those routes on the map, from here up into Cambodia, Thailand, Laos? I checked the date on one or two papers in the office. Nothing later than April, 1975 – nearly five years ago.'

Liane nodded eagerly. 'I think that is right, Donald. I remember reading in *Time* magazine that they flew in agents, supplies.'

'Right,' Carter said. 'Well, you can't get anything more secret than this place. As far as I can see, the only way in or out is by air – those cliffs around the valley are almost unclimbable, I'd say.'

Liane said hesitantly: 'The aeroplane – Colin says it will not fly . . .'

Carter repeated his verdict. The girls looked disappointed, as indeed he was himself. Or was he? He took a long, slow look into his own soul and recoiled from what he saw there: the truth was that he was glad, damned glad, that the old beast was beyond repair. Better spend the rest of his life here than kill himself trying to coax that heap of junk into the air.

The Asian girl said softly: 'I wonder how long he lived, after they left him here.'

'The guy in the office? Maybe they didn't leave him. Maybe he was the anchor man, detailed to clear up after the rest. Perhaps the plane they sent for him never made it. From what I know, the last few weeks of the war were pretty chaotic. Maybe he'd just made a start on fixing that engine when the snake got him . . .'

'Poor, poor man,' Liane said sadly.

'Stranger things have happened,' Carter pointed out. 'They found Jap soldiers in the Phillipines thirty years after the war in the Pacific ended. But I'm not giving up as easily as that. I may be able to get the radio working. Colin – how about tracing the electrical supply from the office? They must have had power from somewhere. You girls have a look round the hangar and see what you can find.'

He walked stiffly round the tail, climbed into the open cargo hatch. Clearly the DC3 had been loaded and ready to go – the crates and boxes were lashed down, leaving a walkway along each side to the flight deck. He grimaced, nauseated: suddenly he detected a rank, squalid stench, unlike any so far, permeating every corner of the old aeroplane. Unable to make any sense of the stencils on the crates, he shook his head and moved forward into the cockpit.

He recoiled, sickened and afraid.

The cockpit was festooned with cobwebs, layer on layer of them, all alive and jerking with the passage of unseen, scuttling creatures in dark crevices; in the port seat was the macabre caricature of a man, wearing a peaked cap green with mould upon a naked skull, leaning on the seat back. One skeletal hand rested upon the centre control console, the bones of the forearm showing through the decomposed fibres of a flying overall; a wristwatch hung gruesomely loose on an eroded metal strap.

The webs, sparkling with water droplets, gleamed in the reflected sunlight from the hangar doors. By the same light, Carter saw that a green snake, as thick as his wrist, was coiled around the starboard control column, its head aimed directly at him. The long black tongue slithered out, waving sinuously, disappearing and reappearing in the square, scaly jaws in loathsome warning.

Carter gulped, took a pace backwards; another – and another; then, with infinite care, closed the door behind him. Question, Carter: you find a bloody great snake four feet away from you, beside a dead man. What steps would you take?

Bloody great big ones . . .

Reaching the cargo hatch and the alloy steps to the ground, he got his feet on solid concrete and tried breathing again.

'Donald?'

He said sharply: 'No one goes near this aeroplane until I say so, Liane. And Debby – tell Colin what I say. There's a snake in there I don't like the look of at all – and another dead man. I want you all to stay away. Understand?'

The girls nodded, shaken considerably. After a pregnant pause, Liane spoke. 'There is some sort of machine behind the hangar. Debby thinks it is a . . .'

'Generator,' the younger girl said firmly. 'Can't be anything else, Don. Lots of cables going in and out. We looked inside.'

'That sounds like it, Debby,' he agreed. He stopped, looked at her sternly. 'What's wrong? Spit it out.'

'The aeroplane . . . If it was fixed, could you fly us out of here?'

He sighed irritably. 'Debby, my love, it's out of the question. That plane's been standing here rotting to pieces for more than five years. Besides, I've never flown a Dakota before. And the air strip is overgrown. It would take months just to clear it. I don't think we should waste time even thinking about it. Now –'

Liane said abruptly: 'I think if you wanted to fix it, Donald, you could do it.'

'Now, let's get one thing straight!' Carter said furiously. 'I'm positively not going anywhere near that damned wreck – it's nothing but scrap! I don't want to hear any more about it!' He stalked out of the hangar, leaving them standing in stunned silence.

Presently, Debby said, 'Liane, do be careful. He's got a lot on his plate . . . and he does know about aeroplanes. Give him time to work it out.'

The stewardess stared discontentedly at the section of valley framed in the hangar doors. 'I do not think he wants to leave this place, Debby. He has no wife . . . His son is married and

84

does not need him. What has he to go back to? I think he will want to stay here forever.'

The boy and girl looked at her with ill-concealed dismay. 'Look,' Colin said carefully, 'it's early days. He's done so much . . . getting us down from that aeroplane . . . organising things here. Let's leave him alone for a day or two – let him settle down. Agreed?'

The girls nodded reluctantly. 'Okay. I'll go and see if he wants help with the generator. And remember – no talk about the Dakota. Not just yet . . .'

Carter was on his knees, checking the machinery. He looked up at Colin. 'I might be able to get this thing working. It's a two-stroke motor, and there's plenty of fuel in these drums. Let's find some tools . . .'

The engine wouldn't turn at all. They took off the cylinder head, heated some engine oil over a Tilley lamp and poured a mixture of oil and petrol into the cylinder bore. Carter levered away at the turning handle, and the crankshaft turned a few degrees. Fifteen minutes later, he primed the cylinder, gave the handle a swing and the little motor bellowed triumphantly, bringing the girls running and sending every bird in hearing distance squawking into the air. Within the hangar, half a dozen lights glowed, dispelling the shadows. Carter stood up, beaming, all his temper dispelled.

'Now for that radio shack.'

He wasted hours before admitting defeat. The set was old, damaged beyond repair by water and corrosion; there was a yawning hole in the roof of the radio shack, and the rain had poured through on top of it. He stood up at last, shaking his head.

'It's buggered completely,' he said disconsolately. 'Short circuits all over the place; some of the tubes are shot. It's so old it doesn't even use transistors. Worse, it's medium wave WT – sends Morse, not voice.'

Debby, her voice breaking, seemed to lose control.

'The way you talk, you don't want to get home! Well, we do! You keep saying this is no good, that's broken, this won't work . . .'

Gently, Carter laid a hand on her shoulder. 'Debby . . . why on earth should I want to stay here? I want to see my family again, the same as you. But I won't go raising false hopes. You have to trust me. It'll take time, but I'll get you home – you'll see.'

She stared at him, tears welling, shrugging away his hand. 'I don't believe you! You're useless . . . A stupid, useless old man, and I hate you!' Her face was twisted, ugly with emotion, and she whirled round stumbled away towards the line of huts.

Liane ran after her, calling her to wait; Colin walked away, face set and angry.

Could it be, Carter asked himself, that she was right? After all these sterile years, he had a chance to prove himself, yet there was something about this place, something that drugged the mind, blotted out memories; it was a little Eden, his own kingdom, with only a girl and two teenagers to dispute his right to rule. Be honest with yourself, Carter: if that thing in the hangar was ready to fly, would you try it?

He sat down heavily on the edge of the generator housing and pondered. Maybe he would, and again, maybe he wouldn't. What the hell was the big deal in getting back to civilisation? A lonely house? Empty, futile jobs? Soaring prices? He was happy here. Suppose they had to stay – would that be so bad? He was fifty-seven, old by some standards, but he was fit; a few weeks here would shift the spare tyre round his waist. There would be problems, yes: those two kids, for instance. Something to worry about in a year or two, maybe less. That Colin was a well-built lad, Debby mature and developed for her age. If she got pregnant . . . He cringed mentally before an image of Debby lying on a bed made out of rushes, screaming, gushing blood . . .

For Christ's sake, Carter, easy . . . easy. He'd have to have a talk with Colin, make sure the young fool kept out of Debby's pants. And then there was Liane. She could waste her best years in a place like this, trapped with a schoolboy and a tired old man – and if the kids were making it together, it would put a hell of a strain on her. Not that he'd be much good to a woman like that. It was nearly four years since Jean went on ahead – four years of subduing his need for a woman. It was true, he thought absently, people said you needed it less, the older you got. True that they said it – not true, in fact. He sighed again. God only knew what the future held . . .

Thoughtfully he got up and walked back slowly towards the

huts; crossing the strip, he looked at it again with the eyes of a pilot.

It would take a bulldozer to shift that little lot. He turned his head to stare down the valley, where some strange beast bellowed once, twice, and was silent. No use brooding: no one was going any place. Not for a long time. He turned his eyes up to the brazen sky, caught in the arc of the escarpments. Some day, someone would fly over the valley and find them. But for now . . .

He shrugged, walked onwards, head bowed.

In the quiet ward, Carter shook his head, avoiding my eyes. 'It wasn't that I wanted to stay, really. I just – wasn't all that keen to leave. There's a difference, Mr Napier – you know?'

I thought about that one for a moment.

'You may be right, Mr Carter. But you're here now. What changed your mind?'

Evenings, invariably, they spent around the mess table, under the naked electric light, the generator thudding comfortingly in the distance. Debby found a pack of cards in the storeroom, and they rotated the games often, to avoid boredom. But despite his efforts, the talk always centred on their predicament, their chances of rescue, until Carter angrily tried to put an end to the speculation.

'Listen,' he growled, 'all this talk about rescue – forget it. You're only making things worse. You go over it again and again. I tell you, I'm pissed off with the whole damn business. I want out of here as much as you.' They glowered at him defiantly. 'I know what you think, but you're wrong. Look at our options: forget that plane, for a start. Take my word for it – it's finished. And forget about walking out for the moment. You know what it was like, the day we came down from the mountain; it took us all day – and that was downhill! Besides, we've no compass, no suitable maps, no travelling rations. We'd need a truck to carry what we'd need for three months – and that's how long it would take us to walk to Saigon.'

He sat in seething silence for a long time. 'Two other possibilities. We may be spotted by a passing aeroplane – or we may be found by people who've been alerted by a plane seeing our fires or lights at night. And that's it – nothing else.'

Colin wasn't so sure. 'We've checked the escarpment this end, Don – I doubt if any climber could get up there. I think we should check out the rest of the valley – especially where the river goes to.'

Carter nodded. 'Makes sense. Okay, we'll go take a look-see tomorrow. You girls be all right for a few hours? Good. And when we get back, we're all going for a long short walk.'

He grinned at their expressions. 'I just remembered, talking about being spotted from the air. Way back, in the RAF, we were taught how to survive in winter. Part of the drill was treading out a big 'SOS' in the snow. Well – we'll do the same on the strip.'

Debby held a hand to her head. 'I don't understand. A long short walk?'

'Sure. One man can make a path by walking the same route five hundred times. Or a hundred men five times, five hundred men in one go. We mark out our 'SOS' and spend an hour a day at it – letters a hundred feet across that an aircraft can see fifty miles away.'

Debby clapped her hands in delight. 'Oh, yes! Smashing, Uncle Don!' She flushed, finger at her lips. Carter smiled with pleasure. 'And one more thing –'

They waited, expectantly.

'I said no walking out – and I meant it. But when the rains end, I'll walk out myself. No' – he held up a hand in check – 'I mean it. I can get along better alone. I've had training in escape exercises, years ago. And alone, I stand a better chance if I run into any awkward sods in the forest. I'll have that gun, and as soon as I make contact with any kind of civilisation, there'll be a helicopter on the way for you. I can't do it in the monsoon, so if we're still here in September, October – I go. And no arguments.'

Colin was making his bed. The girls had retired to the bunkhouse, where they slept; Carter and the boy used the office hut.

'Colin – come and sit down for a moment. I want to talk.'

'What about?'

'Your grammar's awful, boy. Missing too much school. Sit down, for Pete's sake.'

They sat facing each other across the desk. Carter gave him a cigarette and leaned back, debating the best approach.

'Supposing,' he said slowly, 'supposing we didn't get out of here for a long time.'

'More than six months, you mean?' Colin said anxiously.

'Years – three, maybe four years.'

The boy considered. 'We'd get bloody hungry.'

'I don't mean that,' Carter said patiently. 'Look – if we were back home, how would you feel about Debby as a girlfriend?'

'She's all right, I suppose. We get along. For a girl, she's bearable.'

'Girls get to be women, Col. Supposing you wanted to get married; would you choose Debby?'

Colin laughed shortly. 'Give over. She's okay as a pal, but I have my own thing going back home.'

'In school?'

'Hell, no. She's eighteen – works in a travel agency. I met her when I helped organise a school trip to Orleans last year. Right little raver, I can tell you!'

The older man grinned. 'I bet. You're a bit of a tearaway yourself, I reckon. Prefer older women, do you?'

'Well,' Colin said defensively, 'I'm big for my age. Connie – that's my girlfriend – says I look nearer twenty than sixteen. Act like it, too.' There was smug satisfaction in his voice.

Carter looked uneasy. 'Well, that's fair enough, but it doesn't solve our problem. Before long, Debby and you are going to start feeling frisky. Know what I mean?'

The boy flushed. 'Like I feel now, looking at Liane? She's quite a woman . . .'

'And you're quite a boy – which brings us back to our problem. Look Colin, I'll be blunt. I don't care what you do as long as Debby doesn't get hurt. I couldn't stop you, anyway. But if she gets a little bit pregnant before we get out of here, she could die. She's very young. Even if there were no complications, we couldn't handle babies here. So watch yourself. Have all the fun you want, up to a point. Go too far, and I'll break your back. Got it?'

Colin gulped. 'Yes –'

'Okay,' Carter relaxed. 'Look, I don't want this to be too much like school.'

'How do you mean?' Colin said faintly.

'You know – notices everywhere. "There'll be no this" and "there'll be no that". We have to trust each other and stick to the rules. Of which there is only one that concerns you – keep your nose clean and your hands out of Debby's pants. Understood?'

Colin stared, red-faced. 'I wouldn't do a thing like that – Debby's my friend. Anyway, how do I know you're not after her yourself?'

Carter exploded with laughter.

'Good grief! I'm pushing fifty-eight. I lost my wife years ago. Since then I've been the original trier – trying to do all night what I used to do all night without trying... Forget it, Col. Just worry about Debby, and take care of her. Do that for me?'

'I will, Don. Sorry...'

'For what? We men have to stick together. Now off you go and crawl into your pit.'

They left camp early in the morning, sniffing the cool, fresh air; there was a trace of ground fog along the strip, but the air was filled with the rich smells of flowers and shrubs, the sky a pale china-blue bowl overhead.

They had heard odd animal noises again during the night, coming from far down the valley, and Carter took along the rusty .45 just in case. It was old, but it worked, and had a kick on it like a Welsh half-back. At the river, Carter stopped and they filled four Cola bottles with clean water before moving on downstream along the bank. The stream was broad and clear: fish were plentiful, as were the wading birds that fed upon them. Towards the end of the valley the ground fell away gently and the river descended in a series of natural pools, flanked with the familiar red sandstone slabs, before wandering around a stand of dwarf pines and entering a region of heavy undergrowth. From here onwards, progress became a dogged process of trying suitable short cuts, getting lost, abandoning them, trying again, until finally towards noon, they glimpsed the towering grey wall of the escarpment above the trees, and Carter began to encounter boulders of all sizes, clearly the results of past landslides; the stream twisted through mazes of small canyons between rock walls, and the going became dangerous.

Carter was never absolutely certain how it happened. One moment, he was edging carefully along a sandstone ledge ten feet above the frothy green torrent, Colin a few yards behind; the next instant, he was deep in cold, surging water and being swept along at enormous speed for some twenty yards into a wide pool dotted with rocky outcrops. It was all he could do to keep his head above water, until suddenly his body drove hard into a rock slab standing feet clear of the torrent. The massive force of the water pinned him to the rock, bent forward as if in obeisance. It was as if he was in a straight-jacket: he could neither see or hear, and his mind was stunned by the welter of water breaking over him. He was held as if in a vice by a vast yet impersonal force, a giant hand that, as yet, had not killed him, but gave every indication of doing so.

Carter knew that if he was to go on living, he had to get out of the water very quickly. For one thing, the uproar and tumult was destroying his capacity to think; and for another, he had never imagined the water would be so cold in the tropics. And once the feeling left his limbs, he would be as good as dead.

One arm was under water, jammed into a crevice by sheer weight of water; the other was half-free; grotesquely, he could feel the warmth of the sandstone and the heat of the sun on his forearm. Cautiously, he explored the surface of the rock until he found a crevice, a narrow crack which accommodated four fingers, full length. Gripping hard, he began pulling up on his right arm, seeking to slide it around the rock, rather than lift it free. The weight of water was terrifying, but inch by inch, the arm came round and up, until his hand crawled out of the water inches before his eyes, and he stopped, sobbing for breath.

There was time now for a hasty glance towards the shore: he glimpsed Colin, running hard along the ledge back towards the valley, and groaned, a sneer of frustration and disillusion twisting his lips. He jerked at his trapped right leg again and again: it was caught fast. The left seemed rather better: it was partially shielded, and he dragged it upwards, inching his way, until he found some outcrop on which he could get leverage. Painfully, like a drowning seal, he fought his way upwards, until he lay with his upper body flat on the sandstone slab; then his head went down between spread arms, and he lay quiescent, the roaring torrent raging all about him in frustrated violence.

To Colin, it was as if Carter had vanished off the face of the earth: for an instant he had taken his eyes off the man in front to check his footing, and in that instant Carter was gone. The boy let out a great cry of anguish, rushed forward, saw the broken section of rock on the ledge; he plunged forward recklessly, following the stream until it debouched into the side rocky pool – and he turned pale. At the bottom of the pool, fifty yards away, the river entered a stark 'V' of rock which ended almost instantly, the black water flowing under a shelf and disappearing entirely. Colin's tears flowed freely; searching the seething expanse of the pool, he visualised Carter already a mile away in some underground drain, his drowned body battering against the rocks.

And quite suddenly, in the pool, a rock moved. No – not a rock . . . He stood transfixed, watching Carter drag himself from the turmoil like some wounded animal, to lie exhausted across the sandstone slab. And quite suddenly, Colin Todd knew that somehow, he was about to pay his debt to the society which, for sixteen years, had comforted and cossetted him. With Donald Carter alive, there was a chance, however slight, of getting out of this dreadful place. Without him, Colin would be left alone, to care for two girls who, like himself, had no experience of such catastrophes.

He worked his way downstream, to stand on the shore where he could yell and scream at Carter, twenty feet away from him across a boiling maelstrom. He might as well have addressed the cliffs behind him: Carter made no move of any kind. For a long, desperate moment, Colin thought he was dead. Then a hand flexed, moving crab-like upon the rock and he sobbed thankfully, before haring away upstream to the bamboo grove they had passed – was it only minutes ago?

Sweat streaming from every inch of his body, he manhandled a heavy four-inch fallen bamboo trunk down river, dragging one end waist-high, inching it around the sharp bends of the ledge, until he reached Carter once more. This time, the head turned, and the hollow glowing eyes opened wider: the slim brown hand on the rock lifted an inch or two in salute, fell back exhausted.

The boy surveyed the torrent anxiously. Bloody hell, Todd, *think*! He saw at once that if he simply allowed the twenty-five-foot bamboo trunk to fall across the stream, it would be swept away. Worse, it would be smashed down onto Carter's unprotected body in the flood – and there could be only one end to that.

Colin slapped his head, turned and ran back into the valley, searching frantically; the vine he selected was a tough, twisted growth, some thirty feet in length. He coiled it over one shoulder, hurried back to the pool and tied one end to the thinner tip of the bamboo, eyeing closely a second rock which protruded from the torrent six feet upstream from Carter, and another four feet out into the pool. Moving with almost exaggerated care – he knew he would get only one chance at this – Colin jammed the thick end of the bamboo into a recess between two rocks on the shore, grasped the vine and pushed the top end of the pole out into the flood, taking the strain on the vine. Foot by foot, he paid out the rope, fighting to prevent the river from snatching the pole away from him. As the bamboo caught more and more of the pressure as it extended, the boy had to dig in his heels and battle for every inch.

With the pole a bare three feet upstream of the target rock, Colin allowed it to surge free and jam in position; he now had a bridge of sorts to the furthest rock, with Carter held prisoner six feet downstream.

Next, Colin took up a second length of vine, fashioned a rough loop around the bamboo pole and entered the water, pole against his chest, facing downstream. Gingerly, holding on tightly, he edged outwards, pushing the vine loop before him and fighting for breath with each step. Inch by inch he made his way towards the centre of the span, his only fear being that the bamboo might bend too far under the pressure and break, until eventually he reached a position directly upstream of Carter. Playing the vine gently, he brought it against Carter's body; Carter, half-drowned, searched with his left hand, found the vine and pulled it tight. Colin watched in a fever of anxiety as, with painful sluggishness, Carter found the loop which he had tied in the end of the vine and got his head and arms through. Then the boy began to move again, further out towards the anchor rock against which the pole rested, taking the end of the vine with him: he knew the bamboo would never stand their combined weight.

He reached the rock, straddled it, flexed his fingers, then jerked the vine slightly; Carter's head turned the other way, to stare at him glassily. The boy waved urgently, beckoning Carter to move; then he set his feet hard against the rock and began hauling.

It seemed an eternity to Colin, but no more than five minutes elapsed before Carter reached up a trembling hand and grasped Colin's wrists; in a single convulsion of muscles the boy heaved him almost clear of the water and they lay together, fighting to draw breath and still their pounding hearts. Presently, they worked their way back across the bamboo span: Carter first, secured to the long vine which Colin paid out slowly as he went, then the boy himself, until at last they staggered forth onto the small beach and collapsed face down, feeling the blessed warmth of the sun on their backs.

'That,' Carter said thickly, 'was a bit too bloody close for comfort...'

Colin nodded weakly. As far as he was concerned, it was the understatement of the year, but somehow, it didn't seem to matter. The sand and gravel were warm and comforting under his shaking hands, and a great wave of mind-sapping exhaustion swept up over him, carrying him into sleep almost as swiftly and inexorably as the river had taken Carter.

Yards away, a long-stemmed wading bird lifted its head, regarded the two recumbent bodies with incurious eyes and began searching again for the tiny fresh-water shrimps it adored.

When they started back in the early afternoon, the rainclouds were already stacking up in the north-west, and it seemed to Carter that they would never reach home again. Four miles of ceaseless trudging lay ahead of them as they followed the winding river back up the valley – and with only half a mile to go before they reached base, the monsoon rain suddenly swamped them with insane, mindless ferocity, washing out the game trail they were following across a river loop. By sheer luck, Colin recognised a clearing where he and Debby had gathered fruit the previous day, and they stumbled into camp at dusk, barely capable of movement or speech.

The girls ushered them into the hut, white-faced and concerned. Colin collapsed on the bed, stunned with fatigue and exhaustion, and Carter, stripping quickly, snapped out instructions.

'Get those wet clothes off him, Liane; wrap him in a blanket and rub him down hard. Debby – hot coffee, as fast as you can. Where in hell are those brandy miniatures?'

The fiery liquor revived the boy considerably, and he sat on the edge of his bed, watching Liane dry his legs, Debby staring with no little interest. Colin flushed, grabbed the blanket quickly. 'Here – do you mind? I'm starkers!'

'Idiot,' she said scornfully. 'We were worried. Relax. No need to get worked up about a little thing like that –'

Carter began to laugh helplessly; Debby stared, realised what she had said and blushed furiously.

'It was no little thing Colin did for me today, Debby,' said Carter. 'That boy saved my life.'

'Donald!' cried Liane, her face stricken. 'What happened?'

'Let's just say I fell in the river – and Colin hauled me out. If he wants to tell you any more, that's up to him. But I'll tell you this – when we get out of this place, Colin will never pay for a drink in any pub I visit.' He turned and looked at the boy, leaning forward out of his blanket to light a cigarette from the match Liane offered.

Colin looked up, grinned. 'I'll hold you to that, Don.'

Later, as Liane stood by the fire, finishing her cigarette, watching the sleeping boy cocooned in blankets, there was a strange look of tenderness on her face.

'He looks so young,' she said gently, staring down at the flushed face, tousled hair.

'He did a man's work today, Liane. Which reminds me: I had a talk with him last night. About Debby. If we have to stay here any length of time, those two are going to get into deep water. Soft nights, full moon, not many clothes . . . We could have big trouble. I warned him last night to keep his distance.'

'Donald!'

'They start young these days, Liane. Hell, they're on the Pill at eleven or twelve. And that boy's been looking sideways at you, too. Give him half a chance and he'll be all over you. So – don't give him any reasons. Try to keep your shirt buttoned, swim only with Debby, don't be alone with him. You understand?'

Liane's lemon cheeks darkened a shade. 'I will be careful, Donald. But . . . I am much afraid when you talk this way. As if we will be here always.'

Carter sighed. Life was so damned complicated. 'Look – I've covered most of the valley, and there's no way anyone can get in here, short of flying. There's nobody here but us chickens.'

'Please?'

'Never mind. Just remember about Colin – okay?'

The stewardess sat down heavily on Carter's bed, hands clasped in her lap, looking up at him apathetically. There was little that he could offer by way of comfort: it was best that she knew the truth and accepted it. But there was still a deep pain within him, which had been refined and reinforced by the events of the afternoon – pain and sadness that she and the others should be trapped here, with almost no chance of rescue. He tried to imagine spending thirty, perhaps forty years in this isolated valley, and shied away violently from the prospect.

For him, it was simple: another ten, twelve years and he'd be out of it for good. But Liane and the rest? It didn't bear thinking about.

After a little while, she went away. Carter put out the light, stretched out on his bed, trying to find some ache-free part of his anatomy to lie down on. He left the door open, but sealed with mosquito netting for ventilation. The last light was fading along the rim of the escarpment – a black, brooding wall. Dully he reflected that walls were built for many reasons – to keep people in, to keep people out. The valley was large, beautiful, a pleasant place in which to live.

But a prison, nonetheless.

He sighed, rolled over, drew the single threadbare blanket close to his chin, and slept.

NINE

Anguished, Yasovarman came to a decision. In the early evening he addressed his men. 'You know of the Cham treachery,' he rasped. 'Our plans must be changed. Escape is impossible while we carry the great treasure. You know, too, what happened to the boatmen to ensure their silence. And you are afraid – for yourselves.'

They stared at him, fascinated, spellbound.

'Have no fear,' he said calmly. 'Here we shall make camp. The princess and I will continue tomorrow with but a single man, exploring this land in search of a resting place for the treasure. That done, you shall return to the great lake, taking with you half your reward. The last man, when I dismiss him, will follow, bringing you the remaining half. Thus all shall know that the word of Yasovarman is good. And the treasure of the Khmer kings shall remain hidden until it is needed once more, to bring justice back to the land of Angkor.'

So it was done. And on the fourth morning, the three riders came to a mighty ridge, a plateau across which ran many busy streams; one of these they followed north and east until it disappeared into the earth in a mighty cave. Beyond the cave, Yasovarman rode to the brink of an escarpment, there to find a hidden valley, formed, he thought, in the beginning of time when the valley floor sank many hundreds of feet. Surrounded by towering rock walls, it was girt about with a sea of green bisected by a single glinting stream. Immediately below him, the lost river emerged in a green tongue from an aperture in the cliff, dispersing into white spray in its fall to the pool a thousand feet below.

The princess was afraid, but Yasovarman laughed, grasped her wrist and they entered the cave, along the bank of the flowing stream, leaving their guard alone with the horses to stare at the many wondrous rainbows saluting the waterfalls *all round the valley. Below the soldier, the fall surged and thundered, casting a spectrum of magic colour against the morning sun. He shifted uneasily, one hand on the pommel of his curved bronze sword . . .*

Dr Singh met me in Reception next morning at the hospital. He smiled briefly and asked me to come into his consulting room.

'Mr Napier,' he said quietly, 'I would be grateful if you are not seeing Mr Carter today.'

I raised my eyebrows. 'What's the matter? Has he taken a turn for the worse?'

He said, 'We are wanting to do some tests on Mr Carter's back today. You know, when he was flown down from Khota Baru, he could not walk?'

I stared at him. 'No, I didn't know that. He's been in bed each time I've seen him. Is it serious?'

He tightened his lips. 'We are finding severe bruising of the lower back muscles, Mr Napier. Also, a slight misalignment of the spinal column, but we are relieving that successfully by traction this week.'

'Caused when he crashed?'

The doctor shook his head. 'We do not believe so, Mr Napier, sir. We are asking Mr Carter and he is not telling us anything about that at all. But I think he has carried something heavy on his back. Something very heavy indeed.'

I could not quite see where this was leading – and it seemed to me to be none of my concern: I had already established to my own satisfaction what happened to All-Orient Flight HK 108. But I wouldn't have been human if I hadn't been fascinated by Carter's story, and I wanted very much to hear the end of it.

I said: 'Have you asked the others? The stewardess and the children?'

He leaned back and steepled his fingers. They were long, spatulate and probably very strong. 'I am hoping that you would do that, Mr Napier.'

I sat in silence for a moment. I could see that it might look bad if a doctor had to ask other patients how Carter had injured himself: doctors are paid quite large sums annually to find out things like that for themselves. I thought, uncomfortably, that it was rather going behind Carter's back – but on the other hand, it was for his own good.

'All right, Doctor. What do you suggest?'

'The young people's parents are arriving on a scheduled flight from Hong Kong today. I doubt you would get much sense from them. But the girl, Liane Dang Ko, is very well now. We are letting her get up this morning, and in a day or two we are discharging her.'

'You think I should talk to her?'

'Yes, please. But I would not be rushing things too much, Mr Napier. She is well enough physically, you understand, but she has been through much strain. Just talk with her – and do not be letting her think she is being made to give evidence. Do you see?'

I nodded. 'I understand. Don't worry, Doctor – I won't upset your patient.'

Her room was a pleasant one, looking out onto the hospital grounds with the harbour in the distance; there were flowers, tastefully arranged, and the windows were open, carrying the scent of the blooms through the room. She was the only occupant. They had found her a neat white blouse and a blue skirt a little on the short side, it seemed to me, showing a considerable length of slim brown leg. Carter had told me she was beautiful, but that, I thought, was an understatement. Her body, while well-proportioned, seemed thinner than it should have been – or perhaps she was exceptionally tall. The high cheekbones cast shadows on cheeks which should have been softly rounded; her long black hair, secured by a wisp of blue ribbon, hung unobtrusively over one shoulder, and she was playing absently with the loose end with one hand while turning the pages of some magazine lackadaisically with the other.

She stood up when I came into the room, slim, straight of back, composed. I held out my hand.

'Good morning. My name's Napier – from the Ministry of Aviation. Miss Dang Ko?'

She nodded gravely. 'Yes.'

I said cheerfully: 'I understand they'll be letting you leave in a day or two. You'll be pleased to go, I've no doubt. I'm handling the enquiry into the loss of your Boeing – All-Orient Flight HK 108. Do you feel up to talking about it?'

The girl smiled. The facial transformation was startling – there are few people who can inject genuine pleasure into a simple smile of welcome, and I could understand why Carter had spoken so warmly of her.

'Of course, Mr Napier. Will you sit, please?'

'Thank you.' Her English was really very good, the accent barely discernible. I offered her a cheroot, which she refused, laughing – despite my assurances that they were very mild and commonly smoked by ladies. She opted instead for a cigarette, which I lit for her. She relaxed, pointing a bronzed knee at me.

'I have talked with Mr Carter,' I began, 'and he has told me much of what happened to Flight HK 108. It seems to me that you were very lucky to escape, Miss Dang Ko.'

'Liane. Please – Liane. Yes, we were lucky. If Donald – if Mr Carter had not been there, we would have died with the rest. I could not believe this thing could happen like that. And I could not see how he *knew* it would happen.'

'He was a very good pilot himself, Miss – Liane,' I said carefully. 'And I, too, have found that most survivors have been seated in or near the tail of a crashed aeroplane. But the odds against striking the mountainside at exactly the right angle . . . I've only heard of one comparable case.'

She leaned forward, her eyes intent. 'Please tell.'

'A man who jumped from a burning bomber in the war, over Germany. He had no parachute, but he landed on a hillside covered with snow and little trees.'

She nodded, keenly interested. I went on.

'Tell me . . . What sort of a man was Carter? Out there in the mountains?'

It was curious, she said, how her feelings towards Carter changed during their time in the valley. In the beginning, he was more of a father figure – the kind of person she dreamed her own dead father might have been. He organised them, protected them, told them what to do with a quiet firmness that brooked no argument; even Colin and Debby, locked sometimes in internecine warfare from sheer ennui, rarely opposed him.

For many days after they landed, she was stunned, dazed, suffering from delayed shock which erased much of her memory of recent events. But that was a temporary phase and she was able to hide her confusion from the others until she regained a semblance of normality. But during that early period, Carter's personality had impressed itself deeply upon the absorbent surface of her mind, cushioning her against reality and relieving her of the need to rely upon her own strength. It wasn't long before she began to rely slavishly upon the tall, spare Englishman, falling in with his every wish, anticipating his every need.

As the weeks drifted by, she found the group was welding itself together in close companionship, and her dependency upon Carter began to diminish. She threw herself into the business of finding food, briefing the others on edible fruits and plants, building fish traps, collecting the wild rice which grew in profusion along the river. They even selected a flat, muddy patch, built a dam and diverted water into their own paddy field. At the time, hardly any of them really believed that they would still be there in three or four months, when their first crop was ready. It was simply a game, something to pass the time – and there are much worse ways of doing that than paddling around knee-deep in warm, muddy water under a hot sun.

But the Dakota haunted Liane.

In those early days, when Carter had demolished with sheer logic all their hopes of flying home in the old aeroplane, she had accepted it without question: it was a matter of regret to her, but if Donald said it would never fly again, that was that. Her belief lasted less than two weeks.

Most airline employees eventually pick up a smattering of aircraft technology, particularly aircrew, and Liane was no exception. There was nothing very magical, she reasoned, about aeroplanes; she had once heard them described as 'large collections of spare parts going in the same direction at the same time.' Breakdowns were a part of life: sometimes they occurred in flight, which was worrying at the time, but in the main, defects were found during inspections on the ground. Mechanics knew how to deal with such things: they repaired the defective item, or they took it off, threw it away and fitted a new spare part.

It seemed to Liane that the stores available in the valley were more than enough to meet the Dakota's needs – in fact, far more than one little aeroplane would need. Why, then, did Carter baulk at the suggestion of repairing it?

She spent long hours thinking about this. She also began making quick and secret visits to the hangar when Carter and the boy were out somewhere in the valley, and she looked at the aeroplane critically.

Naturally – and quite illogically – she figured that if the larger faults could be rectified, the smaller ones wouldn't matter too much. She checked the replacement tyres, stripping off part of the protective plastic covering, and found them as new. What next? She stood precariously upon the servicing platform, staring at the partially-dismantled cylinder, ready and waiting.

She climbed down, examined the engine cowlings: they seemed complete, undamaged.

Four days passed before she found the courage to approach Carter again, but when she did, she recoiled from the stark, bleak anger in his blue eyes. They were alone in the hangar, out of the blazing sun of the afternoon; the multi-hued birds were back in strength, and she had asked Carter if he would find some eggs for her.

She asked him again, falteringly, about the Dakota. He rounded upon her viciously.

'For Christ's sake, Liane! I told you before! There's not a bloody hope in hell of repairing this junkheap! Goddamit, do I have to go through it all again, or are you too bloody thick to understand? If you don't stop needling me about it, I'll . . . I'll . . . I'll burn the damned thing where it stands! Now – no more. Enough is enough. Understand? Not another flaming word!' And he walked away, stiff-legged, hands bunching into fists with each step, leaving the girl in tears.

Yet once again she almost believed him. Almost. Until he began finding other reasons for staying in the valley. The mountains were too high . . . The cliffs too steep . . . The forest too dangerous . . . Not enough food . . . Bad drinking water . . . No maps for walking . . .

In retrospect, she realised that they were in the valley almost five weeks before she saw the light.

Carter really wanted to stay!

How could she have been so stupid? What was there for him to go back to? Life alone back in England; no wife; family away in Hong Kong for two years . . . She knew about his job troubles, the drinking, the way he had let himself go. They had sat for long hours, talking on the verandah in the evening sunshine. She looked at him now with critical and unbiased eyes. He was probably fitter now than he had been for years: the hint of a paunch had disappeared, the tall, lean body was tanned a deep brown, and he went about habitually now in his only pair of trousers, cut short at mid-thigh for coolness.

Matters were made worse by the fact that she could not talk about her suspicions to the young ones. They were clearly as aware of the situation as she was – but the round-eyes would stick together. If she breathed a word of her suspicions to Colin or Debby, Carter would know very soon afterwards.

Sitting in the cool hospital ward, she turned to me again.

'You see, Mr Napier, it was deadlock. I couldn't get through to Donald; Colin and Debby seemed to believe we would be found in a matter of weeks.'

I leaned forward in my seat. 'But you came out all right, Liane. What happened to change Carter's mind?'

She gave me a long, curious look. 'Has Donald told you what we found in the valley? What we brought out with us?'

I said uncertainly: 'No. No, he hasn't.'

She paused. 'Perhaps he should tell you that himself, Mr Napier. Because that was one reason why he changed.'

I thought about that one for a moment. Then:

'There was another reason?' I said hopefully.

She smiled brilliantly. 'Why, yes, there was,' she said at last. 'Something happened . . . Something quite strange, I think . . .'

They moved slowly downstream, Colin stalking fish in the shallows with a length of bamboo tipped with a knife blade. Sooner or later, Debby thought resignedly, he would catch one – and become even more unbearable.

She perched her bottom on a smoothly-rounded boulder, savouring the lush warmth through her tattered skirt, watching Liane on the far bank, picking berries and fruit. Time had improved Colin in looks, at least, she mused: his body was now deeply tanned, and he was wearing cut-down trousers like

Carter, his hair bleached near-white by the sun. He had matured, broadened out, and since that episode with Carter and the river, there had been a strange aura of . . . authority? No, that wasn't right. Somewhere along the line he'd lost that casual schoolboy banter, that juvenile sense of humour she had always loathed so much. She began to realise that a stranger might so easily take him for a man, not a boy.

She sighed. If only he wasn't such a beastly bore. And lately, she'd caught him looking at her in the *oddest* way; he would flush, turn away, even avoid her for a time. It was most peculiar. Was he going a bit queer in the head? She had always abhorred people who got sick in the head.

Colin stood knee-deep in the clear, fast-running water, spear at the ready. Why couldn't he have been another girl, she mused. True, there was Liane – but it wasn't the same. For the thousandth time she thought of her parents in far-distant Hong Kong, and the tears welled hot and stinging. Impatiently she brushed them away. She was too old for crying now – although those first few lonely nights with Liane in the bunk-house had been different. She scowled, raised her eyes to the jagged rim of the escarpment, wrapped in sadness and a great longing for her family.

'Debby?'

She started from her rêverie. Colin was twenty yards further downstream, on the brink of a little sandy beach.

'Take a look! Here!'

Debby waded down through the shallows, eyes narrowing against the myriad reflections of sunglare. The water was cold and soothing, her feet and ankles deliciously numb, until she climbed out onto a hot sandstone slab.

The boy knelt carefully on the coarse sand. There were imprints – large, flat, round depressions, and nearby, a massive heap of droppings.

'It's a bloody elephant, Deb! Liane – what do you think?'

The Asian girl waded knee-deep through the water towards them, holding her fruit before her in the fold of her skirt. Her slim legs caught the sunlight as she climbed out onto the small strand of beach, to examine the spoor.

'It *is* an elephant, Liane, isn't it? Maybe that's what has been making all those queer noises we heard. Do you see what it means? If an elephant can get in, *we* can get out!'

Liane smiled at his excitement. 'Maybe. Maybe, Colin. Let me see . . .' She knelt carefully, still holding the fruit before her. 'It is a big one, I think. There are many elephants in my country – though not so many since the war. They work in the teak forests. This one, I think, is wild. We must be careful.'

'I don't think we should go anywhere near it,' Debby said anxiously. 'Maybe we should fetch Uncle Donald?'

'Oh, bugger Uncle Donald!' Colin exploded. 'This is the best thing we've found so far. I just want to take a little look at it.'

'You swear so much, you don't even know you're doing it,' Debby said angrily. 'Anyway, it could be miles away by now – and there may be lots of them.'

Colin disagreed. 'We've hardly touched this end of the valley. There must be ten square miles of forest here. Look, we won't go looking for them, but we'll keep our eyes open. I want to take another look at the big pool by the waterfall. Come on, you two.'

They began to move upstream, leaping from rock to grassy bank and down into rippling shallows, driving clouds of brilliant birds into the air. They were careful to check for small black leeches; these made the girls shudder in horror and look away, and Colin had to be called upon to apply a lighted cigarette to make them fall free. The sun was now almost overhead, and they stopped frequently to sluice themselves in the brawling torrent. Soon, the brush became more dense, standing in a green wall along the water's edge, long black roots snaking down the clay banks. The stream narrowed, and they waded thigh-deep through the dark, shady tunnel, out into the sunshine and the soaring rainbows of the waterfall.

Hard under the base of the cliff, the air was filled with fine spray, the two-hundred-foot cascade feathering out randomly according to the vagaries of the air currents. The water fell onto the surface of the pool as a constant shower of fine rain, whipping the water into a great semicircle of froth and foam covering half the surface of the pool.

Colin walked slowly along the brink, examining the sandy areas where animals came to drink: there were tracks aplenty, but none of elephant. He stood at last on a little promontory, shading his eyes, staring at the arras of falling water and the cliff beyond.

'If this was an adventure story,' he said wistfully, 'there'd be something behind that water — maybe a cave. I think I'll swim over for a look-see.'

Debby raised her voice above the thunder of the fall. 'Be careful!'

He grinned, revelling in the superiority of an extra year in age and six inches in stature. 'Nothing in there to harm anyone, Deb. Tarzan wouldn't think twice about it.'

'You're not Tarzan!'

'You not Jane, either. Go get some bananas for lunch.' And with that he was gone in a long, surging dive, ploughing across fifty yards of water in an untidy, thrashing overarm crawl. He slowed, approaching the edge of the water curtain, and went on cautiously, disappearing in the welter of foam and water vapour.

Anxiously the girls watched him go. Then: 'He'll be all right,' Liane said cheerfully. 'He is a very strong boy, I think. Come, Debby — we swim too.'

They stripped quickly, two garments proving little hindrance, and Liane, clad in threadbare white pants, slid into the water with hardly a ripple, down into the green world of silence, where the noise of the fall subsided into a distant drumming. The water was glass-clear, luminescent in the sunlight filtering through, and small bubbles escaped from her mouth as she glided down the smooth, sandy slope into deeper water. The bottom shelved on the far boundary of vision, yellow sand serrated by water currents. There was an ache in her chest, and she was about to thrust for the surface when a small, glowing light on the floor of the pool caught her eye. She pushed downwards, grabbed a handful of sand and shot up into the sunlight, uncertain if she had managed to grasp the tiny glittering object.

The air was cool and sharp in her lungs: she trod water, gasping, laughing, fighting to draw breath and slow her pounding heart. Debby was nearing the shore with her slow, hesitant breast-stroke, and Liane thrashed in behind her. Together, they hauled themselves out onto the flat sandstone ledge and lay back, laughing, feeling the burning sun on their naked bodies.

Liane sat up, water dripping from distended brown nipples, and opened her palm, allowing the wet sand to filter out. She bent forward, staring at that which remained. She leaned forward again, dipped her hand into the water and brought it forth, drawing a quick gasp of astonishment.

'Liane? What is it?'

'I . . . do not know, Debby. I do not understand. Look.'

The ring was a heavy loop of solid gold, adorned with a garland of small rubies. The setting formed a flat mounting almost an inch square, in which rested a single enormous emerald, carved by some long-dead hand into the form of a flat square. Inlaid into the glowing stone was the image of a war elephant in black obsidian; on its back was the outline of a fighting turret in delicate silver filigree, and round its legs, spiked anklets to create havoc at close quarters; the tusks were picked out in white ivory, topped with silver points. It was a miracle of miniature beauty in immaculate proportion. Debby also gasped, incredulous.

'Liane! It's marvellous. Did you find it in the pool?'

'Yes. But I do not understand, Debby. I am afraid.' Liane spoke hesitantly, her eyes deeply troubled.

'Silly – what is there to be afraid of?'

Liane was silent for a moment. Then she stood up, tall and slender in the sunshine, turned her back on Debby and slid down her panties an inch or two.

'What do you see?' she said, looking down over her shoulder.

Debby stared. At the base of the long, smooth back, just above the swelling curve of the buttocks, she saw two deep dimples; between them, an inch or two above the delicate crease, there was a mark. At first, she thought it was a scar, but no – surely it was a birthmark? It was raised slightly above the skin, in dark, almost black pigmentation: an outline without detail. But it was staggering in its implications. Perhaps two inches long, an inch high, facing left, it was an image of the war elephant identical to that displayed on the ring.

It was quite impossible. Debby's mind spun in disbelief, grappling with a paradox to which there was no answer, fighting to produce some rational reason to explain the inexplicable . . .

Liane pulled her clothing back in position, slipped into her skirt and sat quietly, gazing out across the pool, turning the ring over and over in her long, slender fingers. The younger girl came to sit beside her, silent and thoughtful. At last she spoke.

'Liane, what does it mean?'

'I do not know. I am much afraid, Debby. I have never been here before – and yet I know this place so well from my dreams. It is beautiful, and yet it holds much sorrow for me. I want to run, yet I know I must stay. I look around and it is all different, yet nothing has changed. Only I . . . Only I have changed.'

Debby shivered involuntarily; despite the warmth of the sun, it was as if some cold hand had laid itself briefly upon her heart.

Liane turned to look at her, understanding. 'Do not be afraid, Debby. There is no danger here for us. That much I know. There is much to be told, much that remains hidden. If the Lord Buddha so wills, we may be told the meaning of this thing. See – Colin is there, on the far shore.'

Beyond the thunder of falling water, in the calm backwater under the cataract, Colin slowed, breathing hard, moving into the shallows with a few quick strokes. The air was humid with spray, and cold. He hauled himself up onto the rocks, shaking violently in the sudden chill. The cliff towered overhead, soaring up into the green-white mists, patchy with fern, fungus and moss. The fall itself seemed almost solid, overpowering in its intensity; around the edges of the curtain, the water sparkled and danced with refracted sunlight, creating a multiplicity of rainbows, and the air was filled with noise and movement.

He stared upwards, dazed and disappointed. There seemed to be no cave, no concealed highway leading out of the valley. The rock face wasn't quite vertical, leaning back slightly from the shoreline, and the fall issued from an aperture in the rock some twenty feet across, about two hundred and fifty feet above the pool, plunging in a long, sweeping parabola to meet the surface close to the shoreline.

The boy felt his neck stiffening, and rubbed his nape, scanning the cliff face systematically. At this point, it seemed to be eight or nine hundred feet in height; the upper half near-vertical, split into great slabs by dark cracks and crevices. He reckoned it might just be possible to climb as far as the top of the fall itself.

Halfway through a horizontal scan his head jerked suddenly

upwards. Was it possible? No – no, it couldn't be . . . But I wonder, he thought greedily, *if that is what I think it is . . .*

The shadow was indistinct in the spray-heavy air, some fifty feet below the fall's exit point, but the more he looked at it, the more convinced he became that it might indeed be a cave of sorts. But it would be no help to them – no way of escape.

But the fall, now – what about the fall? Would it be possible to follow the flow back to the high lands from which it came? He stared again, shrugged. Then he came thrashing back across the pool, to drag himself out with a great porpoising and blowing, throwing back his long hair in a wild spray.

'Nothing. Not a damn thing. Except there might be a – . . . Just a minute. What's up with you two?'

They looked at him, wide-eyed. Debby was unusually pale. He leaned forward, touched her arm. 'You okay?'

Liane held out the ring in the palm of her hand, a hand that trembled a little. He steadied it, picked up the ring.

'That's nice. Where did you find it?'

Debby answered. 'In the pool, Col. But that's not all. It's the strangest thing. We don't understand it at all. It's scary . . .'

He took a deep breath. 'For God's sake, Deb – *what*'s scary?'

'Show him, Liane.'

The tall, honey-coloured girl stood up, turned her back and remained motionless for a long moment before sitting down once more. Colin started, dragging his whirling emotions away from the image of golden flesh against white cloth.

'Good grief. That's fantastic, Debby . . . Liane – that thing on your back: have you always had it?'

'Yes, Colin. I did not know until I was five or six and started the learning of the dance. I could not see my back, you see. But the exercises and movements – they had a mirror in the dancing school.'

The boy considered that briefly. Then: 'You don't know if your mother had the same mark?'

'No. I have never seen it again until today. I see many pictures of the elephant – some pictures on the body.'

'Tattooing?'

'I think so. But no elephant like this. Do you see? It is a fighting elephant – the tusks made to sharp points with bronze, the spiked war anklets, the war tower filled with soldiers.'

Colin looked up sharply from the ring. 'How do you know, Liane?'

'Please?'

'About the tusks being tipped with bronze. Have you ever seen a war elephant?'

She smiled indulgently. 'Is a joke, Colin. No war elephants now. How could I see one? Perhaps in a museum – I do not know. But it is not important. We have talked too much. Now we go home.' And she stood up, slipped into her skirt.

Debby opened her mouth, avid with curiosity, caught the look on Colin's face and remained silent.

Colin gave the ring back to Liane. 'All right – let's see if we can find *our* elephant on the way back. Did you find any decent bananas, Deb?'

They moved towards the pool outlet where the river began. The heat was oppressive, and they kept in the shade, stopping to rest and eat on the tiny beach where Colin had found the elephant spoor. While he wandered around idly, eating the small green bananas, Debby turned to Liane.

'This is your country, Liane. It's beautiful. But we don't want to stay here always, Colin and I. Do you think we shall ever get out?'

'Perhaps. Much depends on Donald, you know. And I do not think it is good for him to walk to Saigon himself – even if he could climb the cliffs. And he cannot go the other way, not now. There is great hunger in my land – many die. When Pol Pot drove the people from the cities onto the land and into the forests, none knew how to grow the food they needed. And when other countries send money and rice, the government takes it for itself. No white man is welcome in Kampuchea now.'

Colin, joining them, heard Liane's last words.

'She's right, Deb. Besides, Saigon and the delta are nearest, and even they're a bloody long way away. Hundreds of miles through that forest. He'd be mad to try it.'

Debby stirred restlessly, and Colin caught the gleam of a tanned breast in the neck of her shirt; he flushed, turned away, disturbed and embarrassed at his own reaction.

'Come on, you two, time to go.'

He stood on the bank of the little river, staring along the game path used by the elephant, bamboo staff at the ready for probing the shallows; the stream provided the easiest and most pleasant way home.

'Look,' he said persuasively, 'it won't do any harm to explore a little way in. What do you think, Liane?'

'I think we should go back,' the girl said uneasily. 'The elephants of the forest are dangerous.'

'Deb?'

'I don't know. It scares me a little. Those noises we hear at night . . . I do want to go back now – really.'

Grumbling, he gave up the battle, turned to the river. Just as he was about to move, he stopped, one foot raised.

'What was that?'

'Oh, do get on . . .'

'No, Debby, I heard something . . . Listen!'

From somewhere close by, there came the sound of branches being shaken and snapped; an odd muffled groaning. They stood transfixed, eyes round with surprise.

Without warning, the long, deafening fart reverberated through the forest, and they clung together in silent laughter, spluttering with mirth.

'Well,' said Colin cheerfully, 'we seem to have found our elephant. And by the sound of it, he's in a bad way . . .'

TEN

They came at last to a deep, silent chamber within the mountain, filled with black water, leaving only space to walk upright among the surrounding boulders. Yasovarman, bearing a makeshift torch aloft, flung a wood chip into the smooth water; it circled slowly, drifted towards the far wall, accelerated and plunged from sight. 'There,' he said intently, 'the water flows beneath the earth, to emerge as the waterfall. But it was not always thus. See.'

The tunnel showed as a dark, sinister mouth, and Indi hung back, uncertain and afraid. At the entrance, the tunnel roof had collapsed, forming a wall of rock that had dammed the stream, forcing it to find a new outlet by way of the cataract. Climbing the barrier, they followed the low passageway, dripping with water, ever downward, hundreds of feet, until they emerged into the confines of a large, dry cavern. At the far end, a green semicircle of light flickered and glowed, and the hiss of falling water was very loud.

Yasovarman, excited now, hurried to the brink, to gaze at the green curtain of falling water, the frothing pool far below; he peered upwards: the waterfall emerged from the cliff some fifty feet higher than the ledge upon which they stood. He caught at Indibaraja's hand, smiling exultantly. This was it: that special place for which they had searched. Here they would bestow the treasure of old Angkor ...

Thirty yards across the little glade, a wrinkled grey back, floppy ears and a prehensile tongue were visible above the lush grass and fern. They watched the beast stripping fresh young leaves from a branch. Colin whispered: 'Smell him? We're downwind – he can't smell us. Phew! What a pong! Careful, now. Let's get a little closer –'

Debby shrank back. 'Colin —'

'Oh, come on. It'll be all right so long as we're careful . . .'

They moved forward into the shelter of a small jacaranda. The beast stood quietly, munching stolidly, trunk now sweeping the ground, now lifted in alert sensitivity. It was a male, with small tusks, some ten feet at the shoulder, wiry black hair sprouting around ears and busy, mobile mouth. It moved ponderously to the right, and Colin stiffened with excitement.

'Debby! Liane! See that? On the hind foot?'

They could see — but so too could the bull. The boy's sibilant whisper had alerted the animal. The huge head turned, trunk lifted in interrogation of the afternoon breeze, sampling the odours of the air. The leathery ears twitched spasmodically, turning to detect the slightest sound, and they crouched together in the brush, Debby holding Colin's hand in a tight grip.

The elephant lifted a hind leg. Now they could see the chain and iron anklet clearly, dragging as the beast moved. It rumbled deep in its throat, looking directly at their hiding place.

'It's a tame one, Liane — a runaway! Do you suppose . . .?'

'Stay away from it, Colin. When these elephants return to the forest, they soon forget. They are made to work very hard in the teak forests and they become wild again very soon.'

'Well, it certainly looks gentle enough, but we'd better get ready to run, just in case. I want it to see me. If it bolts, run like hell back to the river. Okay?'

'Colin — *no*!'

'Hang onto Debby, Liane. Here goes!'

The boy stepped out into the sunlight, moving very slowly. He stood quite still: the great bull raised its trunk higher, rumbling angrily in its belly, rocking from side to side. Colin could see the small bright eyes, faintly pink, and tried to recall if the rocking was a good sign or bad.

For a tense moment, elephant and boy watched each other across the width of the clearing. Then the beast blew a great angry breath and trumpeted in clear warning, the sound echoing around the valley. Debby remembered the noises in the night and shivered.

'Colin! *Please* . . .'

'It's all right. Calm down,' the boy hissed irritably. 'Liane –
what do you think?'

He turned, receiving no response. The golden-skinned girl
was silent, her face tense, and he saw that her eyes were
suddenly glazed, almost as if she were asleep. She stood, tall
and slender, twisting the great ring upon her finger, mouth set
and determined.

The elephant exhaled again, a great menacing gust.

'*Colin!*'

'It's okay, Debby. I think he's going to . . . *Watch it!*'

The grey mountain moved with incredible speed, feet
pounding the earth, charging half the width of the clearing,
and Colin dodged into thick brush, gut constricting in cold
terror. The beast stopped, breathing hard, barely fifteen feet
away, towering over him: its side heaved, trunk questing, head
weaving from side to side.

'*Colin!*' Debby's voice was a terrified whisper. 'Come away!
It'll kill us all!'

'For goodness' sake,' the boy hissed impatiently, 'let him
cool down a bit. Liane, what do you think?'

But instead of replying, to Colin's astonishment the Cambodian girl walked slowly past him out into the bright sunlit
glade, raised an arm imperiously, and called to the bull in some
strange tongue, her voice incisive and full of authority. Again
she ripped out the command. The elephant's head swung
sharply round to face her. He trumpeted again, quietly, as if in
plaintive question.

Liane said something softly to the beast, and the trunk
descended slowly. She picked up a length of bamboo, strode
forward and tapped the right foreleg; it lifted, forming a step,
and the trunk came to form a looped handhold. The girl swung
lithely up onto the broad, grey back and tucked her knees in
behind the twitching ears.

The bull rumbled contentedly, and Liane rapped smartly
with the bamboo, moving the animal forward to the very edge
of the glade. She blinked once or twice and laughed, but it was
an odd sound with little merriment in it.

'It is all right now, Colin. He will not hurt us.'

They emerged nervously, eyeing the beast with ill-concealed
distrust. The Asian girl laughed again, amused now. 'Come
on!' She spoke a word or two, and the elephant made its knee;

Colin helped Debby up, clambered aboard himself, grinning all over his face.

'Liane, that was amazing! I didn't know you could handle elephants.'

She turned to stare at him, uncertainly. 'I – I cannot, Colin. I was never on an elephant before. It is strange . . . It seemed that I knew what to say, what to do. See!' And she kicked her heels gently, coaxing the bull with soft-spoken words; instantly the elephant responded and they moved off towards the river.

They made good speed, following the stream, and once accustomed to the rolling ship-at-sea motion and the sliding skin of the back, they even began to enjoy the ride. Colin leaned over, pointing to the dragging chain. 'We'll have to get that thing off the old boy, Deb. But just think what Donald'll say when he sees us!'

The young girl turned to him, whispering. 'What did you make of that? Talking to the thing like that?'

'Search me. What with the ring, and that birthmark – and now this. Something's going on. But I'm damned if I know what . . .'

Carter, dozing in the afternoon sun on the verandah, heard them coming down the air strip, and held a hand to his head, incredulous.

Liane tapped the elephant's great head with her cane and the beast stopped five yards from the hut. The three slid to the ground and came clamouring around the man.

'Isn't he fine, Uncle Donald?'

'Liane can talk to him!'

'He's tame – a runaway!'

Carter walked slowly round the bull, and it followed him impassively with small wise eyes, as he bent to look at the drag chain.

'That's been on there a long time; it's rusty as hell, and he's got an almighty callouse under it. Poor old chap, he'll be glad to get rid of it. Colin – nip over to the hangar, will you? A hacksaw, some blades, a hammer – you know the score. Now, let's see . . . Easy, old boy . . . Easy . . .'

He tapped the hind leg with a bunched fist; it lifted, and he pulled the chain from beneath the huge pad. The ankle ring was of rusted iron, two sections hinged together, ending in flanges through which a screwed bolt had been inserted tightly.

'We'll never get that loose,' he said flatly. 'Have to cut it off.'

Half an hour and three hacksaw blades later, the restraint finally gave way. Colin hefted the heavy iron curiously.

'There's something stamped on the ring, Don. Wait a minute: "KHAN 62". Well, now. I suppose Khan must be his name — I like that. "62" — could that be a registration number?'

'Could be 1962 — maybe the year he was born. That would make him seventeen. Is that old for an elephant, Uncle Don?' asked Debby.

'Haven't a clue,' said Carter. 'Liane's the expert. I *think* they go on to around ninety.'

The tall, golden-skinned girl stepped back and stared up at the sculpted head, silhouetted black against the afternoon sky. 'Khan! Khan. *Come!*' The beast rumbled deep in its belly, tossed its head, raised its trunk and trumpeted exultantly, moving towards the girl. The sound echoed around the valley.

Carter blinked. 'Poor old lad. Must have been years since he heard his own name.'

Colin frowned. 'That's just it, Don — how *did* he get here?'

'Huh?'

'I mean, if an elephant can get into the valley, surely we can get out?'

Carter's brow wrinkled. 'That makes sense. But maybe the Americans brought him in by air, to clear the strip — their C130s can land in open country if necessary. Perhaps they sent men in by helicopter first, then, when they all got out in a hurry at the end, they left him behind.'

Debby said sadly: 'How lonely it must have been for him . . .'

'Maybe,' Carter nodded. 'He'd have had plenty of food and no enemies, but he'd miss his own kind — elephants are gregarious by nature. No wonder he was so pleased to see you.'

Khan moved away to the edge of the strip to browse; Carter grinned. 'You've got yourself a job for life there, young Colin. But no feeding him. Maybe the odd lump of sugar, nothing else. He's got the biggest cafeteria in the world right here in this valley. You listening, Debby?'

'Yes, Uncle Donald.'

'Okay. How did you find him anyway?'

Debby snickered. 'He made a — a sort of noise. *You* know. A loud one. He was a bit scary with Colin at first, until Liane spoke to him.'

'Until *what*?'

'Don,' Colin broke in, 'how about some coffee? We can tell you all about it.'

Carter pushed his empty mug away and lit another cigarette. 'That's the strangest thing I ever heard. And this is the ring?' He held it at an angle for a better view. 'That'd fetch a few bob in London. But it's the sheer coincidence that gets me. The ring, and . . . Liane – would you show me your birthmark?'

She nodded gravely. Turning, she undid her skirt and inserted her thumbs into the waistband of her white pants, drawing them down an inch or two. With a grunt of astonishment, he held the ring close to the skin blemish, comparing outline and detail.

'Okay, Liane . . . Thank you.'

The Asian girl dressed, returned to her seat, accepted a cigarette. 'Well, Donald?'

He shook his head, utterly confused. 'There's no logical explanation. Birthmarks are common enough, yet . . .'

He paused, deep in thought. The ring itself was no mystery – although the odds against finding it must have been astronomical. Technology capable of producing such workmanship had existed throughout the world for centuries. Gold? That was common enough – and he knew that precious stones had been mined in South East Asia when Ancient Britons were still painting themselves blue. It was the link with Liane that baffled him completely.

Carter shook his head, uncertain and troubled in his mind. All his life, he had abhorred anything connected with the paranormal. To him, all spiritualists, palm-readers, clairvoyants were out-and-out fakes. Most unusual occurrences, in his view, could be explained as simple coincidences, the rest imagination. But how far could imagination be stretched? Where did coincidence end and the supernatural – *if* it existed – begin?

Then there was that damned business with Khan. Liane had refused to talk about it, with a firm but gentle insistence, but the fact remained that she had somehow known how to handle the beast and had established an instant authority over a bull elephant which had spent five years running wild. It made no damned sense at all.

He sighed, stubbing out his cigarette, half-listening to the conversation around him.

'Uncle Donald?'

He jerked out of his day-dream. 'Debby?'

'It's a pity you can't fix that plane. I mean, with Khan to help us, we could clear the strip in no time, couldn't we, Liane?'

Liane's dark, shining eyes remained shadowed, withdrawn. 'I think we should talk about bed, Debby, not aeroplanes. Donald says it cannot be mended.'

The child stared mutinously at the pilot. 'My Dad would soon make it work. At least, he'd try!'

Carter took a long, deep breath, gritted his teeth and made for the door. They watched him walk away, stiff-necked, heading towards the hangar.

Bloody women. Damned insolent kids . . . He ground his teeth in angry frustration, stalking through the long grass to the hangar door. Keep away from them as much as possible. How about a nice accidental fire? He grinned, despite his temper; no – it was too damned hot already in this place.

That filing cabinet in the office: time he got that open. Could be all sorts of things in there. And those crates in the Dakota – and the dead man. Time he sorted that lot out, too. He had left the door and all hatches open, weeks ago; with a bit of luck, that snake would be long gone.

There was no sign of a key for the filing cabinet: it might have been in the pockets of the dead man in the office, but there was no way he was going to check on it. In the end, he jammed a long steel bar into the top drawer and levered until the lock broke.

Bingo!

Ten cartons of Marlboro cigarettes: two thousand, just when the storeroom stock was running low! Eight bottles of Harper's Bourbon – the old-fashioned type with the square glass stoppers. Carter hefted a bottle in his hand, debating whether to try a sample. He decided against it. The ease with which he made the decision pleased him: all at once, he knew he could take it or leave it. He left it, went on probing.

There was a crumbling set of aircraft documents, fragile with age and decay; he lifted them out with exaggerated care, laid them on the metal desk. Beneath, at the bottom of the drawer, he found a large buff envelope marked 'STATE DEPARTMENT – TOP SECRET – BY HAND ONLY.' He took it over to the desk, sat down under the single light bulb and opened it carefully.

The first few documents were copies of Operations Orders detailing certain aircraft for flights to widely-separated destinations, and they were dated from January, 1975, onwards. The targets included Phnom Penh, Da Nang, two airfields in Java, several more in Cambodia and Laos. There was an original of an order with two copies, scheduling a special night flight to a point in Western Cambodia in the mountains beyond Phnom Penh. This contained detailed instructions on landing strip identification, the lighting to be provided by Task Force Baker Five, the recognition signals to be expected. Carter stared: the date was April 30th, 1975 – very close to the end of the Vietnam War, the time of the American Dunkirk from Saigon. Commander of Task Force Baker Five was given as Major Carl F. Macbain.

The receipt attached to the Operation Order completed the picture. Like St Paul on the road to Damascus, the scales fell from Carter's eyes and he knew, with absolute certainty, what was in those crates, stacked in the silent Dakota. Face pale and drawn, he put the documents back very carefully and closed the drawer.

He walked to the door, checked his watch, listening to the thunder of the inevitable rain on the hangar roof. An hour before dusk: it would ease up soon. He shrugged, turned back towards the old DC3. No use putting it off. Might as well do it now.

Carter lit a Tilley lamp, climbed aboard, moving up cautiously to the flight deck. He peered around apprehensively. No sign of that damned snake, thank God. He closed the door, got out his knife and worked on the fabric webbing of the lashings; the wooden crates were intact, solidly made, unaffected by the moisture and decay which attacked most timberwork on the base. He began unstacking, moving each case near the door, checking the contents and moving on. Presently, Liane walked into the hangar, realised he was totally absorbed, and went away: he didn't even notice she had been there.

Three cases of M1 rifles, ten to a box, in mint condition. Two crates of BARs – Browning Automatic Rifles, .45 calibre, five to a crate. Two cases of grenades. Carter took one out gingerly to check: it was still live, pin in position, made safe for transit with adhesive tape. He went on.

Forty boxes of assorted ammunition followed the weapons out of the door. And there was an unexpected bonus – sixteen cartons of US Army 'K' rations: the standard field issue of canned meat stew, hard biscuit, sweets, coffee and powdered milk, cigarettes, gum. He grinned. No doubt Liane would be able to make something of that lot – especially if they had to walk out. His face darkened ... On second thoughts, it seemed good sense to stash the 'K' rations out of the way, under a heap of camouflage netting in the corner of the hangar.

Forward, near the flight deck door, he found three strong timber boxes, painted black, metal-bound at the corners and spot-welded shut. He took the receipt copy from his pocket, checked the serial numbers on the crates and nodded with satisfaction.

Finally, there was a single metal container, eighteen inches square, twelve deep, painted olive-green; the lid was stamped with the State Department seal, the lid welded shut, the whole lashed down very tightly. Carter cut the bindings, tried to lift the box: he could have been trying to lift the Dakota itself. It was extraordinarily heavy. He nodded, face remote and ex-pressionless, lashed the crate down again and went aft, to sit in the open cargo hatch, looking far out across the valley in the fading light, through the open hangar door. He smoked a cigarette, thinking very deeply, oblivious of the occasional bird returning to roost in the roof members.

In the end, he got up, threw away the butt and set about the last and worst job of all, carrying a plastic bag that once held a dozen 'K' rations containers. Carefully, and with a strange sense of reverence, he gathered up the remains of the man in the pilot's seat. The flying overall was as brittle as burned paper, decayed and rotten, but not enough to hide the two bullet holes in the back. Carter sucked in his breath sharply, leaned round to look at the back of the seat. The two holes in the metal were neat and round, still gleaming dully at the edges where the bullets had penetrated.

Sombrely, he carried the pathetic burden out of the hangar,

down the side path, past the busy little generator and into the underbrush; there, he found a soft spot beneath a banyan tree, scraped a hole and did what he had to do.

On the way back to the hut, his face was set in a frown. What in God's name had happened here in those last few days of the evacuation? Perhaps he would never know. But the contents of those boxes could have had a great deal to do with it. He walked on slowly, deep in thought. Major Macbain: was he the dead pilot or the man in the hut? It made no difference: Task Force Baker Five had screwed up their last mission when the Dying Whore had blown an engine.

The others were grouped around the table in the mess hut. He set down the M1 in the corner, dumped the cigarettes on the table. 'Don't smoke them all at once,' he said lightly. 'There's a few more where they came from, but no more than five a day each. They should last a fair time. Where's that beast of yours, Colin?'

'Khan? He's around. Keeps trying to climb on the verandah. We're going to have to make a few new steps.'

'Oh, great,' Carter grumbled. 'That's all we need – a house-trained elephant! Listen – I just finished unloading the Dakota. I couldn't see that snake, but we'd better assume it's still around, so keep away from the aeroplane.'

Later – much later, he told them about the Dakota cargo. Predictably, it seemed to mean little or nothing to them, faced with the greater realities of survival. What was the use of money here, in Lost Valley?

Ten days passed, in deceptive peace and quiet. Debby and Colin were working on a guitar, knocked up from plywood taken from spares crates. Colin carved the fingerboard from a single teak sapling, breaking four hacksaw blades and as many fingernails in the process. Carter was surprised: the finished article was excellent, agleam with glossy aircraft-grade varnish and inlaid with a mock-veneer of aluminium foil in a cubist motif. Debby made the strings from strands of control cable, pre-stretched to remove the kinks. Colin turned out to be a passable player, and Debby's voice was young, immature but strong. They spent hours writing down what they could recall of pop song lyrics, the songs of the western plains, country music.

Carter produced the 'K' rations a case at a time – given the chance, the kids would have eaten nothing but candy for weeks – and for a long time, the days passed very pleasantly. They were in their seventh week now; a number of aircraft had passed over, all at high altitude, pushing out contrails and almost invisible. Their SOS sign had produced no results, and they knew now that no other living person existed in the valley. Worse, they had checked every inch of the escarpments: only one location gave any hope of being climbable, at one of the highest points, and it involved a climb of almost a thousand feet over soft, crumbling sandstone.

The storeroom yielded a new stock of playing cards: Carter started a Bridge training course, but the youngsters were impatient, unruly, unwilling to learn stupid conventions they might never have to use. He stood up finally, told them to forget it and suggested to Liane that she might like to amble down with him to switch on the generator.

The sun was a fire balloon rolling along the rim of the western cliffs; cloud remnants were breaking up. It promised to be a clear, warm night. The sky was a clean antiseptic blue overhead, fading into deep cobalt, against which the escarpment loomed in black silhouette. The first few stars glowed eternally. Together they trod the well-worn path, hand in hand for companionship. Liane strode along contentedly at his side, the worn blue skirt hacked off at the thigh, patched with lengths of string. It was her one sorrow that no needles or cotton existed on the base, for by now her only uniform shirt, washed scrupulously every morning, was as fragile as wet newspaper.

Carter felt an extreme sense of exaltation this summer night. The heat of the sun was gone, and a sky like some mediaeval canvas spread over the valley. He halted a moment, gazing up at the valley rim, listening to the insect chorus, the sighing of the wind through the bamboo thickets.

'It is beautiful, Donald.'

'Mm – mm. As if the rest of the world didn't exist. Reminds me of Shangri-la.'

'Please?'

'A story in a book. About a valley lost in the mountains in Tibet, where people lived forever and the sky was always blue. But it was only a story – not real, like this.'

She turned her face towards him in the dim light, her hair catching the fading gleam of the sun. 'You would like to live here forever, Donald?'

He was silent for a long moment. 'I don't know. At home, there was always trouble, problems. Money. Houses. Bills, more bills. Prices going crazy . . . Unions crippling the country in order to bring in a half-baked system they dared to call democracy. Yet you go on; I suppose you don't have much choice. And it's not easy – unless you have someone with you.'

Liane hesitated. 'I – I think you loved your wife very much, Donald. I think, maybe, you still love her.'

'Maybe I do,' he said wonderingly. 'Strange – you love people even after they've gone, but in a different way. You get a feeling they're still alive somewhere, if only you can keep them fresh in your memory. When you forget their faces, it's as if you've murdered them all over again.'

Liane looked shocked, but Carter continued. 'It's true,' he said fiercely. 'I killed her, sure as I stand here. For half a lifetime, she worked to care for me and Gavin. I could have helped; maybe got her a home help, or an au pair. I could have found myself a decent job, given her a real home, so that she wouldn't have had to work so hard. And when that . . . thing . . . caught hold of her, began to eat her alive, she said nothing. Not a word. Just went on working and caring.'

'Donald . . .' This time there was a world of understanding and pity in her voice.

'It's no lie. Up to the day they took her away, she worked . . . And I let her. And then, when they sent her home to die . . . God, Liane, they were the worst three days of my life. Because I could do nothing . . . nothing to make it up to her. And before she died, she said she was sorry to leave us by ourselves, to cope without her. Christ, Liane, she actually felt guilty. Sneaking off before her time, she called it . . .'

They stood in a silent vortex of emotion, a million light years from the rest of humanity, alone in a mountain valley in the forest uplands of South East Asia. They could as well have been on the second satellite of Alpha Centauri.

Liane, tears on her cheeks, reached up and drew his head down to her, and the dam broke: he buried his face in her shoulder, his arms holding her with an intensity which took her breath away. Suddenly he felt her lips pressed close to his ear, whispering words he did not know in a tongue he would not understand, her voice lilting and musical, almost as if she was singing softly to him. He kissed her without thought. It was a kiss devoid of emotion, yet immediately he felt the fear and anger and uncertainty and unhappiness draining away, cleansed and purified. Her fingers ran lightly through the hair on his neck, and as they did so, he caught her distinctive fragrance.

That first kiss had been without passion; but soon her body relaxed, softening against him; she became aware of him as a man, knowing guiltily that she had spent long weeks looking upon his body, even that of Colin. Her lips opened to him, and the gentle exploration began.

Within moments they were on the cool grass of the pathway and her clothes were hindering him. Beneath the thin shirt she wore nothing: it fell away, and his hands closed over her breasts.

He was beyond thought now, swept away on a flood of sensual urgings he had long since thought dead. She was moving against him, under him, until suddenly he felt her writhe away from him desperately, her head avoiding his lips, hands thrusting him away from her.

He broke free, sank back, breathing hard, and gazed at her dark figure crouched beside him, her face buried in her hands, resting on drawn-up knees.

'Liane . . .'

She shook her head in the gloom. 'Please, Donald . . . go. I will follow you soon.'

He shook his head in silent frustration, got up and stumbled away, unhappy and filled with remorse. No need to wonder why: he was nearly thirty years older than the girl. Yet for a timeless instant, he had been young again, had felt the surge and the need and the urgency again . . . Since Jean had died, in all the saddened years between, he had consciously sublimated his emotions, drifting from job to job, drinking – anything to black out her memory. And now . . . He found his hands were shaking, and he had to force himself to concentrate on the task of priming the generator, swinging the handle, waiting until the lights came on in the huts.

Colin was alone when he returned. He looked up when Carter came in.

'What's wrong with Liane, Don?'

The pilot avoided the boy's eyes. 'Got a bit upset. Nothing to worry about. Has she gone to bed?'

'She and Debby both. Was she on about that aeroplane again?'

'In a way,' Carter said heavily. 'Forget it. Listen – I may have been quite wrong, Colin. It needs proving, one way or the other. We'll start work on the Dakota in the morning.'

'What? Hey, that's fantastic! I –'

The pilot broke in sourly. 'Don't get all psyched up till I finish. We'll check it over, make a list of the work needed, what spares we have. Find out what we need, if we have it or not. We'll do the thing properly: produce a full breakdown when we've finished . . . Then – *maybe* – you'll all stop pestering me about the damned thing!'

'And if we find it can be fixed?' Colin said breathlessly.

'If pigs could fly,' the pilot said caustically. 'All I'm going to do is prove it's impossible. If you want my opinion, it would be easier to shove a pound of butter up a cat's ass with a hot hatpin. Do you read me loud and clear?'

Colin grinned. 'Where do we keep the butter?'

ELEVEN

By the third day, the treasure in the sandalwood boxes had been laid securely within the lower cavern. Yasovarman now returned to the loyal guard who waited at the end of the ravine.

'You have done well, Norodom Sarin,' said the prince generously. 'One day we shall return, and on that day I shall honour you with land and riches and a house of many rooms. But I am troubled lest you allow avarice to overcome your loyalty and reveal the secret of this place. How can I be sure that this will not happen?'

'Lord,' the guard said fearfully, 'my life is yours. I have served you eleven years. I have killed more than sixty men, and it was I that slew your assailant during the battle for Poipet. How could I ever betray you?'

Yasovarman stared at the man, fingering his beard. 'Very well, Norodom Sarin. I accept your fealty. Kneel to me for the last time and pledge obedience in a prayer to Siva.'

Trustingly the man knelt down, palms flattened on the lush grass of the plateau bordering the busy stream. Yasovarman's sword freed itself noiselessly from the scabbard, and he raised it high so as to get the full power of his broad shoulders behind the stroke. The blade was keen: the man's head jerked from his body to land, face upwards, in the grass. For the space of a man's breath, the body remained kneeling, a bright scarlet stream jetting six feet into the clear mountain air. The eyes in the severed head widened, blinked once and closed forever, and the corpse toppled sideways like a felled tree.

Looking back, Carter blamed himself entirely. He had recognised a potential problem, taken preventative action – and failed to follow through, to monitor the situation. From the moment he started work on the DC3, with Liane fighting on the domestic front, he had left Colin and Debby to their own devices. He might as well have waved a green flag. He was alone most of each day, Liane avoiding him wherever possible, speaking only when circumstances made it unavoidable.

Unknowingly, Debby herself started it. She had fashioned a simple shirt from parachute nylon, after her own disintegrated, along with her bra. Through it, her young breasts were clearly visible. Her plain skirt, too, was barely decent, serrated and raggy edge an inch below her crotch. As the days passed, she grew accustomed to near-nudity, and there were times after swimming when she would forget to slip into her shirt. As a result the shape and movement of her breasts became agonisingly familiar to Colin.

Naturally she was aware of the danger, and of the fact that lack of clothing increased it tenfold. But familiar dangers lose their bite in time, and she became forgetful. Colin's odd behaviour was no surprise to her: like any other girl of her age she had experimented with heavy-breathing boys behind sports pavilions and in the back seat of cars. Without really understanding why, she knew that boys liked to grope around, and she was also aware that the things they did pleased her too. Perhaps if she had found a boy she really liked, she might have let them go considerably further. The trouble was, they all had pimples and spots and bad breath and sweated profusely.

One day, she and Colin rode Khan far downstream, searching for wild rice. By early afternoon they were back on the soft grass near the fall, relaxing after a meal of fruit and a leisurely swim. Khan grazed contentedly nearby; Debby lay on her back beside Colin, a blade of grass between her teeth, gazing up into the blue sky through a tracery of leaves and branches. Colin meanwhile slept peacefully, arms and legs akimbo, head turned away from the sun. His cut-down trousers – the only garment he possessed – were tied loosely at the waist with a loop of cord, buttons by now being a lost and amusing memory.

She turned towards him, studying the strong, deeply tanned limbs, the hair bleached almost white by the sun. He had grown in stature, in body and in mind, and the young hairs on his chest gleamed silkily. Her eyes wandered down, and she could see the dark pubic hairs in the parting of his clothing.

Gazing at him, she felt a dull, inexplicable ache in her groin and an almost painful tenderness in the tips of her breasts. She shrugged off the clinging shirt, welcoming the warm, fragrant air, the heat of the sun on her body. Her nipples hardened; she squeezed a breast, suddenly lost in a storm of sensation. Between her legs, she throbbed, became moist, itched abominably. Hardly aware what was happening to her, she felt her eyes being brawn irresistibly to Colin's loins.

Tentatively, she stretched out a hand, undid the cord loop, reached inside and took the smooth softness of Colin's penis in her hand; drew it forth. It stirred, and her breath caught in her throat, her heart thundering in her ears. She glanced fearfully at the sleeper. He slept.

The head darkened, the phallus swelled before her eyes, suffused with dark purple blood: it assumed frightening proportions, standing stiff and erect. Her fingers encircled it, her wrist moving as if with a life of its own.

Colin groaned, woke, reaching sleepily for that which constricted him, found her hand, stared, mouth agape, until she bent to kiss him, still holding, still moving . . .

Afterwards it seemed to Debby that something magical had happened. Not the first time – no; that was a clumsy affair, involving considerable pain and not a few tears. But later, after a cooling swim – *that* was magic indeed.

Riding home, they let Khan find his own way, and sat close, saying little. It was very queer, Debby thought: she didn't really feel very different at all. Aching, hurting a little, perhaps – but the same person as before. Oh well – it had to happen some time; better with Colin than anyone. She hugged herself luxuriantly, sitting behind his broad back. And best of all, there shouldn't be any complications – not if Liane's advice was good. She regretted nothing, except perhaps the discomfort of the heat, the unavoidable slickness of skin upon skin. Next time . . . Next time, they would find a cool place, a cool time, in the long, dark hours of the night.

Three days passed before I next saw Donald Carter. His back was responding slowly to treatment, X-rays having disclosed no fractured vertebrae, but he was still in traction to correct strained muscles and some pressure on the lower spine.

When I walked into the ward, he seemed despondent and disinclined to talk. But he softened after a while. I think he valued the company – the medical staff were rarely free for a casual smoke and chat.

'I talked with the stewardess, Miss Dang Ko, a few days ago,' I said, as casually as I could. 'She's leaving hospital soon. Has she spoken to you?'

He raised a hand in disclaimer – it was still painful for him to turn his head quickly. 'No – and I don't think she will. Things were . . . difficult when we left the valley.' He stared at me. 'What did she say?'

I smiled. 'Nothing bad, Mr Carter – quite the reverse. She seemed to think you performed miracles.'

'That's a load of balls,' he said sourly. 'I had my own reasons for wanting to leave, in the end. And they all helped with the work. I don't care what Liane says, I *did* want to get out of that place.'

I said carefully, 'I think you did – in the end. But it must have been a wonderful place – peace, quiet, plenty of food . . .'

He looked at me, eyes heavy. 'It wasn't that, Mr Napier. Not that at all. I'll tell you what it was. I was just plain bloody scared – frightened out of my wits. The first time I took a really close look at that old wreck, I was absolutely pissed with fright. I didn't *think* it would never fly again: I *knew* it wouldn't.'

He stood alone on the concrete hangar floor, paper and pencil in hand, at a loss to know where to start. The main wheel tyres were shot completely, but there were new spares available. Luckily, the brakes had been left off, so with luck the wheels would turn all right, provided he could get the thing jacked up. There was one tripod screw jack, but it would be a pig of a job getting it under the wing with both tyres flat. Maybe it would be better to put two complete new wheels on. In the remote event that the plane ever moved again, he would have no brakes: the metal hydraulic lines were solid with congealed fluid, flexible pipes perished and decayed.

Main shock-absorber legs collapsed . . . The air in the combined air/hydraulic cylinders had long since escaped. The glands would be shot, too, which meant taxying on solid legs.

Christ – he must be crazy! Suppose they used the elephant to tow the thing down to the end of the strip? Brakes wouldn't matter, and they'd have the full length of the strip before the wheels caved in from the pounding.

Great heaps of gopher shit, Carter! What the hell are you *thinking* about?

Start from scratch. Aim for an irreducible minimum of services for a one-way flight. Brake system – scratch. Flaps? They could take off without, but needed them for landing – if ever they got that far. Undercarriage? 'UP' system only: it would have to be a belly landing – easier than slaving for weeks on undercarriage hydraulic systems.

Even a bird wouldn't fly in a thing like this. The guy they wanted was Pontius – he was an early pilot. Electrics? The engines would hand-start on the inertia system, and they'd be going in daylight, so no instruments needed. The radio was shot anyway. So who needed electrics? *Who wants to be a millionnaire*, he hummed gently. *I do*. He looked at his list and grinned, despite himself. Shit – he wasn't about to put the old bird into airline service. The engines would run fine on magnetos, without a battery; all he needed was an altimeter and an airspeed indicator and a compass. Of course, the whole enterprise was bloody mad – but he had to admit there was a certain quickening of the blood, something long-dead coming to life within him . . .

Christ, if he could only bring it off!

He started jotting down notes, lit a cigarette.

On the flight deck, he found the hydraulic reservoir and sight glass. Contents: nil. What else? He found a stick, went back and used it as a dipstick: it came out of the tank thick and yukky with a brown jelloid substance – all that was left of four gallons of hydraulic oil. Who cared?

The tally spread to four sheets – but who was counting? He checked the controls from the cockpit: all were free, but accompanied by shocking grating and squeaking noises. Back near the tail, he found himself glowering at a collapsed tail-wheel assembly, and the stark and ludicrous insanity of the whole business reared up and swamped him. He stepped back, looked again at the sagging wreck, laughter bubbling in his guts. He leaned on the guano-encrusted tail plane, clutching his sides, until the storm blew out.

Carter walked out into the sunshine, shading his eyes with the sheaf of notes. That strip, shoulder-high with brush – could it be cleared? Maybe they could bodge up some kind of harness for Khan so that he could drag a log behind him, or something ... Or burn the stuff down first ... It *could* be done, one way or another. *Sod* it! Everything was against him.

Supposing, just supposing, they got the thing running, in reasonable shape. He'd never flown a Dak before. He had no flight manual. Maps – yes, plenty of them. Once out of the valley, he'd know where to go. But that take-off ... He began cataloguing the hazards. No brakes – he'd have to keep it straight on throttle until the tail came up. Once airborne ... He turned slowly, eyes searching the rim of the cliffs. He would have to make a screaming, climbing turn on take-off, gain at least fifteen hundred feet before heading out over the mountains. He began sweating profusely – not from the heat.

If he lost an engine in that climbing turn, it'd be curtains. There was a minimum speed below which the rudder couldn't hold the plane straight against the pull of one engine. The Critical Speed ...

Carter shivered. Suddenly the sky seemed to weigh him down. Brushing the back of a hand over his brow, he walked back slowly to the hangar office, slumped down at the desk, shoved his notes aside irritably. His head ached, and he felt confused. Liane ... How bloody stupid can you get, old man? Of *course* she'd wanted to run away from you – who could blame her? And that damned aeroplane: half of him wanted to set fire to it – anything rather than risk a nightmare flight ending with a last horrific plunge into the ground, Liane and Colin and Debby all screaming, seconds away from death ... And yet at the same time, how he craved to be free from this place! Free of this desperate yearning for a girl half his age. For a fleeting moment he saw the years of misery stretch ahead, and groaned aloud at the prospect.

The sooner they got away the better ... But then the pendulum swung again: that old, hideous fear gripped him in a vice, twisting his guts until he laid his head on folded arms in a fruitless attempt to blot out the world and all its problems.

Sweat trickled down his back and legs. He got up, seized by an impulse, opened the filing cabinet drawer and took out a bottle. He sat down carefully at the desk, placed the Bourbon front and centre, lit a cigarette and sat back, looking at the rich, gold liquid behind the cut glass.

Carefully, he broke the seal, opened the bottle, sniffed gently. There was little aroma. He tilted the bottle, let the smallest drop rest on his palate and held it there for a moment, savouring the smooth, rich taste. It resembled an old sherry wine – until the first big swallow came to rest in his belly. Suddenly he coughed and spluttered, guts on fire, eyes watering, and put the bottle down smartly. Christ Almighty! Talk about rocket fuel!

The next one, Bourbon and water in equal parts, went down more easily. He relaxed into his seat. It had been too bloody long. It was better than anaesthetic, this stuff. He got up, rummaged in the filing cabinet, found a handful of cigars packed in moist leaves; they were soft, pliable, tempting. He threw away the cigarette, lit one, planted both feet on the desk and poured himself another shot.

Of all the goddam lunatic ideas . . . If they thought he was moron enough even to *think* about getting that thing into the air . . . He'd string 'em along for a while, of course. Produce his little list of problems, spares shortages, perfectly good reasons for staying put. There were, of course, those boxes on the Dakota: if he ever got out of here, he could afford a bottle like this every day – maybe two. But on the other hand . . .

There was a faded map on the wall, and he got up, drank deeply again, wandered over to take a look. With those boxes aboard, Vietnam was a non-starter. Those crazy bastards there would take the lot, probably shove the four of them into Ho Chi Minh pokey, and throw away the key.

It had to be somewhere else, preferably with the shortest sea-crossing, given the state of those engines. Hong Kong? No way. Four hundred miles of rain forest, six hundred miles of sea. More than seven hours' flying time – and in the monsoon. How about Thailand? Across the Gulf of Siam? Sheee-it. If they had to cross all that water, better off heading for friendly turf . . . Like Malaysia, fr'instance. That north-east coast . . . Koora . . . Khota Baru. Whatever. Goddam foreign names . . .

He took another stab at the Bourbon. Five hundred miles – four of 'em over the sea. Say, four hours' flying, allowing for a bit of wind . . . He burped gently, smiled at the pun. Four hours . . . Oh, God, that bagga nails wouldn't last four minutes, never mind four . . . an' the sea full of sharks? You gotta be jokin', Carter . . . Hey, no life-rafts either! Kids'd tried them for skylarking on the pool — damn things were rotten.

Suppose they lost a motor on the sea crossing? Suppose you change the bloody subject, Carter? The old pig'd fly on one engine well enough — do maybe 100 knots. With the live engine at full bore — but how long would *that* last?

He wiped his streaming face on a fragment of towel, found a mug, half-filled it with Bourbon, topped up with water. Not nice, drinking from bottle. Only bloody drunks did that . . . By God, that was good.

There was plenty time. He could still be workin' on the junkheap six months from now. An' as long as he was workin', they'd leave him alone . . . Show willing . . . That was it. Show bloody willing. He chuckled, balancing an inch of ash on his cigar. Couldn't do that sober, Carter.

Getting pissed in daylight always seemed strange. Remember that time in Yugoslavia! They'd delivered a dozen old Mosquito bombers, flying through a blizzard to the Yugoslav base at Placo . . . Landed in a six-foot trench dug by a thousand men in ear-muffs . . . Piled into the snowbank at the far end with engines stopped . . . Hairy as hell.

He drank again, remembering. That tin bath on the perimeter track, filled with fried chicken . . . A bottle of grog for everyone. He'd pulled a bottle of Slivovitz — local firewater, by God, an' not a patch on this Bourbon. Standing there in sunlight on a frozen road, unable to stop laughing, pissed as newts . . . The pilot of the transport Valetta, bottle in hand, staring at the trench he'd landed in. Saying they'd never make it off the ground in the 32-seater . . . Laughing like a drain when everyone agreed . . .

Staggering aboard, Carter finding himself asleep before take-off, waking up over Vienna an hour later, not really convinced he was still alive . . .

Something wrong with this bottle — must be a hole in the bottom. Empty. Another cigar — thash what he needed. An' music . . . Missed music . . . Dining-in nights in the Mess, crowded bars full of drunks, high cockalorum, lounge football . . . He grinned lopsidedly, maudlin, remembering. The songs round the piano . . . How did that one go?

'Airman told me before he died –
Dunno whether the bastard lied –
Knew a girl with a thing so wide,
Said she'd never be satisfied.
Built her a tool of stainless steel,
Driven by cranks, muckin' great wheel,
Two brass balls, both full of cream,
Whole muckin' issue driven by steam.
In an' out went the tool of steel,
Round and round went the muckin' great wheel,
Until at last the maiden cried,
"Enough, enough, I'm satisfied."
Now here comes the tragic bit:
Was no means of stopping it,
Until from her ring to her thing she split,
Whole muckin' issue covered in . . .
SWEET VIOLETS . . . pom-pom . . .'

Carter bellowed. He took a deep breath:

'Sweeter than all the roses . . .
Covered all over from head to foot –
Covered all over in –'

'Donald!'
'Huh?' He lurched round, mug in hand, grinning crookedly.
'Liane, ole girl . . . Drinkies?'
'Oh, sweet Buddha . . . He's drunk!'
'Incorrect. Pissed as coot, ole girl. Temporarily unner the affluence of inkerhol . . . *Sweet violets, pom-pom* . . . Listen, you know this one?'
The girl shrank back against the wall. 'Where did you get that bottle?'
'Plenny more where that came from, girl . . . Wanna li'l drinkies?'
She shook her head. 'I think you have too much now, Carter. I come to see if I can help with the aeroplane.'
Carter sniggered. 'Call that heapa crud an *aeroplane*? You're blind . . . Blind an' daft. Should be inna museum. *I* should be inna muckin' museum, too . . .' And he began laughing uncontrollably.
Liane frowned, edging towards the door. 'But you said you would try to fix it.'

'Try? Course I'll bloody try. Lots work, though . . . Lots spares we ain't got. Lots mechanics we don't have . . . Sure, we'll fix it.'

Carter found himself kneeling at the filing cabinet, trying to get the drawer open, climbing it as if it was a ladder. Liane saw the bottles, whipped one away from his groping hand just in time. He bellowed with rage, clutching at her; instinctively, she raised the bottle and broke it over his head. He went down like a felled oak, without a twitch of movement, and she stood paralysed for a long time, realising that she could have killed him.

But he breathed, albeit shallowly. His face was a sick, grey colour. She found water and a cloth and wiped away the blood from the matted hair, the sweat from his face.

The others were away, up at the waterfall: whatever had to be done, *she* would have to do it. She found an old engine cover, made a pillow, turned his head so that he couldn't choke himself if he vomited. That done, she resigned herself to wait.

The long, tedious hours of the afternoon passed slowly; his condition changed little, but Liane took comfort when she began to see a little colour return to his face. The pulse was fast, intermittent, to her inexpert touch. If was her fault and hers alone – she knew that now. In refusing him the comfort of her body, she had made it impossible for him to stay; yet his fear of flying prevented him from leaving. No wonder he sought refuge in a bottle . . .

She leaned forward, tenderly wiping away the sweat from his neck. She lifted one of his eyelids, shrank back, repulsed by the glazed, unseeing eyeball. It was wrong of her to have rejected him. It was little enough to give in exchange for the lives he had saved. But over the long weeks, she had come to feel for him as a father. And fathers did not do what Carter had tried to do. In the way of her race, Liane believed that she had lost face, yet she knew she would lose more face by apologising to him. She would have to find some other way. *If* he lived.

If he lived, things would be different. If he was at peace with himself, he would work well upon the aeroplane – and she would bring him that peace. She would help him overcome the fear which gripped him – *if* he lived. And if he died? Great Lord Buddha, spare this man, she thought despairingly. He is not young. He has done many things, some of them bad, but he is a good man who will climb up to the Six Blissful Seats in the fullness of time – for he tries to do good, for the simple love of goodness. Lord, if he must die, help him place a foot higher on the Celestial Ladder. And if he is to live, let me comfort him . . .

She sat there quietly in the fading light, watching the pale, lined face, the touch of grey in the stubbly beard, the thinning, sun-bleached hair. Soon Colin and Debby would return and come looking for them. They would help her watch over him through the night.

Donald Carter lay silent for a long time, his head moving restlessly on the hospital pillow. He had talked for a long time, and I knew I would soon have to leave.

He turned his head to me. 'I was a bloody fool, Mr Napier. I should have left that booze alone. I was out for nearly eight hours, and I could have died. Thank God they worked on me, all three of them – got me over to the hut and into bed. Made me sick, filled me with black coffee, make me walk round that damned hut until I was dog-weary. And I came out of it in the end. But I wasn't worth a damn for days after that. They were marvellous, all of them: they needed me to get them home, depended on me, trusted me – and I'd blown it. Worse still, they couldn't see it that way. Couldn't see that I'd been prepared to let them rot in that valley.'

I said slowly: 'It seems you owe that girl a great deal, Mr Carter.'

'You're right, there,' he said bitterly. 'Yet all I did for her was let her down. Same as . . .' His voice broke and he turned his head away, embarrassed.

I stood up. 'I'll leave you now, Mr Carter. If you decide you don't want to talk any more, I'll quite understand.'

After a pause, he looked at me in an odd manner. 'You still fly, Mr Napier?'

I told him I still had a private licence for small aircraft, up to the size of an Apache or an Islander. He was very interested in that. 'Is there an airfield up at Khota Baru?' he asked.

'Yes – but it's more of an air strip,' I said, curious. 'The Malaysian government run a daily service into there. Why do you ask?'

He stared at me, undecided. Then: 'Look here,' he said, 'can you spare a little more time?'

'Of course. If you're not too tired.'

'I'll tell you when I get tired,' he said grimly. 'First, you have to promise that what I'm going to tell you goes no further. Can you do that?'

I smiled at him. 'I think I can do that. Providing it's above board.'

Carter nodded, glanced towards the door. 'Fair enough. Look – check outside for me, would you? See if there's anyone there.'

I thought it best to humour him. There was no one there, of course.

'Now,' I said drily, 'perhaps you'll tell me what it's all about.'

He smiled, for the first time that day. 'Hold onto your hat. When I get out of here, I want you to fly me up to Khota Baru, in something capable of carrying a decent load – say, eleven or twelve hundred pounds. Could you do that?'

'I could – if I knew what the load involved. Malaysia is a foreign country. But surely an Islander could carry that load easily enough, with two or three passengers?'

He said slowly: 'Money is no problem. I'll tell you why. We brought something out of that valley, Mr Napier. Something the Americans left there five years ago – something of great value. Why it was ever left there, I don't know; maybe things were happening too fast – perhaps the pick-up plane never made it. The CIA used that strip for agents penetrating Thailand, Cambodia, Laos – agents who carried money for bribes, supplies, you name it. Money was their main weapon: given enough, they could and did buy governments, start revolutions. You only have to look at Chile and Allende . . . I want to bring out that load, for a very special reason.'

'What are you trying to tell me?' I said curtly.

'I brought out two boxes of mixed currency – dollars, Sterling, Swiss francs, local currencies from half the countries in the Far East. Plus a box of gold ingots weighing four ounces each – six hundred of them, weighing a hundred and fifty pounds, near enough. That's how I did in my back. After we landed on the beach, I sent the others on ahead, into the town, moved the stuff away from the aeroplane before anyone could get there. Near the edge of the forest. I must have passed out after that, because the next thing I knew, I was here, in hospital.'

I looked at him very hard. 'That's a very remarkable story, Mr Carter. Do you realise what you're saying? Two thousand four hundred ounces of gold . . . The current rate is around $400 an ounce, I think. That's nearly a million dollars!'

He smiled complacently. 'You've heard nothing yet. There was nearly ten million in dollars, used bills, and perhaps another four in other currencies. If you said $15 million, you wouldn't be far off. And it's still all there, up on the beach at Khota Baru. Waiting to be picked up.'

I took a deep breath. 'I . . . I don't know what to say, Mr Carter. And it won't be as easy as that, if what you say is true. The government here will have something to say.'

'True,' he said reluctantly. 'Look, Mr Napier – there must be some way we can bring that money back. Hell, Singapore can have a fair share – but I want the bulk of that money. I want to help the kids, Liane, the families of those lost in the Boeing.'

'And yourself?'

'No way,' Carter's voice was harsh, determined. 'I have to go back for those boxes, because I need the money for something much more important – something I can't keep to myself any longer than I have to. That's why I have to have your promise of absolute secrecy. Well?'

My thoughts were in turmoil. 'I don't know what to say to you, Mr Carter. After all, I'm an official of the Singapore Government. Tell me – does anyone else know the money was there, in the valley?'

He grinned, but there wasn't much humour behind it. 'You know,' he said finally, 'you have a habit of getting to the $64,000 question. Maybe that's because it's your job – asking questions, I mean.'

I leaned forward in my seat expectantly.

'You'd better switch that recording machine of yours on again,' he said, amused. 'You won't want to miss any of this next bit.'

TWELVE

Prince Yasovarman leaned on his sword, breathing hard as if he had run a great race, his face upturned to watch a great eagle soaring along the escarpment. Presently he dragged the body to the cliff, where a needle of rock jutted out from the brink. Staring down at the pool below the waterfall, he nodded in satisfaction, lifted the dead man and hurled him into space, leaning forward to follow the body's trajectory; then the head; then the curved bronze sword. Soon the waters below were once more smooth, undisturbed. Finally he moved away, down into the cavern of the black pool to join Indibaraja – and not a moment too soon, for just then the skies behind him opened up to the black violence of a monsoon storm greater than he had ever seen in all his life. As he progressed, the boom and hiss of thunder and wind outside slowly gave way to the sound of the fall, where Indibaraja waited.

'Let us wait out the storm,' he said gently, 'and then journey north to China, where we shall find a home until Angkor calls us again.'

But in the upper cavern, a great flood of water suddenly surged in, raising the level of the pool until a massive section of the roof caved in, sealing off forever the only way of escape. Yasovarman, worming his way back up the tunnel, needed but a single glance at the rock wall facing him to see that their fate, too, was sealed.

Together, surrounded by the wealth of an entire kingdom, they made love for the last time, with great enjoyment, until finally Yasovarman lifted up the princess, naked save for the great Elephant Ring of the Khmer kings, and approached the edge of the cave. They kissed once more, and together took a single step into Eternity . . .

The sun was hot on their skins as they lay on the grassy bank of the waterfall pool, their feet dangling idly in the cool water. Debby's face was covered with a square of fabric that had once formed part of her shirt, now long since disintegrated. She was naked to the waist, the remains of her skirt tied between her legs to form rudimentary shorts, and her tanned, pert breasts were rising and falling in slow cadence.

Colin leaned forward, blew gently upon a quiescent nipple. It stirred slightly, and he blew again, directing a thin feather of air at the brown-pink rosette. Debby opened one eye, lifted the corner of her facecloth, poked out an inch of tongue at him.

'Behave yourself.'

'Ah. Yes. Of course.' And he bent, kissed the tip of her breast and retreated a discretionary inch or two, half-expecting an angry reaction. He wasn't disappointed.

'Don't mess about, Col.'

'I'm not. I'm deadly serious.'

'Fool. If Donald could see what you're doing now –'

'– he'd be green with envy,' Colin interrupted, leering. He sucked greedily, and she pulled away irritably. 'Just think – we could be on our way home soon, now that Don's working on the plane. We won't have much time for –'

'Doing what you've got in mind?' she said sharply.

'Yes.'

'Think of something else.'

'Sure. Mm-mm . . .'

'Stop it now, Colin. And stop poking me with that – Ah . . . Colin . . .'

Debby lay stretched out, with Colin's solid, comforting weight upon her, drowsily staring up at the dark leaves of the trees, silhouetted again a china-blue sky. I just hope, she thought lazily, that Liane's patent baby-barrier works. So far, so good. She smiled: in fact, so far, very good indeed. She could feel Colin still inside her, but depleted now, drained . . . How much better it was, she mused, to be a woman, not a schoolgirl. She would never go back to school. Not after the valley . . . And *this* . . . She contracted a muscle experimentally, and Colin groaned softly in her ear. She smiled then, secretively, over his shoulder,

140

her eyes moving along the rim of the escarpment, climbing halfway to the sky.

Suddenly Debby stiffened, throwing him away from her roughly, scrambling to her knees. Colin rolled over clumsily, opened his mouth to complain, then saw her raised head, staring eyes, the hand held to her mouth in sudden alarm.

'Colin . . .'

Then he saw them too: a group of tiny figures moving along a clear rim of the cliff to the left of the falls. Too small to identify at such a distance, but he sensed the sameness of clothing, the carefully measured distance between each tiny figure.

Soldiers . . .

Debby got to her feet, frantically pulling on her clothes, sobbing with excitement and fear.

'Who can they be, Colin? What do you think?'

The boy spoke with new-found authority, his voice calm and unruffled. 'I think we may be in trouble. They're soldiers, of course – a patrol. They could be Vietnamese, Cambodian – anything, in this part of the world.'

'Can they see us?'

'Don't think so. We're under the trees, and Khan is back in the brush somewhere. Listen, we're ready for this – we've been ready for months. Donald's drilled us often enough, God knows. And the first thing we do is keep cool. I want you to get back to Donald just as quick as you can. Don't take Khan – you'll make better time without him. And stay under the trees – keep out of open space, OK? I'm going to stay here and watch them.'

'Will they come down?'

Colin considered. Strange, he thought, that now that it had finally happened, he felt quite undisturbed. He was more annoyed than anything – what a time to choose!

'I think they've been up there for some time, Debby. They'll have seen the hangar, maybe our lights at night. There's only one place they can get down – right here. If they can get down to that part level with the fall, where it's not quite so steep, they're home and dry.'

'Yes . . .' She bit her lip.

He drew her close, in the way she liked. 'Don't worry. Just

141

get to Don – he'll know what to do. He'd better bring some guns – but he'll know about that.'

'You mean we'll fight?'

'Bloody right we will. You think Don and I will let a gang of bloody Chinks get their hands on you and Liane?' the boy said truculently.

She turned white as a sheet. 'Oh, God . . .'

'Stop worrying. Get going as fast as you can. Take care.'

She kissed him swiftly, turned and was gone.

He lay motionless, his vantage point affording a view over the whole cliff face. If only he'd brought their one pair of binoculars. They were up to something over there, that was for sure. Messing about with sticks, or – trees? It was a long way up, and those sticks looked to be getting on for five or six inches thick. He scowled, shading his eyes against the sunglare. Of course! A tripod – they were building a tripod of sorts, sticking out over the cliff-edge. His heart started pounding. The bastards were coming down!

The hot afternoon drifted past, until the sun was an hour above the western escarpment. Donald's voice in his ear was welcome indeed. Colin turned, grinned widely.

Carter said calmly: 'So, we have company, eh?'

Liane and Debby were crouched behind him, all three regarding Colin with more than a modicum of respect. Carter said: 'Well done, Col. You did exactly the right thing. What are they doing up there?'

'Knocking up a tripod, I think, so they can let a rope down. I think there are seven or eight altogether.'

The older man nodded. 'I think you're right. That's how I'd tackle it, provided I had enough rope. And that's interesting – how did they *know* they'd need rope?'

'Because they've been here before?'

'That's one explanation. Another is that they may be a local unit who spotted us some time back and returned to their base for equipment.'

Debby crawled forward for a better view. 'It's awfully high, Uncle Donald. How will they get down?'

'Rappelling. They'll hang a single rope from that contraption, come sliding down in no time at all.'

Colin licked his lips nervously. 'And then?'

The pilot frowned. 'That's where it gets a bit difficult. Look at the options: if they've come for that American money in the Dakota, they won't want to leave anyone alive to tell the tale. Also, there's the girls . . .'

Colin said thickly: 'I already thought of that.'

'Right. Which doesn't leave us much choice. It's going to be rough, but I can't do it alone. You're going to have to do what many men go through life and never do –'

'We're going to kill them.' It was a statement, not a question.

'It's them or us. Now, we can do this two ways: either you take the girls away down the valley and go to ground . . .'

'No!'

Carter grinned. '*Or* we all work together to set up an ambush. We've a lot going for us: we're a good three miles from the base, and with luck, they'll think they can get down to ground level without being seen.'

Colin looked up at the group of busy figures working away on the edge of the cliff, far above, and he shivered, not entirely from excitement. He didn't like the look of this at all. Donald kept treating him like a man, and he wasn't – not really. But then he thought back to what he and Deb had been up to before all this happened. It seemed to be time for paying bills. Ever since he had saved Carter from the rapids down the valley, he'd stopped feeling like a schoolboy. And he wasn't one, not any more. Besides, plenty of people his age had done braver things.

'What do you want me to do?'

Carter said defiantly: 'I want you to do murder, Colin. No – I mean it. This isn't going to be any fair fight. Give those swine up there half a chance and they'd crush us like a steamroller. They're professionals. Our only chance is to hit them from cover with everything we've got. I brought along four M1s with plenty of ammunition, and a box of grenades. The girls did fine – they carried a hell of a load. So, we're only going to get one shot at this, so we'd better get it right. I've shown you all how to handle grenades – we'll try to get into position before dusk. When I give the word, we each throw four grenades as quick as we can: the girls get out of it quickly, head back to camp and hide nearby. You and I, Colin, will open up with the M1s right after the grenades, and keep firing until two of them are empty. Then we get out fast ourselves. Is that all perfectly clear?'

Three frightened faces nodded.

'One more thing,' Carter said bleakly. 'None of us have experienced anything like this before. I was in the 1939 war – but not on the ground. It's not going to be easy, and we may get hurt. What we *do* have on our side is surprise – and we also know the valley from end to end. There's only one real danger: that one or more of them may get away. We won't stand much chance in a real fight, and I wouldn't try it. Now – I don't think they'll tackle that rope at night, and there are still a couple of hours before dark. They'll come down as soon as they're ready, probably early in the morning, and start off down the valley. We'll wait until they're bunched together, ready to move off, then open fire . . .'

Colin found his mouth was strangely dry, and he swallowed hard. Carter didn't know that he, Colin, had attended several OCTU camps over the years and that at least they'd taught him to use a gun. But killing? He glanced at Debby, who was now on her knees, peering up at the escarpment. He remembered her as she'd been that afternoon, and found his jaw clenched tight in determination. He'd do what had to be done . . .

Keeping well under cover, Carter recced the area around the base of the cliff, at the side of the fall. The soldiers' ropes would bring them down the vertical face to the point where the vertical cliff bellied out, level with the fall. From that more gentle slope, they would then climb down, angling away from the pool, gaining ground level in a small natural clearing, some fifty yards from the scree slope. Carter moved around cautiously, taking in the ground contours, possible arcs of fire. Satisfied, he went back to the others.

'I think we've got a good chance. But I want you three to stay under cover here for the moment; there'll be plenty of time to get into position later. They may send a couple of men down to check out the area, in which case we're in trouble. Also, they may keep some men up top, and even if we write off the main party, that spells more trouble. Christ, there's so many different ways they could play this . . .'

Liane, thus far, had been very quiet. She had every reason to trust Carter; but killing was against all her natural instincts. On the other hand, she had spent enough years working in a man's world to know what would happen if the soldiers up there got their hands on her. Oddly, that wasn't what was uppermost in her mind.

'Donald,' she said tentatively, 'if all goes well . . . there will remain a rope hanging from the top of the cliff?'

'So –?'

'Could we . . . Will it be possible to climb it? To leave the valley?'

Carter said thinly: 'I don't need to answer that, Liane – look for yourself.'

High on the rim, a coil of rope arced out, unwinding as it fell, reaching – with feet to spare – the broken scree at the bottom of the rock face. It hung there, swaying gently, more than four hundred feet in length.

The pilot stared up, with the rest, his face shrouded in thought. 'Well, there's no turning back now. We'll have to play it by ear.'

He was perfectly right, in one respect at least. With perhaps half an hour of daylight left, he sat wedged between two rocks not thirty yards from the danger zone, watching as two figures rappelled down, swinging easily out from the cliff and falling in controlled short pitches until they reached the lower level. Once they left the rope and began descending the scree-covered slopes, he could see them clearly – and grunted in surprise.

One, the leader, was a white man, big, husky, dressed in tan trousers, lumber boots halfway to his knees, a leather jacket swinging open to reveal a leather belt and holster. The man who followed was a slim, dark-featured Asiatic – almost certainly Vietnamese. He wore dark green coveralls, jungle boots, peaked cap, and an automatic weapon of some sort was slung over one shoulder.

With the fall rumbling gently in the distance, the men worked their way down through the scattered boulders and scree until they gained level ground. Carter froze in sudden fear: no more than ten feet away, in the little clearing, they stopped, stripped off the strong gloves they had worn for rope work, lit cigarettes.

'Okay, Tran?'

'Okay,' said the thin dark-haired man. His voice was high-pitched, penetrating. 'My hands . . . Is not easy, the rope.'

'That it isn't,' said the bulky man with a wolfish grin. Carter, watching, studied the pale blue eyes, the square, underhung jaw, strong white teeth: it was a face of quite exceptional strength and virility, and it reflected the unrestrained viciousness of its owner. There was a cruel, sadistic twist to that wide, thin-lipped mouth. Carter shivered involuntarily, his mind an icy cavern filled with fear.

'What now, Macbain?' the Asian soldier said in his stilted voice.

Macbain!? Jesus, thought Carter dazedly. *Macbain! Task Force Baker Five was back!*

'Now – nothing. We stick to the plan. There's not much daylight left. You can bring the team down at first light. We're okay for rations and water. You left your glasses up top?'

'Yes . . .' Carter heard the prolonged, sibilant hiss of Oriental English. 'Sergeant Pak Trang Dok is a good man. If he sees anything, he will throw down stones to warn us.'

'Christ . . . not too close, goddamit.'

'No. Those people – you said nothing of them in Saigon. The money – you think it is still here?'

The big man scowled. Carter found the face hard to read in the fading light. The shadows were longer, darker now. 'Jesus H. Christ, Tran, do we have to go through all this every time we talk? I told you the money's here, in the valley. I'll tell you where when I'm good and ready, and not before.'

The Vietnamese officer said bitterly: 'Still you do not trust us, Macbain.'

'You're goddam right I don't,' the big man snarled. 'I didn't work my guts out for five years getting this thing together, for a bunch of fucken gooks to cut my throat before we even got out of Saigon. Christ, I spent fourteen months in this Godforsaken hole with the CIA. I'd rather have done the time on Alcatraz. Workin' all day in the sun, rain for weeks on end . . .'

'You said you were last man out of the valley. Why you not take money with you?'

'I took what I could carry, damn you – and I had one hell of a time for five years. You wanna know what happened? I'll tell you what happened, you little gook bastard. We got four ships out of here after Saigon fell; I was with the last, waiting for the gooney-birds to bring in the field men and their war-chests. Then we got shot up by your goddam Migs, and I missed the last plane out. You listening, damn you?'

'I listen.'

'There were three of us left here – Simmonds, the pilot; Garvey, the mechanic, and me. The ship was in the hangar with a blown cylinder head, or it would have got shot up too. No way it was going to be ready in time. Then the last chopper came in: a Huey with long-range tanks and room for one guy only.'

'You?'

'You betcha ass, Tran. Here – you wanna snort? I got half a bottle left here –'

'No. What happened?'

'Well, I guess it don' matter a pinch of shit now. Simmonds wanted to argue – I hadda kill him. Right there in the plane. Garvey, I figured, was no use to me: he was no pilot, so I left the sonofabitch there to rot. I filled my pockets, got into the Huey and made tracks.'

'Why,' the Vietnamese officer said coldly, 'why you no tell me this in Saigon?'

'Because you'd have called in your secret police. Because they'd have boiled my balls in molten lead to make me talk, if they'd got a scent of the dough. It took me a long time to find a guy like you, Tran, but you came well recommended. I knew you'd prefer half a million bucks to working in a goddam paddyfield.'

Tran said in the thickening gloom, 'You were a brave man, to come back to Vietnam. We do not like Amis very much.'

'Which was why I came to you, instead of the government. And why I told you as little as possible. Shit – all I had to do was whisper half a million bucks out of my money down there.'

'*Our* money,' said the high-pitched voice from the darkness.

'Okay. I'll tell you where it's at in the morning. Your guys know what to do, right?'

'They know. Pak will send the six men down at first light, staying on top with the radio. You go first, with one man – we follow. Is right?'

'Is right, you little yellow bastard. And tell those guys to keep their gook hands off the women. They're white – and

147

they're mine. Plenty of squint-eyed whores in Saigon for your boys.'

'I tell. You have another American cigarette, yes?'

'Shee-it!' Macbain's voice was filled with exasperation. 'All the way up-country, you've smoked my cigarettes. Maybe once we get our pinkies on that dough you'll buy your own. I never met a gook yet who didn't bum a smoke every time you spoke to him.'

The Asiatic soldier laughed. 'First, I think I buy an air ticket to South America, my friend. Then cigarettes.'

'Yeah? You mean, you don't like your cosy little Commie state now you've got it?'

Carter, listening, grinned broadly.

'Communism . . . Capitalism . . . Two names, same thing, I think. Already, we have boss class in Vietnam – people with money, power, influence, people in authority. People with big cars, new houses, plenty food, money in foreign banks. Why you laughing, Macbain?'

'Oh, holy shit . . .'

'So. What different from capitalist country, hey? You tell . . .'

Silence. Carter eased his stiff body a little, listening.

'You 'wake, American pig?'

The man in the rocks heard a muffled snore and grinned. Macbain had nodded off. *Well, you bastard,* thought Carter, *sweet dreams.* I hope you dream you've shot your balls off – and I hope your dreams come true. He began working his way back towards the river. So, he thought grimly, *that* answered a whole lot of questions. It solved the mystery of those two poor sods back on the airstrip. Just possibly, guys, I might be able to square the account for you. We'll see. We'll see . . .

Half an hour before dawn.

Carter moved with painful slowness, rubbing his numbed leg muscles to stimulate the circulation. There was a faint pink glow in the sky to the east, and the shadow of the escarpment projected onto the far rock walls left a brilliant band of sunlight along the western rim. Even as he watched, the shadow slid downwards. He groped cautiously for the M1, checked the safety off and hoped to God Colin was awake –

assuming he'd managed to sleep. He was a hundred feet off, deep in a bamboo thicket with the girls.

Last night they had talked for an hour about the task that lay before them. It would have been easier, Carter reflected, if Macbain had opted to stay with the main group. The surprise attack he and Colin had planned would alert the big American out there in the valley. He'd debated trying to silence Macbain first without sending the balloon up but that was a job far beyond their capabilities; the CIA man could probably handle all four of them without getting out of breath.

He refused flatly to allow the girls up front. They were well capable of throwing a grenade up to forty yards, and that was as close as they would come.

'None of us,' he told them acidly, 'have any experience of action – so we play it as simply as we can. No one plays the bloody hero. As soon as you girls hear the first bang, you throw your four grenades at the same place and get the hell out. Col will be on the right, me on the left, so you don't have to worry about hitting us. Get back to the tail unit on the hill and wait for us there. Colin, you know what you have to do?'

'Okay. I fire off the full magazine, shooting low, chuck the gun away and run like the clappers back here. We pick up the spare M1s and ammunition, and go after Macbain.'

'Very good. I think that's it, then.'

Liane said anxiously: 'And you, Donald?'

'I'll be okay. From my spot, I can see the whole clearing. I'm counting on getting most of them first time round. But I'm not stopping to check – we *have* to get Macbain. With him out of the way, we can deal with stragglers. Colin?'

'Huh? I'm fine. Bloody terrified, of course.'

'You and me both, pal,' Carter admitted. 'I'm too old and you're too young for this game, but what the hell. Like the man in the film said, "You wanna live forever?" '

'Yes, please –'

Carter grinned in the darkness. 'You'll be fine. Get some sleep. When we let rip, they won't even know what's hit them.'

He was wrong there.

Lieutenant Tran Van Dang, toughened veteran from Hanoi, with years on the Ho Chi Minh trail behind him, hit the deck at the first roar of a grenade, and Carter's burst from his M1 went over his head with an inch to spare. All around, Tran heard his men screaming, falling. He hurled himself forward through the low brush, wriggling deeper, hands scraping the ground, burrowing, burrowing. The second grenade exploded yards to his left, followed by an endless stream of the things: there seemed to be no pattern – it was as if they were falling at random. One fell at his feet, rolled to a stop. He picked it up, hurled it from him, dived for another, drew back his arm . . . Almost made it . . .

The bomb travelled the first two feet of a short parabola before it clicked and exploded in his face. He was aware only of a great rushing wind and blackness that picked him up and swept him into eternity as if he were made of rice paper.

Carter stood frozen, legs apart, listening to the echoes rebounding down the valley and the faint groan of a wounded man away to the right. Suddenly, he found himself sobbing with pent-up emotions – terror, anger, and a vast, swelling bubble of exultancy at the havoc they had wrought within those few short seconds. He had lost count of the grenades in the continuous overlapping explosions, and even now there was an angry high-pitched whine of protest in his ears. He stood still, lean and predatory in the early sunlight, gun at the ready.

Nothing. Far away, shocked birds were screeching anxiously, and down the valley, Khan trumpeted stridently twice, three times.

Carter walked forward stiffly, slipped a new magazine into position, set the gun to auto and moved out into the clearing with almost painful care. There had been seven men in the team, excluding Macbain. Macbain – what was going through his mind now? Carter walked round gingerly, counting heads – or what was left of them.

He whirled. Something had stirred in the brush. Panicky now, he shoved the gun forward, the action moving the trigger, sending a long, searing burst into the undergrowth. The rifle stopped firing, on an empty shell, and he heard an odd sound, as if from a heavy weight being thrown into a bush. Then silence.

Shit. Supposing there were more of them? And here he was, standing in the open like a great prick . . . Wanly, he managed a grin of sorts and moved forward, eased round a small thicket – and stopped. Turning away, he let the gun fall, dropped to his knees and puked helplessly, time and time again. Presently, he wiped his face, ground his teeth together, checked out the area. Seven? He shook his head. There were enough pieces to make seventeen. Now he knew why the Americans talked about 'head-counts'. He found six, in various states of disrepair, including the lieutenant – which meant that Macbain *had* taken one man with him, dammit.

That, he thought bitterly, made things just a little more difficult . . . He turned and found himself staring down at the remains of the officer. Two legs were joined at the hip by something unspeakable. Above that – nothing.

Carter kicked angrily at the rifle he'd used for this obscenity, and went away. All the rest of his life he was going to have trouble trying to forget the scene in that little clearing.

THIRTEEN

Over the centuries, the waterfall served the gentle pool. It has always been the custom from prehistoric times for humanity to regard Time as a flowing river, bringing down to the Present the gifts of future events, which exist for a fleeting moment before retreating into the past. Three thousand years ago, Chinese philosophers sensed that the truth was quite different: that Man moves forward through Space, creating Time with movement, and that the only real meaning of Time was Change. Thus the pool and the fall and the valley altered as the years were consumed: here a rockfall, there a subsidence following some deep seismic disturbance. But these were merely different strokes of the brush upon the canvas of history: the valley endured. No so the manifestations of humanity within the cave. As the Armada sailed to destruction, the sandalwood boxes decayed into dust; as death swept the plains of Austerlitz and Waterloo and the Somme, the fading garments on the floor of the cave dissolved into the dust whence they came.

Yet the cave and the fall and the pool and the valley would have given no hint, to a casual traveller, of despair and neglect and isolation. Rather, it was as if they were waiting . . . waiting . . .

Working his way downstream, the tall, spare man limped slightly, thinking very deeply, keeping in cover and shade almost automatically. By the manner of his briefing, he had ensured that Colin and the girls would retreat to the tail section rendezvous after the first clash: Colin, he knew, would not wait, when Carter failed to show up – if the older man was dead, the girls would be his first and only concern. Carter's face darkened, and he gripped the spare M1 tightly, feeling the weight of the bandoliers on his shoulders.

Item: Macbain, inevitably, knew the shit had hit the fan.

Item: Macbain, therefore, was going to be a very angry man – and a very, very careful one. He would understand that he, now, was the quarry, and that he was liable to be bounced at every step. Carter grinned wryly, remembering the fighter pilot slang. All the same, the American, undoubtedly, was a seasoned CIA killer who would use that .45 automatic to good effect.

Item: maybe it was Carter who was on the spot, Macbain who was lying in wait.

So? So he had to out-think the man.

Supposing he was Macbain . . .

For a start, he'd know the hangar complex was empty. Possibly, he knew that only one man, two girls and a young boy opposed him. Ergo, he would concentrate on the man first. Carter nodded as he threaded his way through a bamboo clump. It made sense. He paused at the edge of a stretch of open ground, considered crossing, thought better of it and began working his way round. About a mile to go to the base . . .

'Don!'

Carter hurled himself forward, hit the ground, rolled twice and finished up under a thorn bush, breathing hard. Jesus . . . Who the hell –?

'Don – it's me, Colin!'

Carter raised his head, saw the boy emerge upright from the bushes fifty feet away. He dropped his gun, surged forward, covered ten yards at a dead run, weaving sharply, went in waist-high with a braced shoulder. Suddenly the two of them were rolling deep in the brush, entangled with vines and with each other.

Carter sobbed for breath. 'You bloody fool! Didn't I tell you to go with the girls, if I was late? What the hell are you playing at, for God's sake?'

'Don, I –'

'Shut up, you bloody little turd! Jesus – you could have got us both killed!'

Colin stared at the older man, face ashen, only now comprehending the enormity of his offence. 'I . . . Don, I'm sorry –'

'Oh, Christ, belt up, Colin. Suppose Macbain had been waiting for us here? We'd both have been pork, for sure.'

The boy grinned weakly. 'Pork – that's Treasure Island – Long John Silver . . .'

'Long John bollocks,' Carter said wrathfully. 'It's gospel truth. At least you've got your gun. How many mags in that bag?'

'Four. Did you –? I mean, are they –?'

'We did all right. We only have to worry about Macbain and one man he took with him. There's one more up on the cliff, but he shouldn't worry us. Did the girls get clear okay?'

'I – I think so.'

Carter felt a stab of remorse. What else could he expect? Colin was just a teenage kid, after all. And he *had* done pretty well back in the clearing – Carter had heard his M1 blasting away.

'All right. We've been dead lucky, Col. But now we'll have to watch our step. Macbain'll be waiting for us – and he's a pro. Give him half the square root of one small chance, and we've had it. Understand?'

'Yes,' replied Colin, a little shakily.

'Okay. So you do exactly as I tell you – and nothing more.'

'Right.'

'If we run into trouble, keep your head down and leave the field clear – I don't want to risk hitting you. When it comes to the crunch, my aim's likely to be piss poor. Okay?'

The boy nodded, crouching on his heels in the thick scrub.

'One more thing – and it's important. When we move, I go first, twenty yards ahead; you watch our backs. Don't worry about anything up front. Stop often to listen – you see anything move, let fly. Now, if he's on the base, he'll expect us from this direction, so I'm going to make a big loop round and come in behind the hangar. If we get separated, don't shout: get back to the tail unit and sit tight. All clear?'

'All clear, Don.'

'Right. Talk about Dad's Army. Jesus wept . . . Come on.'

Almost three hours later, the sun was high overhead as Carter parted the fronds of fern in front of him with his gun barrel and stared at the rear of the hangar.

Nothing.

He turned, waved Colin forward, gestured urgently downwards with the palm of a hand. The boy crawled forward, lay prone beside him.

'Don?'

'Not a damn thing. They could be anywhere. Christ, I wish I knew what to do.'

Colin said grimly: 'We've no choice, have we?'

'Huh?'

'We have to go in, look for them. Question is, where? In the plane?'

'Shit, no. Nowhere to run – and there's fuel in those tanks. The huts, maybe – that's what I'd go for. There's a backdoor with a clear view down the strip. Those huts are clear of the ground, two or three feet. If I can make the last in line, I can move down the rest and listen out for them. If you work round a bit so you can see the front walls and doors –'

'I've got it, Don –'

'– you may have a clear shot. Set your M1 on auto. No – like this . . . Good. And sight down fully – it's only fifty-yard range. If I hear them in the huts, I'll put a short burst up through the floor. That should start them moving out the front door, giving you a clear shot. If you miss, they'll be under the hut looking for me.'

'My God, Don –'

'You said it. Pork. You think you can handle this?'

'I can handle it.'

By damn, Carter thought amazedly, I think he can, too, the spunky little bastard . . .

He moved off to the right, Colin to the left, slowly crawling with the M1 across his forearms, the way he'd seen it done in many a movie. Under the first hut, the air was cool and moist, away from the sun. Carter sat up, head howed under the floor, listening. You idiot, how the hell are you going to be able to point an M1 up straight? He grinned, shaking his head in mock despair.

Silence.

He began to worry. Maybe he'd guessed all wrong . . . Maybe Macbain was miles away.

Try the next hut . . .

He got moving again, body sliding very slowly over the rotted vegetation, heading for the bright avenue of sunshine between the buildings. Nothing . . . Carefully, he got his legs under him, came up to a crouch and started across the gap. Behind him, he heard the faintest creak and found time to think about dying before the weight landed solidly on his back, flattening him across his rifle, ramming his face and mouth into the dirt. His neck cringed, expecting the bullet or knife; he tensed, then erupted in a volcanic surge of energy, smashing aside the reversed pistol swung by the soldier. Carter had a brief glimpse of green cloth and staring oblique eyes, before a hurtling body hit the Vietnamese from one side, and the weight came free, leaving Carter gasping like a landed fish.

Colin, much later, confessed that he had no real idea of what happened: when he saw the soldier jump Carter from the verandah, a thick red fog seemed to swim before his eyes. There were clouds of dust and a heaving body under him, and he had a forearm under the man's chin, a knee in the small of his back; his right hand found his left, forming a bar of immense strength. He pulled back savagely in a single, convulsive heave. He heard a crack, almost like a .22 pistol he had once owned; felt the man under his knee jerk spasmodically and dissolve into grisly immobility.

He lay motionless on top of the green-clad body, chin resting on a still shoulder, great shudders of reaction passing down his body in waves; hands were pulling at his arms, a voice in his ear.

'All right, boy . . . Easy, now . . . You can let go. Colin – it's finished.'

He turned his head. Carter knelt close by, easing the boy's forearm clear, pushing him clear of the body. Colin rolled onto his back, looking up at the clear blue of the sky, tears welling; he didn't know if he was crying for himself, or for what he had done.

Carter left him, shoved and rolled the body of the soldier under the hut, reached up onto the verandah and brought down the Kalashnikov with the curved magazine and the exaggerated front sight. The boy needed time to adjust to the shock; reality needed time to penetrate, and that reaction would be a long time coming. Waiting, Carter squatted in the shadow, staring around at the panorama of waving grass, trees swaying in the wind along the strip, the customary noises of birds in transit. It all looked so damned peaceful – and menacing.

Macbain was no fool. He had known they would come looking for him and left a booby trap in the form of a

Vietnamese soldier, a deserter along for the easy money the American had promised.

Colin sat up, nodded at Carter's frantic signal to keep low, stared with dazed eyes at the pair of dirty jungle boots sticking out into the sunshine. He looked away quickly, shuffled over to Carter, sat down, rubbing his right arm.

'It aches,' he said, wonderingly.

The pilot grinned. 'I'm not surprised. Bloody good work, Col. My God, you'll have something to tell your kids about. You learn that at school?'

The boy grinned, his face strained but with an air of quiet satisfaction. 'Played wing three-quarter. Mind you, I'd have been sent off for a tackle like that. Is he . . .?'

'Yes. That's twice you've saved my bacon, lad. I won't forget.'

Colin nodded sombrely. 'We're still a long way from even. What about Macbain?'

'That,' Garter said grimly, 'is a bloody good question. He's not here – if he had been, he'd have jumped in feet first, with both of us close together. But we'll check the place out just in case. You okay?'

'Sure.'

Carter smiled. 'Cocky little bastard . . . Just don't push your luck. Let's go.'

Twenty minutes later, they were in the mess hut, wondering what the hell to do next. Colin was near the window, on watch, while Carter made coffee. Both were uncomfortably aware that despite their search, Macbain could be out in the bush with a .45 pointed their way.

They were not disappointed.

'Don!'

'What is it?'

'Macbain. Out there. With Liane.'

'*What?*' Carter came out of the galley like a prowling tiger. Christ, the man was a devil incarnate. Of course, he would have seen the tail unit from the rim; with the camp deserted, there was only one place to look. But *Liane* . . . The pilot groaned, as if in real pain. He crossed to the window.

The big man had his left arm round Liane, pulling her close to him. With his right hand, he jammed the barrel of the .45 up under her chin, forcing her head back at an acute angle. A white-toothed grin split the tanned face a hundred yards away.

'You hear me in there?'

Colin stared at the pilot, his face grey and racked with anguish. 'For God's sake, what do we do?'

Carter ignored him and kept his eyes glued to Macbain. 'I hear you.'

'I wanna talk. Truce – unnerstand?' Macbain yelled.

The pilot set his teeth, picked up the M1, checked it, walked out onto the verandah where he and Liane had sat watching so many sunsets. Macbain urged the girl forward brutally; and the colour drained from Carter's face.

'Listen, fella – you answer a few questions, or I jerk off the girl and take my chance. You read me?'

'You're doing the talking,' Carter said harshly.

'That firing – my team?'

'– that was,' the pilot said, with some satisfaction.

Macbain scowled. 'And my man here?'

'Gone to join his friends.'

The American nodded sagely. 'For an old guy and a kid, you've done okay. I guess you saw us come down yesterday?'

'We saw you, Macbain. Cut it short.'

Liane squirmed as the big man started. 'How come you know my name?'

'I was . . . handy when you talked to Tran.'

'The hell you were. Seems I underestimated the problem. I suppose the guy up top pulled up the rope when the shit hit the fan?'

'Right again. *Go easy on that girl, sod you!*' Carter's voice was filled with venom.

Macbain caught the inflexion and scowled. 'Listen, don't push it too hard, you Limey sonofabitch. I'm in the driving seat, and don't you forget it. How long have you been here in the valley?'

'A few months.'

'That wreck up the valley?'

'Yes. Get on with it . . .'

Macbain looked down at Liane, grinned savagely. He slackened off his grip, just enough to let her breathe. He stared at Carter. 'You want this broad back in one piece, right?'

'Yes, damn you –'

'Okay. That DC3 – any chance of fixing it?'

Carter said truthfully: 'I'm no engineer. How would I know?'

'On account of you've been spending most of your time in that hangar – we've been watching you for a week while we looked for a way down. Well, that leaves us with a problem, right? We all need to get out – and I've got the girl.'

'Don't bank on it,' Carter said heavily. 'You have to sleep sometime, and there's two of us.'

Macbain said nastily: 'I could soon set those odds right, buster. Look, I'll do a trade: I let the girl go, and we work together to get out of here. And we split the money down the middle. Deal?'

Carter said bluntly: 'No deal.'

'You wanna think that through again?' Macbain suggested.

'No. You want to kill Liane right now, you go ahead. But you'll go the same way ten seconds later. And try to move away, I'll kill you both myself.'

Macbain sneered. 'You don't have the balls, fella.'

'Try me,' said Carter between gritted teeth. 'Try me. And don't get any stupid ideas that girl means anything to me – she's just a stewardess from our plane. I don't have many years left – maybe you'll be doing me a favour, killing me. But you won't walk away from here. Because the boy's got a gun on you too, Macbain. Right, Colin?'

'I'm here, Don.'

Macbain scowled, clearly uneasy. Carter began to fear that he was forcing the man into a corner with no way out. Men of violence react very strongly in such circumstances . . . It all seemed totally unreal, Carter thought, standing here with a loaded gun in his hand, on a day when he had killed six or seven men already. Was it really only a few brief months ago that he was drinking himself to death in Hampshire pubs?

There was so much now that he wanted to do, *needed* to do. Liane's eyes were staring at him accusingly, and time seemed to slow down, stop with a judder.

Few people realise how fast a large elephant can travel in the charge. With no warning, Khan burst from the trees fifty yards away from Macbain, legs going like pistons, ears spread wide, tail ramrod-straight, trunk uplifted. And as he came, he bellowed in fury, the trumpet call echoing round the valley.

The big American jerked his head round, stood transfixed. Dropping the girl, he used both hands to fire the .45, but it was like using a peashooter to stop an express train. Great jagged wounds appeared in Khan's head and trunk; the gun was empty now and Macbain, screaming words incoherently, hurled the weapon at the raging beast, then turned to run.

The elephant caught him in mid-stride; a single fat coil of trunk snaked round his waist, and he was lifted off his feet, legs kicking frantically, while Khan half-skidded to a halt on the very edge of the runway strip. The bull trumpeted again, brought the man to earth, holding him down firmly. With almost ponderous ease and lack of haste, it bent at the front knees, and Macbain disappeared from view into the long grass. Carter heard a single, searing howl of agony, abruptly cut off; then he turned away and walked stiffly towards Liane, a frail figure down on one knee in the dust . . .

They found Debby an hour later, stumbling through the river shallows on her way back to camp. In the late evening, when Carter's trembling had subsided and Colin had returned from his solitary communion with himself, the girl filled in the details. She had moved uphill away from the tail unit to see what she could see in the valley; meanwhile Macbain had moved in quickly, caught Liane, suffering no more than a few facial scratches in the process, and hustled her away. Debby had heard her screams, but could do nothing to help: only when she heard the faint sounds of shots from Macbain's gun did she finally decide to come down from the hills, come what may.

Carter lit a cigarette.

'We've been incredibly lucky,' he said, 'and that's not detracting a damn thing from what everyone did. It could have been a great deal worse if Debby hadn't spotted them up on the rim. I've been asking myself if that really *is* the end of it, and I think it may well be: Macbain left one man up on top, who pulled the rope up when the firing started, but none of his men were real troops – regular soldiers, I mean. I think Macbain had a deal of some sort with the other one, Tran. All in all, I doubt if anyone will be looking for them.'

Debby said tiredly: 'What about the one left up above, Uncle Donald?'

'He can take his chances. He's alone, up in the mountains, with nowhere to go and all his friends gone. I shouldn't lose any sleep over him. How Macbain expected to get the money out undetected, I don't know – maybe he had a helicopter waiting somewhere. Either way, it doesn't matter a damn.'

They sat around the mess table, watching his face. He stubbed out the cigarette. 'All the same,' he went on, 'I think we should move as fast as we can on the aeroplane and get out of here as soon as possible, just in case Macbain has friends who'll come looking for him. And one more thing. I'm not given to making speeches, and Colin's got a big enough head already. But I want to tell you, Col, in front of the girls, that you did well today. Not many lads of your age would have managed to do what you did. But I don't want you to get hung up over those men. You saw what they were like and you know what they would have done. We'd shoot a rabid dog without hesitation – and these were worse than animals. End of speech.'

Debby came round the table, eyes brimming. She slipped an arm round Carter's shoulder. 'You're a very nice person, Uncle Donald. And thank you for saying that about this great lout here – we'll never hear the last of it, I'm sure. You'll have the best meal we can fix up for you. What are you going to do now?'

Carter got up, picked up his cigarettes, jerked his head at Colin. 'Come on, lad. Let's leave them to it. We've got a job to do.'

Outside on the verandah, Colin stopped, a stray lock of hair over one eye. He pushed it back irritably. 'What job?'

'A little digging,' the pilot said sombrely. 'Let's get this place cleaned up.'

Liane said quietly: 'Debby, will you be all right if I leave you for a little time?'

'Why, yes. What is it?'

'I must go to Khan – he is hurt. He saved us all today, I think. Perhaps I can help him now.'

'Liane, let me come with you.'

'No,' the tall, bronzed girl shook her head. 'This I must do myself. It is strange . . . There is an understanding, a bond, between Khan and myself . . .'

She shook her head, confused and disturbed, and walked slowly out of the hut.

PART TWO

FOURTEEN

As things turned out, it was twenty-four hours before I was able to talk to Donald Carter again. This was largely due to the intervention of the night sister, who, with some considerable show of temper, pointed out that it was now evening and that Carter had been talking for a number of hours. She hustled me out very quickly indeed, uttering dire threats against the day staff for their dereliction of duty, and when I suggested that I should return next day, she would only commit herself to an uncompromising, 'We'll see . . . We'll see.'

The rest must have been beneficial for Carter, for when I returned to him at four in the afternoon, he was sitting by the bed, dressed in shirt and slacks, reading a slim sheaf of letters. With him was a burly young man in RAF khaki drill, wearing a pilot's brevet and a look of extreme satisfaction. Carter introduced him as Gavin, his son, newly arrived from Hong Kong on a VC10. Gavin shook my hand, said he had to leave on the instant but would visit his father again later; I went out into the corridor with him.

'Your father's a remarkable man,' I said.

He nodded. 'If only half of it is true, I ought to take my shoes off when I go in there,' the young man said cheerily. 'He seems none the worse for it all. Except . . .'

'Except what?'

'Something's niggling away at him, Mr Napier. I don't know what. He should be as happy as a pig in shit, but somehow . . .' His voice tailed off.

I said carefully: 'Did he give you any indication what it might be?'

'Not a word. But that's normal: he's always been . . . reserved.'

I said I thought that was a fair description. We shook hands again, and I watched the young man start down the stairs. I could see Carter in him quite clearly, Carter as he had been thirty years previously – but of course, I did not say so.

'That's quite a son you have there,' I said when I rejoined him.

He nodded absently. 'Have you had time to think about what I told you yesterday?' he asked diffidently.

'If you mean about those men you killed, Mr Carter, I think you had no choice at all. I only thought it was tragic that a young boy like Colin –'

'– should be involved? I'd have kept him out of it if I could, Mr Napier. Will you have to include all that in your report?'

I smiled at that. 'Certainly not. I don't approve of what you did, but I'm no policeman, nor judge and jury. May I ask you a question?'

'Surely,' he said, surprised. 'Go ahead.'

'When I played back my tapes,' I said cautiously, 'I noticed you said that you needed to get the American money out of Khota Baru because you needed it for something much more important . . .'

He nodded warily.

'You meant, presumably, this idea you had for helping the relatives of those on the Boeing?'

Carter relaxed, smiling, and reached for his pack of cigarettes. I thought that he smoked rather too much, but it wasn't for me to tell him what to do.

He said quietly: 'You said you'd respect my confidence, Mr Napier – does that still go?'

'Of course.'

'Okay. What I have to tell you now has nothing to do with Malaysia, or Singapore for that matter. Hell, your people can do what they like with most of the money – because it's peanuts.'

I smiled at that. 'One doesn't often hear fifteen million dollars referred to as 'peanuts', Mr Carter. But I'll listen to what you have to say: in fact, I'm fascinated.'

'Too bloody right,' he grinned. 'Funny thing. I can't wait to see your face when I tell you. It's not often anyone has the chance to break the biggest secret in history.'

Now he had me. I leaned forward.

'You know the situation in Cambodia – Kampuchea – now?'

'Broadly speaking,' I admitted.

'After the war,' he said calmly, 'the Pol Pot régime took over. Revolutionaries, crackpots with unlimited powers, criminals who committed genocide in the name of Communism. They drove everyone into the countryside, emptied the cities, and told them to work or starve. Well, they've gone now. But they left behind a famine which may kill more than twenty million people.'

His voice faded away, and I waited patiently. I was beginning to have a great deal of respect for Mr Carter.

'Some nations are trying to help – but it's too little, too late. And much of the aid is diverted – stolen – by corrupt government officials. Have you any idea how much money is needed to save that country, Mr Napier?'

I shrugged. 'Millions, I suppose.'

'Far more than that,' Carter said sombrely. 'Unlimited cash – that's what they need. Spent on supplies delivered right where they're needed. Food, clothing, portable buildings, farm machinery, fertiliser. And that's what I can give them, Mr Napier – unlimited cash. Because what we left behind in that valley is worth maybe a thousand times more than what we brought out. It makes the gold looted from the Aztecs look like a piggy-bank.'

I stared at the man, quite bemused.

'I'm talking about the lost treasure of the ancient kings of Angkor. The wealth of an entire kingdom – exactly where it was hidden, four centuries ago.'

In that incredible moment, I have to confess, my mouth fell open in utter astonishment, and Carter laughed aloud in sheer glee. Most people, I believe, regard me as a rather stolid, phlegmatic person, old-fashioned and conservative. Perhaps I am. But at that moment I didn't know whether to laugh, openly mock or simply get up and walk away.

The man in the bedside chair eased himself into a more comfortable position. 'Can't even begin to describe what we found. People talk of Morgan's treasure in the Caribbean, the contents of Tutankhamen's tomb. I tell you, this thing is bigger still – big enough to buy Fort Knox and the Bank of England both. Disposal is going to be an almighty headache. I've lain awake at night here, trying to work out ways of dumping the stuff on the market without debasing the world's entire currency. There's gold there – not much, though. Mostly jewels – thousands of them. Not scratch stuff: each one is a selected and matched gem that would have to be in a museum because no one could afford to buy it. There's one ruby on the statue of Siva . . .'

His voice died away, and I sat there for a long time, watching the play of emotions on his face. Some minutes later, he looked up at me again.

'I need that American money to go back to the valley, Mr Napier. And I desperately need help to work out the best way to help the people of Kampuchea. After all, it's *their* property, no matter how long ago they lost it. You see, I'm not important – none of us is. What matters is the people of Cambodia – Kampuchea.'

I leaned back in my chair. For some unaccountable reason, there was a thickness in my throat.

'I see,' I said very slowly. 'All right, Mr Carter, perhaps you'd like to tell me how you stumbled on this treasure?'

He looked up quickly. 'That's where things get a little involved, Mr Napier,' he said. 'You see, it wasn't a case of stumbling on it. It all started like this . . .'

September drifted into October on the makeshift calendar in the hangar office, and as the list of outstanding work on the Dakota dwindled, so too faded their memories of those fearful days when evil had burst into their paradise. The ingenuity of the girls and Colin surprised Carter every day: when the replacement wheels had been assembled, they brought Khan into the hangar, positioned his broad back under the wing, edging him forward until the old wheels lifted clear of the ground and Carter could slide the screw jack into position. The beast's wounds, he noted with pleasure, were healing cleanly.

Liane and Debby insisted upon taking over the cleaning of the aeroplane, and Carter didn't object; Colin meanwhile rigged up a spare gas burner under an empty forty-gallon drum to produce a limitless supply of hot water, and with it the two girls set about removing the layers of encrusted guano on the upper surfaces of the aeroplane. Slowly the original paintwork began to emerge, the freight cabin was cleaned out, scrubbed spotless, the bullion and cash boxes replaced.

Carter had been surprised at how little impact his discovery of the American money had had on the others. Perhaps it was because they had lost almost every vestige of contact with the outside world; they had now read all the old magazines lying around the base a score of times, and with the total lack of news from outside, everything unconnected with the valley itself assumed an aura of unreality.

There were, on the other hand, serious problems which Carter concealed from them. One was food. Their supplies of canned goods were all but exhausted; the local deer and other animals were too wary of the M1 rifle to come within three miles of camp; the rice in the paddyfield was finished, the natural supplies of fruit waning with the season, and increasingly, Carter had to turn to the 'K' rations. Without them, survival would have been impossible – but if the aeroplane failed them and they had to walk out (assuming they could find an exit) the rations wouldn't be sufficient for any long journey.

But they worked on steadily enough – until the day Carter's worst fears were realised.

The day began no differently to any other. It was noticeably cooler in the mornings now, and the monsoon was drawing to a close, the rains lighter, less frequent. Carter and Colin were abroad early, working on the starboard engine: Carter found an engine service manual for the Pratt and Whitney, and they were leaning over the engine, deeply involved in fitting the new cylinder, Number Seven, high on the front bank of cylinders.

The rocker gear and cylinder head were easily freed, but the piston itself was seized solid in the bore. Carter was reluctant to try freeing it by turning the propeller, which they had already re-fitted. All the retaining nuts had been cleared away. The pilot bit his lip, checking the condition of the bore. It was brown with rust, badly pitted above the piston line. They toiled for an hour or more, cleaning it with light oil and emery cloth – normal engineering conventions had long been discarded from sheer necessity.

Then Carter brought up a length of timber to the servicing platform.

'I daren't start driving wedges under the cylinder to free it,' he explained to Colin. 'We'll put a load of warm oil-petrol mix in the bore, then try levering it up with the four-by-two.'

He found a length of flexible wire, tied it at both sides to the base of the cylinder, forming a loop on top, through which he passed the length of timber.

'Pad these rags on top of the next cylinder, Col ... That's it .. . Now get the timber on your shoulder. When I say 'lift', lift as hard as you can, and I'll start belting the cylinder with the hide hammer.'

The boy poised, then suddenly looked up, head turned towards the hangar door.

'You hear anything, Don?'

'No. Shut up and concentrate. Now . . .'

'Wait a minute . . . *There!* It's Debby –'

And the boy was gone, haring off through the sliding doors, with Carter following ten yards behind. Out in the sunshine, far across the strip, Debby screamed again, arms semaphoring wildly. Colin and Carter ran until the blood pounded in their ears.

'Don, something bit Liane – on the leg . . . There!' Debby's voice cracked.

Carter knelt down, and Liane sagged against his shoulder, grey-faced, eyes half closed. There was a dark-blue patch around two deep punctures on her right calf. Carter reached up and tore away the loop of cord Colin used to secure his trousers. He tied it round the soft thigh, ripping the remnants of the skirt out of the way. Then he poked a piece of wood through the loop and started tightening the tourniquet savagely.

'Knife, Col – quickly, dammit. Debby, get into the hut, fix her bed, get some hot water organised. And something for bandages. *Move!*'

He bent forward, knife poised. 'Hold on tight, Liane . . . This'll hurt . . .'

Gritting his teeth, Carter cut deeply across the bite-mark, cut again at right angles, and placed his mouth over the wound. The flesh felt warm against his lips. He sucked, spat, sucked again, biting hard so as to extract as much blood as possible. Liane screamed, thrashing about, until Colin threw his weight on her.

'Good lad . . . Hold her, now – almost finished.'

The blood tasted salt, with a nauseating metallic rancidity that turned Carter's stomach. He hoped to God he had no open mouth ulcers. *Suck again, spit, suck again ...*

Debby returned with a quart of drinking water. *Thank God ... Rinse mouth, start again ...*

At last he raised his head, sick and shaking. 'Debby – down to the hangar. Whisky in the office filing cabinet –'

Eaten up with fear and doubt, he looked closely at Liane's face: it was pale, with a deep, greyish tint he didn't like at all. She was still now, eyes closed tight. He bent, trying to check the heartbeat. It was there still – a tiny, faint flutter as of some trapped bird.

Debby came across the strip like a homing greyhound, with a bottle and the first-aid kit from the aeroplane. Carter nodded grimly. The girl was using her head. He released the tourniquet, allowing the blood to flow again, poured whisky liberally over the wound. Liane groaned again, as if from a distance.

'We have to get her away now, Colin. Take her feet. Ready .. . *Now ...*'

They started the journey desperately slowly, unable to hurry for fear of dropping her. On the way, Carter asked, 'Debby, what was it? Did you see?'

'No, Uncle Donald. I'm not sure. When Liane screamed, there was something around her ankle. She kicked, and it flew off into the grass.'

Carter bit his lip, looking back over his shoulder. 'Colour?'

'Black, dark-brown ... I don't know!' Debby ended in a wail of terror. 'She's going to die, Uncle Donald! She'll die ...'

The hut was close by now, and he braced himself for a final effort. 'All right, calm down, Debby. You're not going to help her by panicking. Get that door open – fine.'

They lifted her onto the bed. Carter, secretly appalled to find how light she was, released the tourniquet again. If she got over this, by God, he'd see she put some weight on again. They stripped her, wrapped her in blankets, for despite the warmth of the evening, she had begun to shiver violently, making strange, small animal noises that gripped his heart in a vice. She was drenched with sweat, yet her skin was cold.

He straightened up, looked at the boy and girl; it seemed to him that they had aged perceptibly that day. They were ashen-faced, but calm – and very concerned. Carter smiled, concealing the tiredness that gathered around his mind.

'Take it easy, now. The worst's over, with luck. We may have got to her in time. Debby, how long between Liane being bitten and me getting that tourniquet on? Any idea?'

'I don't know. I screamed twice, and that was when you came out of the hangar. After that – two, maybe three minutes.'

'It bit her only once? I can't see any other marks.'

'Yes. She kicked it away quickly. Then she said: 'Get Donald' – and I screamed.'

Carter sat down heavily, while Colin ran a damp cloth over Liane's face. 'I wish to God I knew more about snakebite. I know she mustn't have stimulants – her heart rate's high enough already. Deb, make her some dilute canned milk, plenty of sugar.'

After Debby left them, Colin looked Carter squarely in the eye. 'She's going to die, isn't she? We can't do much –'

'Shut your face,' Carter said aggressively. 'She's going to make it, you hear?' He knelt by the bed, rubbing the girl's cheeks, wrists, talking to her. Terrified to see how quickly she was losing body fluid, he forced her to take the diluted milk. If she became dehydrated . . . He made Debby and Colin bring in relays of soft drink bottles filled with hot water, loaded the slender figure with blankets, made a fire in the stone hearth, until eventually he ran out of things to try.

Colin bit his lip. 'Don? What do you think?'

'I'm past thinking. There are so many variables. What kind of snake? How deadly the venom? Had the damned thing bitten anything else recently that might reduce the strength of the poison? Did we get to her quickly enough? Did I get all the stuff out? Why in God's name did the bloody Yanks take away all the snakebite outfits?'

Colin shook his head.

Carter stood up, looking grim but determined. 'All right. I want you and Debby out of here. No backchat – I saw a guy die of snakebite in America during the war, and it's not a nice thing to watch. Besides, I'm going to need a break later on – someone has to be with her. If she's going at all, she'll go soon – that was a nasty bite. Get going.'

Colin and Debby didn't like it, and said so – forcibly. He overruled them, shouting in sudden fury that sent them scuttling away. Alone, he reached for a cigarette, drank a cup of the coffee Debby had made for him, and sat by the bed. Colin had stopped the generator now, and the single Tilley lamp hissed and glowed on the table. At intervals, he removed Liane's bandages, washed the wound, released the tourniquet. Around midnight he took away the retaining cord: it had done its duty.

After midnight, her condition began to deteriorate. Her hands became restless, fluttering on the blanket, her head turning incessantly. Just after one o'clock she began to run a fever, her skin dry and scaly to the touch and with an unpleasant sheen. When he lifted an eyelid, he was shocked: the pupil was enormously dilated, forming a vast, liquid window into her soul.

By the early hours he was beginning to tire, but still he worked on steadily, sponging down her body, checking the wound, dripping a little cool water between her lips. Towards morning, in those dark hours before dawn, her condition became much worse: her eyes were glazed, and delirium possessed her; she spoke jerkily, frenziedly for minutes at a time, in a language he couldn't understand, the words fusing together in a meaningless gabble.

It seemed to him that she was slipping away slowly, into a land and a time far remote from him. Her heart beat slowed down until Carter began to fear it would stop altogether. He knew that unless something was done, she would drift away into the long night. Agonising that, in his ignorance, he was helping her to her death, he poured a massive dose of neat brandy down her throat and began rubbing her chilled frame with all his strength, using a dry, rough blanket. At intervals, he bore down hard upon her chest, and ceaselessly he talked to her in a low voice, urging her to fight on, calling her back from the brink.

As the first, tentative glow of dawn stained the window facing east, Liane began, with painful slowness, to pull through. Colour began stealing back into the pale, almost translucent skin, and her breathing became easier. Now Carter called in Colin and Debby, had them make a great pot of black, sweet coffee, hot soup made from 'K' ration canned meat, and when the sun was clear above the eastern rim of the cliffs, Liane opened her eyes – eyes that now could see and comprehend.

'Donald . . .' He sat by the bed, holding her hand, swallowing hard. Too much damned pepper in that soup, he thought irritably; makes your eyes water. Debby too was shaking away the tears, smiling defiantly, and Colin was beaming as if he would never stop.

'Liane, how do you feel?'

'Tired . . . So tired, Donald. But it is so nice to be back . . .'

'Back?' said Carter, confused.

The girl on the bed lifted her hand, laid it on his own. 'I have been on a journey, Donald – such a long journey! I can remember cities on fire, great armies fighting, the elephants on the plain, and a tunnel . . .'

Debby said gently: 'Oh, Liane, I'm so glad you're going to be well . . .'

'Debby, I – I remember now . . . The valley, and the snake. Donald, have I been dreaming?'

Carter nodded happily. 'I think you have.'

The Asian girl turned her head on the pillow. 'I remember now: the ring . . . and the cave behind the fall . . . Such unhappy dreams, Donald . . .' Her head sagged a little, and Debby cried out in alarm.

'It's all right,' Carter said softly. 'She's sleeping now. And when she wakes, she'll be much better.' He stood up, swayed and put out a hand to Colin to steady himself.

'Easy, Don! You've been up all night, remember.'

'Yes, – yes, I have.' The point seemed a little academic to Carter. A great weariness was breaking over him like a tidal wave. He stumbled towards the other bed, falling face down, asleep before he could even comprehend the fact.

Colin found a blanket, covered the lean, sun-tanned body, drew back the thinning fair hair from the face. He stared down at the sleeping man with a feeling of compassion that he would remember all his days.

Then, having made sure that both he and Liane were sleeping peacefully, Colin and Debby went out into the morning sunshine, down to the river to bathe and to prepare Khan for the day's work.

In the quiet hut, the sleeping man shifted drowsily into a more comfortable position, engrossed in a dream he would forget on waking, yet which would always be part of him.

FIFTEEN

Three weeks from the day Liane almost died, Carter was lying on his bed, trying to come to grips with the knowledge that all his good intentions had evaporated, just like so many others before them. There was no getting round it: they were beginning to have trouble finding things to do on the Dakota; very soon, he'd be forced to move the old wreck outside and try and start the engines. But before things got to that stage, he promised himself he'd start planning his walk-out. Once he got past that rock face at the fall, he reckoned he could make it in three or four weeks – but he needed supplies. He started squirrelling away candy bars, even whole 'K' rations; found a passable water canteen, spent time surreptitiously looking at maps.

Inevitably, he felt as guilty as hell – a feeling he did his best to ignore. In the beginning, he'd sworn no one would get him up in an aeroplane again, not after that 707. But now that Colin and Debby had almost cleared a usable strip by driving that bloody elephant up and down towing a log, the proposition had become horribly feasible . . .

He frowned. It hadn't helped, of course, the way Liane had blossomed after getting over that snake bite. The kids had made sure she ate properly, took plenty of rest, but the root of the trouble was in Liane herself: the way she kept looking at Carter with a troubled, almost puzzled air. He drew up a knee on the bed, depressed and unhappy. It had been his fault Liane had almost died; he'd warned them about snakes, but that wasn't enough. He should have devised some kind of treatment, ready for emergencies – should have briefed them on what to do. As if it hadn't been enough killing Jean . . .

When Liane came into the hut that evening, he was totally unprepared. Colin and Debby had taken Khan up to the waterfall pool for their evening swim, and the pilot was relaxing after a quick splash in the river.

'Donald?'

'Liane, come on in. The kids back yet?' he said uncertainly.

She shook her head, standing in the doorway, the orange disc of the sun behind her. Shading his eyes, he could see the clean, sharp outline of her body through the worn, patched-up skirt, the shirt fashioned roughly from parachute nylon. She stood with a slim hand upon the door, the other flat on her thigh, the long strand of black hair tied at her neck, hanging free over her right breast. He thought achingly that he had never seen her look so lovely.

She said: 'Not for some time yet. They are swimming. You want to talk?'

'Sure.'

She walked forward slowly, sat at the foot of the bed. He shifted his legs quickly out of her way, clutching the towel at his waist.

'Let me get some clothes on,' he started, and she smiled quickly.

'No need, Donald. You need rest. Stay there.'

'Okay,' he said lightly. 'How's your leg?'

'It is good now,' Liane said gravely. 'It hurts only a little, when I walk.'

He grinned at that. 'Okay. That's fine. What's on your mind?'

'This.' She opened her hand. Carter's stomach contracted; he thought he'd hidden those fuses where no one could ever find them . . . She must have been watching. He stared at her resentfully. 'So?'

'So why do you do these things, Donald? The aeroplane is nearly ready – otherwise you would not have done these bad things. Making the wheels to go flat; hiding little pieces like this . . . I know you become angry when I speak of this, but I must ask. Why do you wish to stay here until you grow old and die?'

'I'm old now.'

'Answer, please.'

He shook his head, aware that she would never understand.

Nor the kids, for that matter . . .

Liane's eyes were hard. 'It is easy to see why you stay. The aeroplane is ready; we have found much money – enough to make us all rich; we have fixed the airstrip with Khan – there are only a few things left to do. There is only one reason we cannot go: Carter is afraid.'

He stared at her, mutely, his mouth working. Then: 'All right. Maybe so. You and the kids want to make it out of here alive. But I *know* we can't make it. You'll go on believing we can do it right up to the time that damned machine goes into the deck and kills us all. I tell you, Liane – if there was even one chance in a million we'd make it, I'd try it. You have to understand that.'

Her mouth twisted. 'You say this, Donald Carter. But I say you lie. It is because you are afraid to fly again.'

Carter shook his head in helpless frustration. 'What can I do to convince you? Will you listen to me, just for a moment?'

The golden-skinned girl shrugged. 'I listen.'

'Okay, I'll keep it simple. *If* we get the engines started, we've no brakes to keep the plane straight until it flies. So I have to use rudder – when we're moving fast enough. But at the beginning, the tail will be down, so I won't be able to see the strip. You follow that?'

'Go on, please.'

'Right. With a wide strip, it might be possible – with a skilled Dakota pilot. Which I am not.'

Liane shrugged again. 'The strip can be widened, Donald.'

'Never mind. There's worse to come.' He took a deep breath. '*If* we get off the ground, we'll need at least five minutes to get enough height to leave the valley – but if an engine stops in that time, we crash. Understand?'

'I am listening.'

He stared at her, disgruntled. 'Okay. And making a single-engined landing without brakes or flap on a narrow strip is suicide. Now – the nearest place to go is Khota Baru, in Malaysia. Know where that is?'

'I have been there sometimes with All-Orient.'

'In that case you'll know it's five hundred miles from here, most of it over water. If a motor stops then, we go into the sea, without lifejackets, or rafts – and the water's full of bloody sharks. Am I getting through to you, Liane?'

'Is there much more?'

He exhaled savagely. 'Yes, there's more, damn it. If we make the coast, we have to belly-land – we'll have no wheels or flaps. And for every single problem I've mentioned, I could list a dozen more: engine on fire, fuel leaks, controls giving way; burst tyres on take-off; runaway propeller . . . Add it all up and you get only one answer: stay here, we live; try it your way, and we die. Very unpleasantly. All of us. You want to load all that responsibility on me, girl?'

Her eyes were filling with tears. She leaned forward, laid a hand on his arm.

'Donald,' she said very softly, 'I know all these things. You have said them before, many times. There are risks – but do you not see we would rather die that way than die of loneliness here? Colin and Debby miss their families. I know you hate me –'

'Hold it right there,' Carter said quickly. 'You've got that all wrong, you know. I could never hate you.'

'I think so. For the thing I did to you – for the way I sent you away that night. I know you wanted me . . . I wanted you too, Donald. But my thoughts were wrong. Can you understand?'

'Damned if I do,' he said roughly. 'But I know why you changed your mind – I'm twice your age, Liane. I don't blame you at all.' He was finding it hard to speak clearly.

She smiled then, richly, white teeth gleaming in the fading light.

'Such fools, men. Why cannot you understand? Since we met on the Boeing, since you saved us, cared for us, brought us here, Col and Debby think of you as their father. It was the same with me. All my life, I had had nothing of my father but memories, a photograph or two – until you came to care for me as my father would. That night I seemed to be two people: part of me was a woman, wanting you so much – and part a daughter, terrified because my father was doing things no father should do . . .'

At last Carter began to understand. He held her hand tightly, in silence. She was very close to tears, and he sat up on the bed, pulled her close to him. Her head went down under his chin and he held her very close. Time became unimportant, and with a strand of the towel, he cleaned away the salt tears, smoothed back the straying hair with a gentle hand, diffidently, as if he were almost afraid to touch.

He said hoarsely: 'I don't want to be a father to you, Liane. I wanted you from the first moment – but I thought it was impossible . . . You – you could have had any man in the world. You were so kind – but I knew all you could feel for an old man like me was pity.'

She sat up, amused.

'Old? You are not old, Donald! Your mind is as bright as the sun; and since we came to this place, you have become strong and hard.' Absently she drew a long forefinger down his chest, and his breath caught thickly in his throat.

'Listen, my only love,' she said very softly, 'soon we must fly away. We may be killed, but I do not want to die until you have loved me. Why should we not be lovers, like Colin and Debby –'

'He straightened up, aghast. 'What?'

'You did not know? For many weeks now. But they are very careful, Donald. I have spoken to Debby many times, and I give her the root of a forest plant to eat. For one week after she eats, she cannot make babies.' She caught his expression and laughed again. 'What did you expect? They are always together – swimming, lying in the sun . . . They are very happy. And I want very much for us to be happy, too –'

The tall, slender girl stood up lithely in a single flowing motion, slipping out of her makeshift shirt and the old tattered skirt with serrated edges hanging halfway down the long thighs. She stood unmoving, one leg slightly forward, palms flat on her thighs, the old, threadbare white pants set against the golden skin, the deep wedge of black visible through the material.

Carter watched her breasts rise and fall with each inhalation. He rose slowly from the bed, to stand before her, gripping her upper arms so tightly that for a moment she winced before lifting her eyes to his own and smiling.

'Liane – God, if you only knew. Why are you doing this? You must know I want you more than life itself, but –' His voice died away, his uncertainty and disbelief yielding to the dawning realisation that a miracle might happen.

Her eyes widened. 'And you must know that I have loved you for many months, Donald. As I have never loved anyone in my life. Women of the East find love only once, did you not

179

know? And they know that love must be tended like the forest orchid – that women must learn the ways of the garden, so that those who come to plant the seed will find the soil prepared.' She paused, looking beyond him at a sun drowning in clouds. 'These women of the West,' she said, 'they know the act of love merely as they know a tree on a hill, seen every day. But they know nothing of the sweet paths that await the traveller, the fruits to be tasted, the flowers to be touched on the way. Hah!' she smiled wryly. 'I talk too much.'

Carter laughed deeply. 'No – I love to hear you talk this way, Liane. I always wanted you – but I was afraid . . .'

She laid a cool hand on his cheek. 'You cannot be afraid now, Donald.'

Liane slipped free of her last constraining garment and knelt at his feet. Carter stared down at her, incredibly moved and excited. Her lips moved along the inside of his legs, kissing the sensitive inner thighs, hands caressing, moving on. He had known nothing so erotic in his life. He picked her up, surprised by his own strength, laid her on the bed and knelt between her thighs, feasting his eyes upon the golden smoothness . . .

He lay down beside her. Time, immeasurable time, passed.

Later, he could recall little of it. For some time afterwards he slept, while Liane, still naked, sat beside the bed with a bowl of water and a towel, gazing down at him, studying the skin tanned to the shade of new leather, the face, once slack and baggy-eyed, but now glowing with health, the sweat of the past hour still glistening on his brow.

There had been other men in her life – casual, greedy men, who wanted to use her but did not want her; men who offered many things – money, houses, clothes, jewels. Some who offered nothing, others who offered everything. None had the intellect, the ability, the courage of this tall, spare man. He was flawed, she knew it; accepted it without fully understanding. Somewhere, sometime, he had been terribly frightened. Now, he was lost, afraid of being afraid, without confidence – but now she knew she could help him. If she could but give this man back the desire to live, to be young again, what could they not achieve together? He could take them from this cursed valley of ghosts . . . away from that tomb beneath the fall, where . . .

Liane stood up convulsively, trembling violently, a hand to

her head in an attitude of terrible enlightenment. *Great Buddha*, she whispered, *what is happening to me?* Why, out of all those half-forgotten dreams of burning cities, clashing armies, senseless flights through dark, water-filled tunnels, *why* should this nightmare persist?

She walked to the door, staring blindly out into the darkness. Broken, indistinct projections of falling rock . . . A dusty floor under her bare back . . . The ring . . . Strong arms around her, and the dream fading into fantasy, the two of them flying like the birds of the forest . . .

Her hand stole behind her, touching for the millionth time the birthmark upon her body, feeling the great elephant ring on the index finger, cool and heavy on her skin. She felt the healing tightness of the scar on her calf, remembering . . . Remembering how she had almost died, and had returned, her mind filled with confused sequences of war and battle and a journey on some sleek vessel . . . Dreams – and like all dreams, they had faded from her memory.

All save one . . .

He slept in utter relaxation, one hand under his head. His phallus lay reduced on his thigh, and she was of a mind to waken him in the way of an Angkor concubine. Her mouth went dry. Lord Buddha, how did she know this thing? Were the nightmares to start again?

Liane moved abruptly, breaking the spell, and bent her head towards him, lips pursed, blowing the finest jet of air into his root, stirring the hair. She blew again: the shaft filled, hardened, and she slipped her fingers beneath, taking the weight, until it stood erect.

Her soft lips opened, and she awoke him royally . . .

Thirty yards away in the bunkhouse, Debby snuggled closer to Colin, sleepily.

'What do you think, Col? Will they make it up?'

'Don'll get a thick ear from me if they don't. Turn over . . .'

SIXTEEN

The hospital staff, I found, were extremely kind. Towards lunchtime I offered to leave, but the ward sister shook her head with some determination.

'Your visits are beneficial to the patient, Mr Napier. If you wish to stay, we can bring you something to eat on a tray. You are, after all, on official business, the doctor tells me.'

Presently Carter laid down his fork, wiped his mouth, set the napkin on his tray.

'You have to understand, Mr Napier, that much of this came from Liane and the boy and girl later. To tell you the truth, I was more than a little worried when Liane first told me about that dream.'

I lit a cheroot, settled back in my chair.

After supper one evening, Carter began, the conversation, as always, turned to means of escape from the valley. They had been over every inch of it, looking for a way out, and they were all feeling claustrophobic. There was perhaps two or three weeks' work left to do on the aeroplane, but by mutual consent, they never referred to it. Debby insisted that the underground river might offer a means of escape, but then she hadn't witnessed Carter's brush with death in the torrent.

'Besides,' Colin said importantly, 'I forgot to tell you something – I think I saw a cave under the waterfall. That day Liane found her ring. I mean, if that stream comes down from the top of the plateau, there may be a way up to the top through the cave.'

Quite suddenly Liane said in a small voice: 'The way is blocked.'

Carter shot a glance at her uneasily. 'What was that, Liane?'

She said diffidently: 'There is a cave. But the way to the top of the mountain is closed.'

Colin and Debby started speaking together excitedly, but Carter held up a warning hand, frowning.

'Shut up, you two. Liane, what exactly do you mean?'

The girl sat immobile for the space of two or three breaths. She seemed to shake herself mentally, trying to shrug off some brooding presence around her. Then she looked up at Carter with a strange, almost surprised expression. 'Donald?'

'Why did you say that, Liane? About the cave?'

She smiled. 'It is nothing . . . Only a dream I had, after the snake . . .' Her voice tailed away, as if she lacked the confidence to go on.

Carter nodded understandingly. 'I remember you were saying all sorts of things. None of it made much sense. What can you remember?'

'Only that there was a cavern filled with black water, and a second cavern beneath the first, with – oh, Donald, it sounds mad . . .'

'Go on, please,' he said intently.

'The second cave had a window in the end – a great window made of green glass. And there was someone . . . Someone . . . I can't remember any more.'

Carter looked at her very hard. 'Okay. Don't worry too much about it. Tomorrow morning we'll go and take a look. Col, how did that rock face look to you? Difficult?'

The boy considered. 'I think it might be possible. I'll organise some ropes; there's lots of parachute cord, bolts we can use to hammer into cracks . . . From the scree line up to where I think that cave is, it's only about two hundred feet.'

Christ, Carter thought with dismay. He glanced at Liane, smiled, and quite suddenly he wasn't afraid.

They reached the pool early in the morning, before the sun began to roast the valley mercilessly. Carter and the boy carried large coils of white parachute cord, as strong as rope ten times as thick, plus bolts, hammers – anything they thought might be of use in scaling a cliff. Carter hated heights, but despite himself, there was burgeoning within him a secret hope that the cave – *if* it existed – might offer an escape route.

At the pool. Khan, failing to see what interested the two-legs so much, snorted, rumbled and wandered away downstream in search of a mud wallow, leaving the others to study the pool surrounds, and especially the great cliffs on each side of the fall. Carter could still see the tripod Macbain and his party had erected, but of the sole guard they had left on the rim, there was no sign: all that remained was a hundred-foot length of rope swinging from the beam. Now that, Carter thought hopefully, *was* interesting . . .

It was very pleasant, splashing around in the cool water, but presently Carter called them to order. They were there, he said sternly, on business. He and Colin, he proposed, would swim under the fall and examine the alleged cave. This suggestion, however, was immediately shouted down by Liane and Debby.

'All right,' Carter said resignedly. 'I'm outvoted. No use trying to instill discipline into this unruly mob. We *all* swim out to the fall, right?'

'We swim slowly?' Liane said anxiously.

Carter laughed. 'We swim slowly, Liane. Just stay close to me.'

Ten minutes later, all four of them stood in a wet and shivering row at the base of the rock face, their backs to the cascade, craning their necks upwards.

'You could be right, Colin,' Carter said critically. 'The fall starts about three hundred feet up. The cave – if it is a cave – is fifty or sixty feet below it, slightly to the left. It doesn't look too bad a climb – not absolutely vertical, plenty of handholds. That face doesn't get up into the vertical until you pass the fall. The rock's wet, though, and that could be a problem. Suppose we tackle the drier section there, over to the left, then work our way across?'

'You're the boss,' Colin yelled, above the thunder of plunging water.

Carter grinned: *that* would be the day, he thought grimly. That boy had a mind of his own.

That view was soon reinforced when Colin said firmly: 'I'll go first.'

'We'll go together,' Carter said dourly. 'The girls stay here until we signal or come down. And you'll do what you're told, boy. I don't want to have to explain to your parents why I let you fall off a cliff.'

Colin cocked his head on one side. 'I won't fall. I've done plenty of rock climbing with the school, in Wales.'

'You have? You didn't mention that before.'

'You never asked. Besides, I didn't want you to get ideas about going up those cliffs. A couple of hundred feet is bad enough, a thousand's bloody impossible. Let's get this rope sorted out —'

The climb was physically arduous, but straightforward: the rock face was uneven, rough, with plenty of foot- and hand-holds. Colin went up thirty feet, belayed the rope around a rock snag and waited until Carter was beside him, red-faced and breathing hard, but otherwise in good shape. Then the boy went on again. At the end of the fifth pitch, they stopped on a broad ledge to rest, wave down to the girls and survey the situation.

Carter stared up and across. 'The cave must be behind that overhand. We can start angling in soon. I don't know how the hell people can do this sort of thing for a hobby.'

'Just don't look down. It's a straight climb from that ledge. Ready?'

'Uh-huh. Bit short of puff.'

'You smoke too much . . .'

Twenty minutes later, Colin climbed up onto the ledge, got three turns of the rope round another lump of rock and helped Carter over the last few feet. They leaned over precariously, waved frantically to the girls below and turned to the cave opening. The ledge was smooth red sandstone, with a central trough which had once accommodated the stream which formed the cavern. The ledge was covered in places by a film of mud formed by spray, and it felt gritty underfoot. Slowly they moved forward into the mouth of the cave: it was some twelve feet wide, seven high at the entrance, widening considerably inside. Once inside, they paused, allowing their eyes to adjust.

Against the left-hand wall, what had once been a long row of sandalwood boxes had disintegrated with age. Protected from the winds, they had formed vague piles of grey dust through which countless stars seemed to beckon. The pilot walked forward slowly, went down on one knee.

'Oh, my God . . .' he said, in a stunned voice. 'Colin . . .'

Some of the boxes appeared sound, but crumbled into dust at a touch; Carter brushed away the détritus carefully.

The custodians of Angkor knew their trade: each box contained a specific type of jewel. Carter recognised the translucence of emeralds, the blood-red of rubies, the silver sheen of pearls, but there were many others – the sheer volume of the stones was mind-shattering. His fingers scrabbled in the encrusted débris of centuries and he saw that he was holding a marble-sized black pearl of such lustre that his eyes seemed to be drawn into the very depths of the jewel. His mind reeled with the unimaginable wealth assembled here. He could hear Colin, alongside, grunt in astonishment, half-mouthing words that died before they were born.

In a fever of excitement, Carter moved on down the line of boxes and came to a double mountain of emeralds, flanked by a scattered board of great Burmese rubies – heavy, fat-bellied wonders, some of them exquisitely carved in the form of dancing girls, elephant heads, beast of the forest . . . The impact was overpowering. With but a fraction of the great store exposed, he rose to his feet, walked out onto the ledge near the green curtain of falling water that hissed past, filtering the sunlight like a stained glass window in a cathedral. *Glass . . .? Window . . .?* He remembered Liane and her dream, and for all the warmth of the day, he shivered involuntarily. There was something about this place . . . He stood there, supporting himself with one hand against the rock wall, eyes lifted up to where the sun splintered into a million diamonds with the falling water. He found his hands were clenching, unclenching, again and again.

Colin came out to join him, his face pale and disturbed. Neither of them would ever be the same again, thought Carter blindly. He grasped the boy's arm.

'Colin, we should bring Liane and Debby up here – but I'm worried about Liane –'

'About that dream of hers, you mean? I already thought of that. You remember she said the way was closed? I'll go down and fetch them up. How about taking a look at the back of the cave? It's just possible that . . .' He left the words unfinished, hanging on the air.

The older man grinned, a strained expression on his face. 'For God's sake, there's plenty of time for that. In any case, we'll need light of some kind – a Tilley lamp.'

'Okay. I'll go down for the girls. I'll lash up some hand ropes on the way down. You'll be okay?'

'Why shouldn't I be?'

Colin smiled. 'Any idea what all that stuff is worth?'

'A hell of a lot. About a hundred times more than the Royal family fortune. Let's just say you could buy New York City and have enough change left to ride on the Staten Island ferry. Go on – get on with it.'

Colin took a long look into the mouth of the cave, whistled sharply and climbed down over the ledge. Carter called after him, 'Bring Liane up first – she's the strongest. And put a rope on them –'

Time passed as if in a dream for Carter. In the half-light of the cave, he worked busily, moving the scattered heaps of jewels into neat piles on the smooth rock, clearing away rotted wood and débris. In a corner he noticed something odd, blew the dust away carefully and uncovered the rotting remains of garments, some leather sandals of a strange design, a curved bronze sword jammed into a jewelled scabbard, the teak handle all but disintegrated. Beside them lay more treasures: a flattened pile of rubies two feet wide at the base, two such piles of emeralds and two of diamonds. Carter's eyes opened wide: he hadn't realised that people of such antiquity as to use bronze weapons also had the skills to mine and polish diamonds. Beyond lay four more great mountains, this time of pearls, pink and white, and the remnants of a leather sack that had contained a bushel or more of matchless black beauties . . .

When the girls finally gained the ledge – they had insisted on climbing together – Carter was cleaning the encrusted dirt and filth from a magnificent statue of a god, twenty inches high; the multi-armed figure stood in awesome majesty, with one foot posed on the silver corpse of a new-born infant. It was surrounded by an arc of lambent green flames – huge emeralds set in a filigree of gold wire like an obscene halo.

Carter turned to see Liane staring at the statue with a face as pale as death. He rose, reached her just as she slumped to the floor of the cave in a dead faint.

'Debby, quickly – there's a gold bowl over there. Get some water from the fall.'

With infinite care and patience, he wiped the sweat and dust from Liane's face, and poured a little of the fresh cold water into her mouth, while Debby knelt beside her, rubbing the thin, cold hands. Presently, Liane opened her eyes and stared up at Carter, uncomprehending for a moment. Then she looked over his shoulder into the cave, and remembered.

'Donald . . .'

'It's all right, Liane,' Carter whispered. Behind his back, Colin exchanged a glance with Debby, smiled conspiratorily. The pilot, oblivious, helped the Asian girl to her feet, and she stood immobile for a long time, staring at the cave and its contents.

She looked at Carter with eyes that were no longer afraid. 'It is the place from my dream, Donald. There is nothing here to hurt us. What is it that you have found? Colin talked about treasure . . .'

'Come and see.'

Liane went with him, kneeling to run slim fingers through the gleaming pyramids of riches. He brought the statue of the many-armed god to show her, and she nodded calmly.

'This I have seen in school, in museums in my country, Donald. It is Siva – the old God, before Buddha came to save us. And these words around the base – they are in the old language of Cambodia.'

'This is all from your country?'

'I think we are in Cambodia now,' she said calmly. 'In the high mountains the border is never marked or disputed. And I will tell you one more thing, Donald – it is no accident that we are here.'

Carter opened his mouth to protest, stopped to think, then blurted out, 'That's crazy talk, Liane – how could that be? That damned dream . . . That snake –'

She smiled tiredly. 'You in the West, Donald, you do not believe. You *cannot* believe, because it would make nonsense of everything you learned as a child. Your coming to Singapore so that you could save us from the Boeing . . . The way in which we came to the valley . . . My dream – all steps on the way.'

He turned his head to look at Colin and Debby. They had drawn close for mutual comfort, disturbed by the presence of something quite beyond their experience. He shook his head stubbornly. 'I can't accept that, Liane. You're saying that the future is already fixed, unchangeable? That time itself... No, I don't believe it. I *won't* believe it!'

Liane laid a hand on his arm. 'Then do not believe, Donald. Just accept – accept the proof that lies before you.'

Embarrassed, Colin broke in with: 'Don – how do we know all these are real?'

Carter started, as if emerging from some daydream. He smiled grimly. 'I wouldn't take any bets on their being fakes, Col. Liane?'

The girl said quietly: 'This is a royal treasure, Donald – and yet also from the temples of old Angkor. Some day we will know the truth about how they came to be here. But for now it is enough that we have found them.' She looked past him, to the green curtain beyond the cave. 'It grows dark. A storm, I think –'

Carter pulled himself together, straightening his shoulders. 'You're right. We'd better get back as quick as we can. Another day, we'll come back and see if there's a way out . . .' He noticed the expression on Liane's face and smiled. 'Yes – I remember how your dream went, but we have to check. Let's take the statue along for now, and leave the rest here. After all, nobody's going to steal it while we're gone.'

Hurriedly they began to prepare for the descent, the statue of the god wrapped in Carter's shirt and tied firmly to Colin's back. None of them would get much sleep tonight, that was for sure, thought Carter as he worked his way down the rock face. He began to wonder about the centuries that must have elapsed since long-dead hands brought the treasure to this place. How long ago? Before Columbus sailed west? Before the Armada sailed? Had Henry finished his sequence of 'separations' from his wives?

Carter was still in a state of mild shock – but it was shock combined with euphoria. He was staggered by the sheer immensity of their discovery. It was impossible simply to say that they were rich: wealth of this magnitude required a whole new definition. But it was not only about wealth that he was thinking as he made the descent; it was also about responsibility.

Reaching the end of the scree, Carter gained the rocky shore of the pool and stopped, watching Colin help Debby over the last pitch. He had an uncomfortable feeling that someone, somewhere, was watching, would be watching his every move . . . Reaction, he told himself angrily. What else could it be? Involuntarily, he looked up at the far rim of the escarpment, watched the storm clouds scudding past.

Easy, Carter; you'll be seeing ghosts next.

Looking back, Carter couldn't recall ever having worked so hard in his life. Using Colin as a fitter's mate, he returned to the task of the cylinder replacement which had been interrupted by Liane's narrow escape from death, and spent three nerve-wracking days refitting the new cylinder over the rings of the piston – a nightmare, because they had no replacement rings, and to break even one would spell disaster. Through the long hours of the day he toiled, drenched in sweat, with Liane constantly at his side, making him eat salt tablets and drink huge quantities of water to prevent dehydration.

Even such simple tasks as setting the tappet clearances – a job a skilled mechanic could have cleared in less than half a day – taxed him to the limit. If it hadn't been for the rotting and mouldy manuals he found in the hangar office, the whole thing would have been quite impossible.

His salvation lay in a profound gift for improvisation. He coaxed the old cylinder off the piston with a mixture of oil, petrol and judicious swings of a hide hammer; he removed the spark plugs of both engines one at a time, cleaning and setting the gaps; he drained the oil from each engine, cleaned out the filters, replenished the oil, and had Colin rotate the propellers with spark plugs out for more than two hours until he was satisfied.

The landing flaps were jammed down: it took him four days to dismantle the 'up' system, clean out the coagulated oil from pipelines and valves, refill the system and bleed it free of air.

Carter drove them all like slaves now – and himself hardest of all. There were times when Liane, taking a late cup of coffee down to the starkly-lit hangar, would find him on his knees against a main landing-gear wheel, fast asleep, a wrench still in his hand.

Slowly, the outstanding items on his list were being whittled down, yet still there were long, soul-destroying tasks that seemed never-ending: the patient tracing of control runs through the structure; checking, greasing, tightening, replacing, tensioning, testing, groping deep into access panels always an inch too small for the average arm, with cutting edges that laid his flesh open like sharp knives.

And corner-cutting. Answers, somehow, had to be found time and time again. Stripped threads in a sparkplug hole on the starboard engine; screwing in an oversize plug and hoping that half an ignition system would cope. Outside now, ready for an engine run – and no petrol reaching the engines: strip the system piece by piece, clean out the rubbery goo and sticky residue of old fuel, and put Colin back to work on the inertia starter, winding that detestable handle all through the long day.

The girls were a revelation to Carter: each time he left the hangar, the strip seemed a little longer, a few feet wider, and from his work on the aeroplane he could see them far off down the strip in the hot sun, urging on Khan and the massive log he towed, mowing down the short brush and stubble. When it became too hot, they would take him down to the river and let him wallow in a pool, while they used the time to burn off great heaps of cleared brushwood.

Through it all, they never lost faith. They talked, not of 'if' they made it, but 'when'. It seemed to Carter that they took it completely for granted that he would get the old wreck into the air on sheer willpower alone. In his darker moments, when he lay awake in bed, too tired to sleep, with Liane breathing softly beside him, he thought fearfully of the hundreds of miles of jungle and sea, the stark, precipitous hills, the thousand-and-one things that could – and probably would – go wrong with the aeroplane. At times, he even toyed briefly with the idea of making a single-handed try, early in the morning, before the rest of them were awake.

Yet he knew in his heart that it would take all of them, if it was to be done at all. So he worked on, in a constant nausea of panic and foreboding, like a condemned man forced to dig how own grave . . .

Carter seemed to be tiring, and Dr Singh sent me about my business for an hour while he went through a complete check-up on his patient. I stayed in the waiting room, making notes from my tapes and sipping gratefully the large mug of hospital tea provided by an indulgent staff. Carter told me that his son paid him a brief visit at that time, before flying back to Hong Kong; there, Gavin proposed to put in for a ten-day leave and come back to spend it with his father, bringing the family with him.

I thought that was a very good idea, and I told Carter so later that afternoon. He agreed.

'It'll be nice to see Shirley and the boy again,' he said, 'and the three-month-old grand-daughter I've never seen.'

I asked him if they'd chosen a name, and he flushed with pleasure. 'Jean,' he said contentedly. 'After my wife – she would have liked that.' He paused for a moment, then looked up. 'Where were we, this morning, Mr Napier?'

'The Dakota,' I said, prompting him.

'Ah, yes . . . There isn't much more to tell really. We got it fixed, and brought her across to Khota Baru.'

'I doubt,' I said drily, 'if it was quite as simple as that.'

He grinned broadly. 'You can say that again. It was bloody terrifying. Yet in a way, it was the most satisfying thing I've ever done, I think. Only at the very last things went sour on me. Your recorder on? Good. Well, it happened like this.'

SEVENTEEN

On the hundred-and-seventieth day of their isolation, they hitched up Khan to the Dakota and towed it out of the hangar into the afternoon sunshine. They had drained the fuel tanks and replenished them from the forty-gallon drums in the compound using a hand-pump – it had taken all the previous day. Now, out in the pale sunshine, the pilot briefed Colin again and climbed into the cockpit to try running the engines. He could see Khan, with Debby perched on his neck, starting yet another swathe down the strip; Liane would come to the plane soon, when she finished her chores.

He opened the side window, peered down at Colin, who was getting ready to throw his weight on the turning handle.

'Contact port, Col. Wind her up, boy!'

It hardly seemed right, Carter thought, calling Colin a boy – not now. There was nothing of the schoolboy left in those hard hands, knotted muscles, set jaw. Steadily the sound of the inertia starter wound up from a low groan to a high-pitched whine, but Colin was tiring visibly; Carter yelled *'Contact!'* and pulled the 'engage' toggle. The noise changed down in pitch, the propeller turning in brief kicks, smartly at first as Carter primed like mad; then, almost at the last moment, the motor fired, stopped, fired again and stopped for good.

'She's almost there, Col. One more time!' Carter yelled.

'Hang on! I'm clapped out!'

'All right. Take five . . . I'll give her a few more primes this time. When you're ready.' Hearing muffled curses below, Carter grinned. *'Contact!'*

She fired almost at once; Carter primed furiously, catching it on the throttle, swore as the motor coughed, missed, fired again and caught, roaring in defiance, smoke pouring away aft as the over-rich mixture settled down. '*Go, you great bastard . . . Go!*'

Below on the gravel, Colin was turning cartwheels, laughing like a maniac and Carter saw Liane come running across from the hut, summoned by the noise. The speed built up to 1000 revs, and Carter chopped it back a little to a steady tick-over, keeping a careful watch on pressure. It seemed okay. He leaned out of the window, stabbed a finger at the other engine.

Trouble. Four times they tried to start the port motor; four times they failed. Eventually Colin staggered off to one side, falling exhausted in a patch of long grass. The fifth time, it caught, fired, but ran very unevenly. Carter switched off the twin ignition switches one at a time to test the dual ignition system – and on the port magneto, the revs fell sharply, from 800 to 450. He groaned: spark plugs, almost certainly – or maybe magneto contact points. Trouble, whichever way you look at it.

The hydraulic pressure built up satisfactorily, but there was no way of testing either flap or undercarriage systems, since he had isolated the return systems in each case. It was, he thought wearily, a case of 'suck it and see' – everything had to work right first time.

If it didn't? Carter sucked his teeth thoughtfully. In that case it would be a case of Vital Action Number One: place both hands together in front of the chest, close the eyes and repeat slowly, 'Our Father . . .' He frowned, fighting the gut-sickness of fear.

In spite of everything, it was an enormously encouraging start. Switching off the engines, he climbed down to ground-level to be met by a babel of joy and enthusiasm.

'So far, so good. Still some work to do on that port engine. But they work – at least they work!'

Liane flung her arms round his neck. 'Donald – we go home soon? Tomorrow?'

'Optimist,' he mocked. 'A week, maybe more. Besides, we've got to bring the treasure down from the cave first, and that'll be two or three days' work, at least. How much more to do on the strip, Debby?'

'One more full-length cut, Uncle Donald – you'll have your hundred yard width by tomorrow night.'

He stared round at the eager young faces. 'Okay. Now let's not get too excited – there's a hell of a lot to do yet. We have to improve that towing gear. Khan will have to pull the Dak down to the end of the strip. There's a few more things to check – but we can start loading in a day or two. Put everything we load into that square I've marked on the floor, Colin; that should keep our centre of gravity within limits.' He stood silently for a moment, looking at the Dakota, wiping his hands upon a piece of rag. It had been one hell of a struggle, but there was a chance – a ghost of a long chance – that they would make it. He took the cigarette Colin offered, watching Liane guide Khan away on another sweep of the strip. He opened his mouth to make a comment, but it was still-born.

The pair of Migs flashed across the valley from end to end, re-heat incandescent in their tail pipes, soaring up into the cloudless sky in tight formation. At the top of the climb, they slowed, went into line astern, rolled over the top gently and came down in a long, slow orbit, tracking along the escarpment.

Carter yelled frantically: 'Under the aircraft, everybody! *Quick!'*

Flat on his belly between the wheels, he could see only the top of the waving elephant grass and a glimpse of Khan's back in the distance. Thank God! Liane had gone to ground. But his heart was like lead within him: those boys were no amateurs – they'd spot the aeroplane, the cleared strip, put two and two together . . .

Two passes . . . Three . . . Carter was terrified that they would do a strafing run which would destroy the aircraft – and the three of them beneath it. But after the third pass, the Migs drifted eastwards in a steep climb towards the rim of the escarpment, the Number Two sliding in beside the leader as they disappeared from view.

Long minutes passed . . .

Behind him, Liane said fearfully: 'Is not good, Donald?'

'Is bloody awful. They were Vietnamese – and looking for trouble. That last man of Macbain's, the one left up on the rim – maybe he got through, spread the word.'

Debby said tensely: 'What'll happen now, Uncle Donald?'

'I don't know. Maybe a ground party trekking in, maybe

helicopters – we're a long way out from Saigon, remember. Most likely they'll drop paras on the strip.'

'How long have we got, Don?' asked Colin.

'No time at all, I reckon. If they use paras, it'll take them time to set it up – I'd guess tomorrow morning at the latest. Not today – unless we're well into Kampuchea air space. But there's been an undeclared war going on for years in these parts.'

Liane laid a hand on Carter's arm. 'Donald – what do we do?'

He hesitated, terrified of what he was about to suggest. 'We have to go – as soon as we can. First light tomorrow morning. I'll have to work all night clearing that port engine, and you'll have to do what you can on the strip.' Carter stared at the stricken faces around him. 'Look,' he said firmly, 'we've been expecting this ever since we got here. What we didn't expect is that the people who'll find us won't want us around to tell the tale – all they're after is what's in those boxes. It's in the lap of the gods now – we *have* to go, and we go tomorrow morning, whatever shape we're in.'

Later, setting up the aluminium platform around the port engine, Carter turned to Colin, trying to sound confident. 'This thing could really go bad on us if those sodding Migs come back and catch us after take-off. We won't stand a chance: they'll blow us away, rather than risk us getting away with it. We have to have some sort of surprise ready for them.'

'What had you in mind?' There was no apprehension in the boy's voice – only a plain recognition of the emergency.

'It'll take hours to fix this engine. But we do have those BARs – point five calibre, automatic...'

Colin failed to hide his consternation. 'Here – you don't mean we're going to fight them?'

'Don't panic, it's just an idea. But we've nothing to lose. Suppose we rigged up a timber frame, lashed half a dozen BARs into it, to fire straight out the aft door. With a wire or something, to make them fire all at once. I wonder what those boys would do if they did find us? Hack us down right away? Not on your life – they want us for propaganda value. Think of the headlines: the Americans back in Vietnam...'

'That's all very well,' Colin said nervously. 'You think they're going to steam up alongside to take a look?'

'Why not? The old Dakota doesn't carry guns – they know that. We may get lucky – blow at least one of the bastards out of the sky.'

Colin grimaced. 'You bloodthirsty old bugger! All right – but what's the other one going to do, meanwhile? Pick his nose? And suppose they send more than two?'

'Cross that bridge when we come to it. Come on, we've a full night ahead of us. First light, remember – no later. Minimum turbulence, cold air for maximum power.'

'All right, Don.' Then suddenly Colin grabbed the pilot's arm savagely. 'My God – we've forgotten the treasure!'

Carter stared. 'Christ on a crutch – I forgot all about that! Well, there's no time to collect it now, Col. We can take the statue, some weapons, the American money. Nothing else.'

The long afternoon was drawing to a close; I placed a new cassette in my recorder and accepted gratefully the cup of tea brought in by the slim Chinese student nurse. It seemed to me that the pilot was tiring fast, and he was smoking too many cigarettes for my peace of mind. I asked him if he felt he could carry on, or if he would prefer to finish next day.

'I'll be all right, Mr Napier,' he told me. 'I'm almost through. Do you really think I could sleep tonight with the rest of this on my mind? I tell you, it's a physical relief to share this with someone else. I've had it bottled up inside me so long . . .'

Colin would never forget that last night in the valley. Carter drove them all on relentlessly, as if to atone for his earlier attitude, working them a straight twelve hours until midnight and ending up with a walking inspection carrying a Tilley lamp on a pole. At one a.m. he had Liane bring Khan round to the hangar, ready for towing. At three, he located the ignition problem, seven hours after he began checking: an intermittent short circuit in the lead from the switch to the magneto. He could have found it within five minutes using the megger appliance he didn't have. It was sheer luck in the end – he spotted the bright sparks from beneath while the engine was running at tick-over and Colin was in the cockpit.

At the first thin streamers of light in the east, they hitched

Khan and began the Herculean task of dragging the aeroplane down to the end of the strip. The ground was soft, and they fought for half an hour before Carter finally released the elephant, started the engines and taxied down to the take-off point, using fuel he could ill afford. Once there, Carter had Colin wedge a piece of wood under one wheel as a chock, belted the starboard engine and got the old aeroplane facing up the strip towards the west.

The girls began ferrying their meagre belongings to the Dakota, riding on Khan's broad back. They had little enough: a few keepsakes, the guitar, Debby's pressed flower collection, Colin's box of bugs. The boy handed the statue of Siva up to Carter who was standing in the cargo hatch: it must have weighed forty-five pounds, and Carter was breathing hard by the time he got it stowed away behind a bulkhead on the flight deck.

'Anything else, Col?' he said anxiously.

'That's the lot — I just have to drag the BARs into position. I hope to God we don't have to use them. Do you think they'll come, Don?'

'They'd be bloody fools not to,' the pilot said sourly. 'Get the girls aboard. It'll soon be light enough, and I don't like the feel of things at all.'

Donald Carter sat in the left-hand seat, settling down, fastening the lap strap. He checked out of the window: it was a fine, unclouded morning, the sun a half-disc above the valley wall, and from his vantage point he could see the dark shadow retreating across the flat valley.

He sat for a long moment, fighting to control his breathing and the pounding of his heart. It was sixteen years since he had flown an aeroplane of any kind. And he had no experience of Dakotas at all. Through the windscreen, the strip ahead looked like the back garden path of a suburban house — too short, too narrow, too rough, too every bloody thing.

The girls came forward and stood behind him, pale-faced and dark-eyed from lack of sleep. Below, Colin stood legs astride, holding the engine turning handle and staring up at the cockpit.

Carter slid the window open.

'All clear?'

'All clear.'

'Stand by to start port engine. Priming now . . . Turn her over!'

The inertia starter began the long, slow build-up through the octaves, from a bass moan to a high-pitched whine. As the speed peaked, Carter yelled '*Contact!*' and yanked the 'engage' toggle, priming like fury. The motor turned, fired, missed, backfired thunderously, then roared in triumph. Carter heard the girls scream ecstatically from behind him, and turned a grimy face to them, smiling wearily.

Starboard now . . . The propeller turned, slowed, turned again, the engine belching clouds of smoke. Carter stopped priming. What a fool he was – the engine was still warm. He'd flooded the damn thing.

They tried again. This time there was no mistake: with both engines at fast tick-over, Colin obeyed Carter's signal, dragged away the chocks, waved frantically at the cockpit and ran for the cargo hatch. Seconds later, he was in the cockpit.

'All right, Don?' he screamed above the engine noise.

'Bloody fine. Get the girls set – Liane here beside me, Debby behind to carry messages, you down back. All right, Debby?'

Her eyes were shining, brimming with tears. She nodded, beyond speech. The pilot turned back to Colin, waiting for the engines to reach operating temperature.

'We've a few minutes yet. Got those BARS lined up?'

'Just have to drag them into the doorway.'

'Remember what I told you. Pull the string, they all fire. Wedge them in tight – there's a hell of a recoil. Check all the safeties off, like I showed you. And don't fire unless you've got a clear shot – I'll send Debby down to tell you. Okay?'

'I . . . I think so, Don.'

Carter glared. 'Bloody hell, don't you go soft on me now. If you have to do it, do it quick – let 'em have everything you've got. Now get back there and hold on – we're going any time now!'

Carter settled himself in the seat more firmly, glanced briefly at the sun swelling over the valley rim, and took a long, shuddering breath. The moment he had feared all these months was upon him: he was entrapped in the pattern of events, as helpless as a fly in a spider's web. The great blunt nose of the Dakota obscured most of the strip ahead; he looked through the side window, at the roughly-trimmed margin barely fifty yards away. It just couldn't be done . . . *Couldn't be done* . . . A vein throbbed painfully in his temple and his mouth tasted dry, metallic. Predictably, he wanted to be sick.

He wound on full forward trim to get the tail up as soon as possible, opened up both throttles before he had time to regret anything, and the old aeroplane surged forward, sluggishly at first, wheels ploughing through the débris of grass and brush. He kept his eyes glued to the strip edge, closing one throttle or the other fractionally to keep straight, stick hard forward. No time to look at the speed indicator. Correct direction again. Pedal hard on the rudder . . . No feeling yet. God – nearly overcorrected that time . . . Engines still running, bloody miracle, thanks, Lord, keep going . . . Was that a hint of reaction in the rudder at last? The tail came up slowly and now he could see the strip – what was left of it. *Jesus!* A few hundred yards, no more . . . He started winding back on the tail trim, keeping the nose straight. Rudder good now, and she felt lighter, bouncing along . . . Controls dreadfully stiff, but working. Thank God there was no wind – bloody impossible with a crosswind. Carter grinned wolfishly: it had been impossible from the beginning!

Seventy knots . . . Eighty . . . She *wanted* to go, with two hundred yards left . . . He hauled back viciously on the stick, and the Dakota lifted, bounced, lifted again and they were away and free, the gear coming up. At first she felt sloppy and unbalanced in his hands, lacking full control – then the speed built up.

They passed over the end of the strip, the escarpment dead ahead, and Carter rammed on left aileron and rudder, grinding her round in a steeply-banked turn, wing-tip scraping the treetops, until the river and strip came into view in the top left corner of the windscreen. Now he began to straighten her out, climbing steadily at 120 knots. He yelled dementedly, banging both fists on the control column, grinning madly at Liane, strapped in the right-hand seat. She smiled stiffly, as if her face was rigid with cold, and he turned back to the side window, checking his position. The valley wall was looming up again: he coaxed the old plane round in a more gentle, climbing turn, keeping the engines running flat out. The oil pressures were holding, cylinder-head temperatures getting a little high: he opened the cooling gills a shade, coming out of the turn to parallel the strip once more.

He stared down at the peaceful valley below: the tiny base, the single hangar, the stream where he had bathed so often, the hut where he had found what he thought never to find again, the source of so much happiness.

He felt a touch on his shoulder. It was Debby, her eyes shining, mouth wide in an exuberant laugh. He winked, shouted above the roar of engines.

'All right, Deb?'

She nodded, beaming. 'Yes – it's going to be all right?'

The aeroplane? Or the pilot? Well, Carter thought happily, it could be a great deal worse. Fifteen hundred feet . . . He pulled back the propeller levers, let the engine speed drop, the noise falling to bearable level. Now the rim of the escarpment was receding, becoming just another ridge in a long series stretching away to the horizon. He reefed the Dakota round to a heading of 255 degrees on the emergency compass, set the old-fashioned gyro and re-checked his heading.

Stretching far away to the horizon, the forest-covered ridges were divided by steep valleys with sparkling streams; he had no idea of the highest ground en route, but it didn't matter – they'd be in the clear, in daylight all the way. He levelled off at 2,500 feet, throttling back to cruise settings, leaning off the mixture until the motors began to run a little rough, opening up again fractionally until they ran sweet and level again.

He groped in trouser pockets for a cigarette, lit one, gave the pack and matches to Liane and concentrated on holding a steady course. He had his head bent over the compass, setting the grid ring, when he heard the sudden thunder of the Migs, flashing over the cockpit. They were terrifyingly close. He jerked upright, staring through the front screen, watching them pull ahead, turning port in a tight pair in échelon.

Carter turned to Debby, his face working with rage and ill-concealed fear. 'Get back to Colin – get ready; keep covers on guns and wait. Got it?'

The girl nodded, biting her lip.

'Okay – get going!'

The pilot held his course, bile acid in his mouth, shaking with helpless rage. After all that damned work! The dark, fish-like silhouettes drifted astern, turning in again, disappearing from sight behind the tail. Seconds later, they slid back into view on his port beam, the leader nearest, his Number Two formating closely on the far side. Carter noticed that they had full flap down: the Dakota's cruising speed was very close to the stalling speed of the supersonic jets. They were painted silver grey, but with no national markings; the leader's aircraft had a large black '06' painted on the side. The fighter's clear plastic hood slid back, and a black-helmeted figure turned to stare at Carter through a dark green sun visor. A gloved hand came up, finger pointing downwards; it stabbed down, once, twice, and then waved in unmistakeable command – 'follow me.'

Carter gritted his teeth. *Like hell, buster* . . . He turned, yelled for Debby.

'Listen,' he bellowed, 'I'm going to try to get them to fall back. Colin has to wait until he can see both clearly. Leave the canvas on the guns – he can fire through it. And don't forget the bloody safeties.'

The girl's face was ashen with fear, grey and drawn, but she nodded vigorously then turned away.

Colin Todd had never felt so alone in all his life. He sat with his back to the vibrating side of the Dakota, facing the open cargo hatch, six feet square. In front of him was the makeshift frame he and Carter had devised – six loaded BARS lashed down into place, muzzles pointing straight out of the hatch. All six triggers were tied with wire to the short length of wood in his hand; the faded green canvas sheet was lashed to the frame, and from outside the aeroplane it resembled stowed cargo.

From the moment the Migs appeared in their opening pass, he knew he was going to have to fight. Carter would expect it, the girls too. He tried to stop himself thinking about what would happen if he managed to knock down only one of them: the furious survivor running in astern again and again, cannon shells ripping through the fuselage . . . Fire . . . Explosions . . .

He had read plenty of war books. He knew what it would be like. He also knew he was so terrified, he was close to losing control of his bowels. He wiped cold, wet hands on his grimy trousers, reached under the canvas and released the safeties on the guns, as Carter had shown him.

Debby came down the cabin between the stacks of boxes, lurching from handhold to handhold; she squatted down beside him, shying away from the open hatch and the terrifying chasm beyond it, quailing in the blast of air swirling around the tail compartment. She gave him Carter's message, and he nodded, almost absently. Old news was no news at all. Debby bent, kissed him briefly, went forward again.

The Migs came round again, sliding up alongside like two monster fish. As they did so, Colin could see the pilots clearly: they ignored the gaping hatchway, moving forward level with the flight deck. The boy waited, stomach heaving as he watched the fighters rising and falling as if on some bumpy invisible road.

Donald Carter glared at the Mig pilot, uncertain, afraid. An immediate refusal to turn could bring disaster, and he couldn't ignore the order completely. In the end, he opened his side window, hunched his shoulders, pointed back towards the tail. If only Colin... The leader looked forward, and Carter saw his oxygen mask moving as he transmitted a message – then he saw him turn back to look at the Dakota. The Migs began sliding back, reducing speed, past the wingtip, almost out of sight. Carter held his breath in agonised silence for a moment, then screamed to Debby:

'They're moving back! Tell Colin!'

The Mig leader was uneasy. He had no training or briefing for such a confrontation, but there was no doubting the tenor of the message from Ho Chi Minh base: this aeroplane *had* to be preserved intact, forced down, its occupants left alive for interrogation. It could be of enormous propaganda value to the Vietnamese people. He *must* not fail.

He stared again at the old guano-stained aeroplane, the missing hatches and panels, one undercarriage wheel drooping down below. *This* was the enemy? He grinned into his oxygen mask, watching the pilot. An old man with no flying helmet – perhaps no radio? And a girl? There was something very strange about this American aeroplane. He decided to delay radioing again until he knew a little more. The old man was signalling, indicating something about the rear of the plane. That cargo hatch was open. He would take a look.

The Dakota wingtip moved up level with his right shoulder as he throttled back fractionally, very close to the stall. A little more . . . Now the dark square of the hatch came into view. Cargo of some kind lashed to the floor, beneath a green cover. Someone sitting behind the cargo – white face, yellow hair. Another American?

He opened his mouth to make a comment to his Number Two, a green pilot fresh out of training school near Hanoi. The green canvas cover erupted into a roaring wall of flame. He died instantly, streams of heavy slugs hosing through the cockpit and the aeroplane structure. His legs kicked out wildly in a dying frenzy: the Mig, already staggering under the pounding of .45 fire, slid sideways into the second aircraft, and in front of Colin's horrified eyes, the sky flared into a nightmare of flame and disintegrating metal, swelling into a fireball of horrendous proportions before falling away astern.

Colin dropped the triggerstick, turned his head to stare at a horrified Debby, and buried his face in his hands. There was a hot, stinging sensation in his groin, and he knew the worst had happened. Slowly came the realisation that, for once in his life, he had done what he had to do – and done it well.

He lifted his eyes to the girl's and stared at her defiantly.

'Well?' he said, above the wind noise. 'Don't just bloody stand there – go and tell Don it's all right'

But as soon as he was alone again, he went to the door, hanging on desperately, gazing down at the distant drifting smokecloud, shaped like a horse's head. 'Jesus,' he whispered. '*Jesus . . .*'

For some moments, Carter had no idea what was going on. He heard the crashing roar of the BARS, which seemed to go on for a terribly long time: a sustained, shuddering broadside followed by something that sounded like a distant street accident. But he could see nothing from the side window. He hauled the DC3 round in a tight turn to port, peering out and aft, and there it was: miles away, curving groundwards, a long trail of grey-black smoke, flecked with débris. He sucked in his breath. No sign of others. Was it possible? *Both* gone?

He continued the turn round to his south-west heading, straightened out, shouted across to Liane, who throughout the action had sat immobile, hands clutching the armrests, face set in a stony grimace of fear. His heart went out to her, and he leaned across, touched her gently.

'It's all right, my love. They're gone. Colin did it! That boy — *he did it!*'

The hours drifted past. Carter could still hardly believe that a miracle had happened. The engines were still turning, the speed a steady 145 knots. He munched candy from a 'K' ration, smoked the occasional cigarette, looking constantly from the map on his lap to the ground below. An hour after take-off, they sighted the coast, the shimmering silver sea beyond, and screamed with delight. He started to climb, explaining to the others, grouped behind his seat, 'We need all the height we can get, once we're over the sea — if we have any problems, it'll give us that much more time.'

Later, Carter wondered about that decision. Was he psychic? Did he know all along, deep down, that they'd never make it? They flew on steadily, climbing up past 6,000 feet, going for 7,000. He checked the fuel. There should be no problem there.

They were some fifty miles out from the coast, cruising in clear sunshine at 140 knots, when the starboard engine let go. There was no warning: it simply cut dead, propeller windmilling, and the Dakota yawed violently to starboard under the offset power of the live engine.

Carter trod hard on the rudder, reefing the tail around into a straight course, jammed his thumb on the feathering button.

'If we can't feather that thing,' he yelled frantically, 'we've had it. Too much drag —'

He tried again, holding the button in hard. The propeller slowed, came to a stop with blades edge-on to the airflow. Carter gulped, wiped the sweat from his face and experimented with breathing again; it felt good, so he kept on doing it.

'Christ almighty,' he said thickly, 'that was bloody close.'
He wound on some rudder trim to take the strain off his left

foot, opened up the live engine to take the additional load. The revs went up to the take-off setting, the single propeller roaring flat out. When he had everything straightened away, fuel cocks set, he sat back to take stock.

'We still have two hundred miles to go – almost as far if we turned back. And I'm damned if we're going to turn back. At this speed, it'll take the best part of two hours – *if* that port engine keeps going. I can take off some of the load by descending when we get close to the coast, but until then . . .'

Colin leaned close. 'What happened, Don?'

'Who knows? We were lucky it went that way. At least there was no fire. Without any extinguishers, we'd have had it. I figure it was probably a blocked fuel line. I'm not surprised, the amount of crap we found in the filters. We'd better look out for ships: if we run into more trouble, I want something afloat nearby. Maybe we could thumb a lift . . .'

It was a poor joke, but they grinned dutifully, found a window each and started looking.

To Liane, the whole situation was horribly reminiscent of the Boeing crash – but this time she knew Donald would take care of her, no matter what. She sat quietly in the front seat, looking down at the endless wastes of ocean below, furrowed and winnowed by the wind.

Ships saw they none. That day the Gulf of Siam seemed as deserted as the sky itself. Visibility was barely two miles into the sun, and Carter knew that the whole Russian Eastern Fleet could be just over the horizon. He sat at the controls in an agony of anticipation, dreading with each passing second the explosion of the overworked engine, a sudden burst of flame . . . It was as if the aeroplane was poised precariously upon a needle-point. They had reduced altitude to 3,000 feet, losing precious height slowly to a level where the single engine could hold the Dakota in level flight. But with each tiny change of attitude, each control movement, they lost a few more feet . . .

At this reduced speed, their time over water lengthened interminably. Five hours had passed by now, and fuel was becoming a desperate problem: the single engine, at full power, was using more fuel than would both engines, throttled back to maintain a steady 100 knots. He had no idea of fuel quantity – the gauges were electric – but his experience told him there was only one possible end: the live engine would stop, and they would all fall out of the sky.

At ten minutes before noon by his watch, with the sun almost overhead, he spotted a long, grey shadow on the horizon which could only be the coast: ordering the others to strap themselves in tightly, he did all he could to prepare for a crash landing. His left leg ached abominably; despite full rudder trim, he had to hold on some left rudder to keep a straight course.

Now, he could see the coast: they would intercept at an angle, the beach stretching from under their left wing, obliquely away into the distance to starboard. He began checking the coast feverishly for a pinpoint of some sort: far away to starboard, he could see the mouth of a river, with buildings on each side of the estuary – a small town sitting in a clearing, surrounded by a semi-circle of forest, thinning out on either side at the beach. The sand was white and glistening in the brilliant sunshine, and far inland, the green hills rose and fell in ridges all the way to the horizon.

Ten miles . . . Five . . . We've damn well made it! he thought exultantly. *We've made it!*

At which point the port engine cut, backfired, caught again, then stopped for good.

For a few frantic moments, he panicked, getting the trim off, feathering the windmilling propeller, getting the aeroplane into a stable glide. It was quiet now, in the cockpit; he found, amazingly, that he could speak naturally to the others, who were watching him anxiously. He heard his own voice, sounding composed and full of a confidence he didn't feel, as he briefed them:

'Sit tight – we're going to be all right. We're only a couple of miles off the coast, with plenty of height. I'm going to put her down on the beach. Get your heads down between your knees, you two – up against the bulkhead in the cabin. Liane, pull that lap strap tight. And hold on!'

Now, Carter, you stupid old sod, just for once in your life, do something right . . .

He checked the descent indicator: they were losing 500 feet a minute. Height: 1,500 – that made it about three minutes to touchdown. And wind? Too far out to see. This was going to be a dead-stick landing with wheels up, but he couldn't have wished for better conditions: the beach was wide, perhaps a hundred yards, rising gently from the water's edge and with a long, harmless curve to the north-west that would give little trouble.

No flap for landing . . . The thought came to him quite automatically. In fact, all the old habits and skills were flooding back, as if he had flown regularly for years. He'd have to come in fairly fast, a flat, shallow approach, keeping the beach in sight until the last moment. At five hundred feet, he began a descending turn to starboard, allowing the speed to build up to 90 knots for safety, keeping the white ribbon of sand high right in the windscreen. Straighten up a little . . . Still curving in gently, like a fighter attacking a target from beam to astern . . . Speed back to 80 . . . Hold it there.

He sat at the controls, relaxed, resisting a ludicrous impulse to whistle nonchalantly, head turning like clockwork: Airspeed . . . Beach . . . Airspeed . . . Beach . . .

It was time: the old Dakota was skimming in over the lines of white surf, a hundred feet, fifty, the waves breaking now under the right wing. He swung the controls firmly, bringing the wings level, trimming back hard, miles of beach ahead, shelving slightly from the left, right down to the water's edge, black seaweed on the white sand . . .

Hold her there! She's trying to go nose-down. Trim back all the way . . . Now, hard back on the pole, airspeed falling . . . Starting to shudder . . . Near the stall . . .

Wham! Tailwheel digging in, he thought fleetingly. Hold her one last second, and –

Crunch!

The impact on the belly of the Dakota was solid, teeth-shaking, but she stayed down. With sand grinding underneath, she skidded slightly port towards the tree line, with Carter ramming on the right rudder which he knew was useless. Finally, she stopped, twenty yards from the trees, nose pointing straight inland, the sea at her tail.

No time to sit and scratch your arse, Carter: the old crate could burst into flames any moment. '*Everyone out!*' he yelled, and with a surge of energy he half-dragged Liane down the cabin to the open hatch, shoving Colin and Debby ahead, oddly astonished that he could step neatly from plane to ground, a distance of eight or nine inches. Together, all four of them scrambled up the beach, collapsing on the dry, hot sand well clear of the Dakota, laughing, crying, finding it quite impossible to believe that they were down, and safe . . .

There was no fire. The pilot sat with head bowed, physically exhausted, mentally stunned, a cigarette burning unheeded in his hand, the healing sunlight warm on his bare back. Carter knew, instinctively, that he was closer to collapse than at any time in his life; Liane sat beside him, an arm round his shoulders, and Colin brought water from the plane, made him drink. His hands refused to stop trembling, and the water failed to refresh him. Debby, still shocked, knelt alone on the white sand, fifteen yards distant, face buried in her hands, shoulders shaking.

Carter looked at Liane wearily. 'Go take care of her, Liane. She's at the end of her tether.'

The golden-skinned girl stared blankly, unfamiliar with the term. She looked at Carter with a strange, distant expression, then did as he asked.

'Don? You okay?' Colin said anxiously.

Carter grinned feebly, punched the boy's upper arm. 'I didn't have time to thank you for what you did back there.'

'The Migs, you mean?'

'Yes – Christ, that guy must have had a shock when you opened up. Did they all fire?'

Colin nodded bleakly. 'I think so. I didn't like doing it, Don. I pissed myself with fright . . .'

Carter nodded. 'Welcome to the club. Don't worry, lad – all be the same in a hundred years. Here – where are the guns?'

'Shoved them overboard when that engine stopped,' Colin told him with some satisfaction. 'I thought the less weight the better – and I didn't think we'd need them again . . .'

Carter nodded absently. 'Sure. Listen – the girls are coming back – we don't have much time. There's a town about three miles up the beach, that way. We're somewhere near Khota Baru, but I don't know where exactly. I want you to take the girls there – no, listen to me: I want to get our cargo stashed away safely, where we can collect it later. I have something in mind, but it's best I'm the only one who knows where it is. I'll explain later. The girls won't go without you, so get going. Tell them no arguments.'

But he had left it too late. Liane and Debby heard the last few words.

'No arguments about what, Donald?' Liane said tensely.

'Colin will explain. There's no time to waste. He'll take you up the coast – there's a town up there. I'm staying, to get the money out – hide it. Otherwise we'll lose the lot. On your way now.'

Liane stood rock-like before him. 'You want us to go – and *you* hide the money? For yourself?'

'Christ,' Carter said in exasperation, 'no, of course not. Look, take them away, Col – *now*!'

The pilot waited until they were three remote specks far up the beach, plodding through the soft white sand, then he turned, went into the Dakota and began stripping away the covers and lashings from the cargo. Fifteen minutes later he was out on the beach, leaning on the money boxes, sucking air into aching lungs. No time . . . No time . . . Tying a length of webbing strap to the first crate, he dragged it fifty yards along the beach to a particular tree, found a piece of sheet metal from the wreck and began digging.

Long before the first hole was finished, the sweat was pouring off his body, and a dull ache was spreading through his chest. The three black-painted boxes went down solidly, and he began shovelling sand over them.

The gold box . . . *God*, he thought despairingly, I'll never move the swine. It was too heavy to drag through the soft, yielding sand. He stagged up the beach, scooped out a second hole, large enough for the single crate. Back at the Dakota, he dragged the steel box to the cargo hatch, spent five minutes hollowing out a shallow trench in which to stand, hauled on the straps. Sobbing in sheer agony, he got the box onto his back and one shoulder; then, bent double as if crippled, he stagged drunkenly up the beach, before collapsing six feet from the hole. After a long time, the sand-encrusted body stirred, moving jerkily and stiffly. Four feet . . . Two . . . At last the box slid into the hole, and he knelt, shoveling sand on top with his bare hands, like a drunken man.

Totally spent, he swayed onto his feet and limped back towards the Dakota, smoothing out the flattened channels gouged out by the dragged crates. He felt his knees buckle. Head on fire from the sunglare, he crawled like a wounded animal into the shade of a wing, and lay quite still.

Carter was silent for a long time. Finally he looked at me pleadingly and said:

'So you see why I have to go back to get that money. Somehow, we have to get that treasure out of the valley, use it to raise money to help the people of Cambodia out of the unholy mess their governments have got them into. With the American money . . . It's not for me, you see. It's for Liane's people. You have to talk to your government, tell them I need help. Will you do that for me?'

EIGHTEEN

I think it must have been the night nurse who came in, at the end, to see why Donald Carter's ward light was still on: I know she was shocked and angry to find that a visitor was still in the hospital as late as eleven o'clock at night. It came as a considerable shock to me, too, to realise that Carter had talked for more than eight hours.

The nurse, I'm afraid, became officious and distant, ignoring our apologies and ordering me out of the ward. I can't say that I blame her entirely.

Carter's face wore a tired grin when I said goodbye.

'I told you it was quite a tale, didn't I?'

'You did indeed, Donald,' I admitted. Somewhere during that day, we had graduated to first names. 'Look here, you'll have to leave this with me – I must talk to my minister. One last point: do you want to see Miss Dang Ko again?'

His mouth twisted cynically. 'Boot's on the other foot, Alan. She doesn't want to see me.'

In fact, he was quite mistaken there. My appointment with Lee Kuan Lok was arranged for the next afternoon: at noon that same day, I was allowed, with some reluctance, to see Liane Dang Ko again – however, the night nurse must have been telling tales out of school because I was strictly admonished to stay ten minutes and no more.

She stared at me without expression when I walked into her little room on the second floor. It was clear that she was to be discharged that day: she was dressed once more in her airline uniform and looked extremely well. Her small valise was open and lying on the bed.

'Hello, Liane. It's nice of you to see me again before you leave,' I said carefully.

She glanced quickly at me, curious, before resuming her final packing.

'What can I do for you, Mr Napier?'

'Would you mind if I sat down for a moment? It's a long walk here for an old chap like me.'

She relented at once, found me a chair and fussed over me for a moment or two. To tell the truth, I enjoyed it, for she was a beautiful and attractive woman and such favours occur all too seldom. I lit a cheroot, and she brought an ashtray to me and sat down on the bed before my chair.

'I saw Mr Carter again yesterday,' I began. The small frown between the magnificent black brows deepened fractionally. I went on doggedly. 'He seems to think that you don't want to see him again before you leave – that you don't wish to speak to him at all. Is that right?'

She turned her head away; I could see a small pulse beating in the hollow of her neck, below the fine gold chain she wore. Her right hand moved absently at her hair, as women's hands do, and I saw the heavy gold and emerald ring on her forefinger. Her voice, when she finally replied, was almost inaudible.

'Mr Napier,' she said slowly, 'how can I tell you how I feel about Donald Carter? What do you say when you find out that a man you have come to love and respect – a man who has saved your life not once, but several times – that such a man is a thief and a rogue, who thinks only of himself?'

I smiled secretly, watching that proud profile in the quiet room. 'I suppose you mean the American money he buried on the beach at Khota Baru?'

Her head swung round and she got up onto her feet, startled.

'He told you?' she said incredulously.

'He told me, Liane. That – and much more. He also told me what he wanted to do with it. Tell me: when you got back to the aeroplane on the beach, did you speak to him?'

She bit her lip, troubled. 'No. We walked a long way until we found the little town more than two hours' walk along the beach. We found a local government officer and he drove us back to the aeroplane. When we found Donald, he was . . . Colin said he was "out cold" . . .?' She looked for confirmation of her choice of words, and I nodded. She went on: 'He could not speak or hear. We were very frightened.'

'I see. And you haven't spoken to him in the hospital?

Because you thought he was going to keep all that money for himself?'

She nodded. 'For myself, I did not care. But the children . . .'

I took a deep breath. 'You'd better sit down and brace yourself, Liane. I have something to tell you . . .'

When I had finished, she got up and walked to the window, turning her back on me. Presently she pulled a tissue from her pocket and blew her nose elaborately. This was surprising to me: I had the impression that Liane Dang Ko was a very calm and collected young woman, not given to tears. It just shows how wrong you can be.

At length, she came back to the bed and sat down.

'I have been a very silly woman, Mr Napier.'

'Yes,' I said drily. 'I think you have. But there's no harm done, fortunately.'

She smiled, though her eyes were still moist with unspilled tears. 'And that was how Donald hurt his back? Carrying those boxes?'

'Yes,' I nodded. 'Now, let me ask *you* a question. What are you going to do about it?' I said shortly.

Her mouth became very determined, the muscles tightening, and she stared me straight in the eye.

'I am going,' she said decisively, 'to ask Donald Carter if he will forgive a very stupid woman for believing he could do something so wrong.'

I nodded again. 'Well, that sounds like a very good start. Then?'

'Then I am going to marry him, if he will have me.'

I thought there wasn't much doubt about that – but she could find out for herself. I stood up to leave.

'One last thing, Liane: you know Donald intends to go back to that valley. I have promised to help him – I think he would want you to help, too. Can you arrange a leave of absence from your job?'

Her smile was brilliant, and she looked lovely, standing there – clean-limbed and slender. I thought that Donald Carter was a very lucky man.

'As from this moment, Mr Napier, I have a new job – a

permanent one. Looking after Donald Carter,' she said earnestly.

I stopped with one hand on the door handle. 'I think you're very wise,' I said at last. 'There are very few like him around.'

A few minutes before four o'clock that afternoon, Lee Kuan Lok came round from behind his desk, opened his liquor cabinet and poured out two glasses of brandy.

'Alan, I never drink as early as this normally,' he said huskily. 'But I have never heard such a story in all my life. If any other man but you had told me, I would never have believed it. If half of what you say is true, there's enough money in that cave to give every family in Kampuchea an income for life. Provided the aid can be delivered where it's needed, it can save a whole nation from starvation. Carter has a tremendous responsibility, Alan.'

I drank a little brandy. It was Lee's prime stock, which I had sampled on very few occasions over the years. He *must* be disturbed, I thought happily.

'Yes,' I said thoughtfully. 'And he's going to need some help, Lee. Remember, everything I've told you has been in strictest confidence. I think what he's doing is right, but you know what governments are. He's afraid that Malaysia may grab every-thing he brought out of the valley, and that your people will have similar ideas. I told him I thought I could probably arrange some sort of deal – two-thirds to the Singapore government, one third to Carter and the others. Of course, he's obsessed with the problem of getting the Angkor jewels out of that place.'

Lee topped up his glass. 'It won't be easy, from what you say.'

'No,' I agreed. 'It won't. I'm not even sure it's possible. For a start, the Vietnamese, who seem to own that part of the world regardless of frontiers, know now that the valley is there. After losing two Migs, they'll go through the place from end to end until they learn the secret. But they won't find anything, of course.'

The Minister chuckled. 'I'd like to have been in Ho Chi Minh City when the news came in. An American aircraft, operating from a secret mountain base near the Kampuchea border, five years after the war ended –'

'The point is, Lee, won't they leave people in the valley, once they know everything there is to know? After two or three weeks, when the excitement's died down? Of course, no plans can be made to go back there until we know the situation.'

'You say there's no way in or out of there, other than by air?'

'So Carter says. It's way up in the mountains, on the border.'

'Well, there's your answer. What good is that place to the gooks now? They have an undeclared border war going on with Kampuchea at the moment, but what good is a base they can't use? Its entire value to the CIA lay in its secrecy, inaccessibility. Which reminds me . . .'

He got up from his chair and walked around, hands clasped behind his back. I settled back in my chair: these thinking sessions of Lee's could – and did – last for a very long time. At last:

'Alan, do you remember Major Winkler?'

'Major who?' I said, startled.

'You must remember him. The US liaison officer at Butter-worth in 1944-45?'

'Oh,' I said. '*That* Winkler.'

'I met him in Washington last year, at the Third World Conference. He was there as consultant for the development of education courses by satellite for the non-aligned countries. India has already started using the –' He caught my eye and stopped abruptly. 'Anyway – I think I could ask him to monitor activity in that valley by satellite. The Americans have all sorts of junk floating around up there. It shouldn't be too difficult.'

I thought he could be right. 'Carter has a map on the plane, showing the exact location of the valley. And the monsoon is over now – they might get good results.'

'I'll get hold of Winkler right away. Alan, we have to be bloody careful, you know. I don't even feel happy about talking over the telephone about this business. I think I should go and see him personally.'

'Look here, Lee,' I said sharply, 'don't go off at half-cock. You have to decide whether you're getting involved as a minister, or a private person. I mean, that American money –'

He stared at me scornfully. 'You surprise me, Alan. That US

money is spoils of war, finders keepers – call it what you will. They wrote it off at the end of the war. Now we don't want to go messing up their bookwork, do we? We'll take a share – officially – without releasing any details; in return, we'll help Carter retrieve his treasure. But *that* belongs to the people of Cambodia – Carter is quite right there, and I'm all for it. What we can do is offer him advice, help, a base of operations – anything he wants. None of us have any claims to the treasure. We don't want it. Alan, I know a great deal more than you about conditions inside Kampuchea now, and they need every penny the world can scrape up.'

I stood up, satisfied. 'Very good, Lee. Carter will be out of hospital in a day or two and I'll bring him along to see you. After that, you're on your own. You can have my report on Flight HK 108 within a week. By the way –'

'Yes?'

'I've an idea Carter may want to get married – quickly. He's not the sort of chap to hang about. I'd be grateful if you could grease the wheels a little.'

He smiled. 'Of course, Alan. Be glad to. Tell me – the Dang Ko girl . . . Is she really as, er, good-looking as you say?'

'Better,' I said slowly. 'If I were thirty years younger . . .'

'Go away and let me think,' Lee ordered, grinning hugely. 'You're a disturbing influence.'

For me, events seemed to move very quickly in the weeks that followed. Carter, it was plain, was beset with impatience and found the waiting intolerable. It was remarkable to see the change in him after he left the hospital. He and Liane were married quietly at a civil ceremony in Singapore, at which Lee and I were happily in attendance as witnesses. Carter's son, Gavin, flew down from Hong Kong, bringing with him the others – Colin Todd and Debby Worthington and their parents, all of whom seemed quite prepared to insist that the sun shone out of Carter's armpit – Gavin's words, not mine, though he didn't exactly say 'armpit'. Typically, Carter had told his son little or nothing of the events before his arrival at Khota Baru, and Gavin had to trap me at the reception, in a private room at Raffles, to learn the truth. Thereafter, he spent the evening walking round Carter in small circles, as if expecting him to vanish into thin air. It was obvious the boy was blissfully happy about his father's wedding – certainly, he and Liane developed an instant understanding and liking.

I have a small holiday home in a tiny fishing village a few miles outside the city. I packed off Carter and Liane in a hired car, with instructions to stay as long as they pleased; the arrangement wasn't altogether successful. He pestered me over the telephone every day about the Dakota cargo, and in the end I brought him back for the recovery operation.

This was a classic exercise in disguised intervention. The boat Lee procured for the job was a fifty-foot sea-going pleasure cruiser, with two massive MAN Diesels and a shallow draught. Carter landed on the beach one morning an hour before dawn from an inflatable dinghy, accompanied by two of Lee's most trusted men. The transfer of the three boxes and the steel crate took rather less than an hour, and before he left, Carter went back to the Dakota for one last time to collect the Siva statue from behind its bulkhead and the map showing the location of the valley. Surprisingly, the Dakota hadn't been damaged by the local inhabitants, who had contented themselves with removing everything that hadn't been screwed down.

Lee, whatever his faults, has a flair for organisation and never misses an opportunity to tell everyone about it. A plain closed van transferred the load to the Williams bank in Palembang Boulevard, where it was counted, checked and deposited in Carter's private account. Lee, through his connections, was able to dispose of the gold at very favourable rates, and two days later, Carter sat in Lee's office with Liane and wrote out a cheque for the largest amount he had ever seen – ten million dollars, US currency, payable to the Singapore government.

The minister took the cheque and laid it very carefully on his desk.

'Mr Carter – Mrs Carter – ' Liane smiled, a little self-consciously. These things took time, I reflected. Lee went on: 'I thank you on behalf of my government for this money. We did little enough to earn it' – he held up a hand against their protests – 'and if we are to keep face, we must do everything else possible to help you. Alan, I have to tell you that I have told the facts of the case to *one* other high-ranking gentleman . . .'

'How high?' I demanded.

'As high as you can get,' he said diplomatically, 'without calling in the clergy.'

I grinned and sat back, satisfied.

'I have full authority to give all the assistance you need, Mr Carter, in recovering the Angkor treasure, short of involving Singapore forces on the Asian mainland. All our resources, other than that, are at your disposal. More important still, Singapore has agreed to grant you indefinite residence in this country for the purpose of administering your proposed Kampuchea Distress Relief Fund. I think we all know what I mean by that.'

Carter flushed. 'Minister, that's far more than we expected. Thank you.'

Lee nodded benevolently. 'Now — we change the subject. Through certain friends, I have arranged satellite monitoring of the valley over the past fourteen days. For three of these, the Vietnamese flew transport aeroplanes in and out of the valley. They then brought in a bulldozer, and now the airstrip is longer and completely cleared. We have some photographs here taken only twenty-four hours ago.' He took them out of a desk-drawer and passed them round, big black-and-white blow-ups of the base area.

'The base, as you can see, has been levelled. I think they decided it was of no use to them, but clearly they were anxious to deny the resources to others. Leaving, of course, the airstrip as an emergency landing ground — I'm told they're a little thin on the ground in that area.'

Carter grinned at that. 'You can say that again, sir.'

'For the last six days, the valley has been deserted. Tell me, Mr Carter, is there any way they could have stumbled on the cave and the treasure?'

The pilot looked at Liane, reached out to touch her hand, looked straight at Lee.

'No, Minister . . . I don't think there's any way they could do that.'

I smothered a sigh of relief. Lee knew most of the story — but not all.

'I understand,' Lee said, satisfied. 'The question in all our minds, of course, is how you plan to go about recovering the treasure?'

Carter cleared his throat hesitantly. 'I've got as far as this: I know what we can do, and what we can't. For example: we *can't* go in by helicopter, because of the distance. If the gooks have left the store of fuel behind, it might be possible – but I doubt it. Again, we can go in, using an ordinary plane, by day or by night. Day is risky – it's two hundred miles in from the coast, another two hundred out again. I don't know how good their radar is, but that would be asking for trouble.'

The minister nodded, sitting back in his tall leather chair, fingers steepled before him. 'Go on, Mr Carter, please.'

'Penetrating overland just isn't on. Even if we could reach the valley, those cliffs are a thousand feet high in places. And there's almost half a ton of stuff to bring out. Which leaves only one solution . . .'

'Which is – ?'

'Go in by night in a light plane, to arrive at dawn. We carry camouflage nets, hide the plane and spend the day getting the treasure down and ready. At dusk, we set up portable landing lights and a radio beacon on a balloon, up to a thousand feet. We fly the main aircraft in after dark, homing on the beacon, use the lights to land. We load up, abandon the light plane – it won't have enough fuel – and fly direct to Singapore.'

Lee Kuan Lok considered this proposition with all the care it merited. I was, I must admit, quite impressed. There were, of course, some obvious disadvantages which Lee pointed out at once.

'We'd have to use an unmarked plane in each case, I think. There must be no apparent connection with Singapore. We can't operate out of Khota Baru officially – but there are ways round that. What does concern me is this: if the Vietnamese have left a security squad in the valley, how do we handle them?'

'You can leave that to me,' Carter said grimly. 'There are a lot of loose ends, I admit – but I think the idea is basically sound.'

'I'm sure it is,' Lee said equably. 'All we have to do is build in some insurance. What kind of planes and pilots did you have in mind?'

'For the first plane, I thought something like a Comanche or an Apache: they're fairly fast. Full night-flying gear, navigation equipment. We'll have to cater for at least three men, to hump all that stuff down to ground level and shift it three miles to the strip. Ideally, we could do with a jeep or similar – but that means using a bigger aircraft.'

I said: 'What about those mini-tractors? The ones that pull small trailers?'

Liane intervened. 'You are forgetting Khan,' she said softly.

'Of course!' Carter beamed. 'What a damned fool I am! Khan could shift the whole lot in a single trip if we gave him some panniers or something. For the second aircraft, I'd like a Caribou, something with a tail loading ramp.'

Lee said he thought that would probably fit the bill. 'Which brings us to pilots . . .'

I hope to goodness he doesn't look at me, I thought hastily.

Lee went on: 'My friends tell me there may be one or two ex-CIA pilots available – men who actually used that strip during the war, flying for Air America. On private contract, of course – for a very good fee, sufficient to ensure their confidentiality. So – the thing begins to take shape, Alan.'

'Indeed. And if we succeed? When we come back with the bacon?'

Lee allowed himself a confident smile. 'This part I have already considered in detail, Mr Carter. There will be a special reception area at Seletar Airport; from there, the treasure will be moved under close escort to your bank, where I have arranged that a special strongroom will be built. From that time on, we will assist in every way to, ah, unload the gems onto the market in such a way as to ensure maximum return. For this, our economists will charge a modest fee. In other words, we can arrange, not only capitalisation of the jewels, but for organising and operating the relief operation in Kampuchea. Mr Carter, have you any idea of the magnitude of the task you intend to take on?'

The pilot nodded. He said uncomfortably: 'I have. And it scares the crap out of me. I'm going to need a lot of people helping in all sorts of ways – but the more people are involved, the greater the risk of supplies going stray. We're talking about hundreds of millions of dollars in food, farm equipment, vehicles, clothing, housing, trucks, ships . . .' He paused, extremely disturbed. 'I don't know how I'm going to cope, Minister, and that's the truth of it.'

Liane spoke in a quiet, firm voice, reassuring, comforting.

'Donald, there are many people in my country who would help us in this work. People who do not care about governments and politics and Communism – people who just want to see our country whole again. We can find them, if we try hard enough.'

'What do you suggest, Li?'

'Let us first of all bring the treasure to a safe place. Then let us build a proper charity organisation, approved by the countries of the world and the United Nations. That way, we can go into Kampuchea openly, to bring help to my people. But we shall also bring hope – for when the people learn that the treasure of Angkor Vat will be used to rebuild their country, they will come forward and help us.'

Carter said doubtfully: 'They may take some convincing.'

'I know,' she said calmly. 'That is why, when we go back to Phnom Penh, we shall take back the proof they need.'

Carter shot her a questioning glance.

'The statue of Siva, from the temple of Angkor,' she said, in a quiet voice.

'Of course.' Carter nodded understandingly. 'They could hardly argue about that.'

Lee Kuan Lok added a note of caution. 'I think this is a good plan, Mr Carter – but you must be most careful. Money buys power: as it flows into Kampuchea, you and Mrs Carter will become very important people. The rulers will have to do as you wish if the aid is to continue, and if some of them are hostile to your plans, you will have the strength and authority to remove them. Do you see what I mean?'

Carter stared at the minister with dawning apprehension in his eyes. 'Christ,' he said ruefully. 'I hadn't thought of that. I don't want to get mixed up in politics.'

'Frankly,' Lee Kuan said, 'I don't think you have any choice. I don't believe you've thought this thing through. You may not like it, but once you start the process, you and Mrs Carter are going to be responsible for the welfare of many millions of people. It is a very great responsibility, and I think you should consider the alternative – of handing over the money to the Kampuchean government, or the United Nations.'

'No!' Liane's voice was emphatic in denial, almost autocratic. She came to stand beside Carter, slipped her hand into his. 'You are of the East, Minister, and you, of all people, should understand. You know of the I Ching?'

Lee bent his head silently in assent.

'Three thousand years ago, the Chinese came to understand that while the paths of the heavenly bodies through space are fixed, immutable, we on earth have a very small degree of control over our own destinies. You know that the I Ching is a very old form of computer – that it can help those who consult the Book of Changes to choose a path in the present that will bring benefit in the future. You know of this?'

The minister frowned. 'I know of it, yes. But I don't see –'

'Please –' Liane held up a slim hand, upon which flashed the great elephant ring. 'The old Chinese knew, Minister, that our lives are planned by Buddha – perhaps by One even greater than He. We can make small changes, but all our lives, we follow the path. Since I was born, I have followed my path – the path that led me to Donald, to the valley, to the treasure. Donald's own path, as was intended, met my own in Singapore, and from that time onwards, we travelled together. Now, the way is clear to see. I think, Donald, that we shall see much sadness, but we shall also bring happiness to many people. It will mean a heavy load upon us, but together we can do it. Will you come, Donald?'

Carter was quiet for a little while after that. My own mouth was dry: I had spent almost all my life travelling the world, seeing many places, doing those things it was possible for a man in my position to do. And it seemed to me, now, that all these things had served only to lead me and guide me to this intersection with history.

The tall, lean pilot turned his head to the woman at his side. 'Together, Liane . . . Together.'

In that moment, I found it hard to swallow. I turned to the window, staring out across the busy streets towards the harbour, but the view was blurred, indistinct. Later, I heard the door close behind the Carters.

When I got up to go some fifteen minutes later, Lee came to the door with me.

'I think you've handled this affair extremely well, Alan,' he said warmly. 'But I doubt if any of us could have foreseen that it would turn out this way.'

I said carefully, 'No. You're right there. Sometimes . . . Sometimes, I get the feeling that Shakespeare was right, Lee; that all the world's a stage, and we're merely the players . . .'

He smiled reminiscently. 'And what a leading lady . . .'

I couldn't argue with that sentiment, and told him so. It was then that Lee, standing with one hand on the door handle, said something very stupid, and I walked out of the room rather stiffly, closing the door behind me.

It was quite ridiculous. I'll be seventy years of age next March.

I couldn't be in love with her myself.